52 SLEEPLESS NIGHTS

SHORT HORROR STORIES

TOBIAS WADE

First Edition: March 2018
52 Sleepless Nights

HAUNTED HOUSE

PUBLISHING

CONTENTS

Devils so work that things which are not appear to men as if they were real.
    —Lactantius

GRIM REAPER'S SCYTHE

There is no fear as potent as the fear of the unknown. No monstrous visage discovered yet is as terrifying as the infinite potential for horror which exists before the mask is removed.

That is why we humans, in our naive misunderstanding of the universal order, are gripped by the mortal fear of death. We think it's the final frontier: the greatest imaginable unknown from whose penumbral shores no traveler may return. And so we cling desperately to even the dreariest and most anguished lives, suffering any known evil over our release into the beyond.

But death is not to be feared, because death is very well understood. We have witnessed it, caused it, measured and recorded it to the last dying spasm of neuronal flickering. Even as I lay dying, it seemed silly to me that I should be afraid of the emptiness which reason promised to expect.

While I was alive I wouldn't experience death, so there is no reason to be afraid. When I was dead, I wouldn't be capable of experiencing anything, so fear still has no cause. That thought brought me great comfort as I felt the last erratic struggle from my heart against the inevitable conclusion I approached. It wasn't until I was finally drifting off to sleep that a final intrusive doubt bubbled in my brain:

What if it isn't death which is to be feared? What if it is what lies beyond?

And so troubled did I slip beyond mortal understanding, stepping into a world as far forsaken by reason as I was now from life. I was still in the hospital room, but the bustle of nurses and the beeping machines lost their opacity as though I was mired in swiftly-descending dusk. It seemed as though every sound was an echo of what it once was; every sight a reflection. With each passing moment, the world was becoming less real....

But all that sight and sound—all that being—it wasn't simply disappearing. It was *transforming* into a figure beside me. The less real my room became, the more real the figure was, until presently it existed in such sharp actuality that nothing beside it seemed real at all.

His cloak was black. Not the *color* black, but its essence. It was as though seeing a tiger after a lifetime of looking at a child's crude drawing and thinking that's all a tiger was. Reality flowed around his scythe like a brush through water colors, and I could see each elementary particle and time itself sunder across its blade.

Surely this, I thought. This is why we were taught without words to fear death. I clutched my hospital blanket, cowering from the intensity of the Reaper's presence, but the once-soft cotton now flowed like translucent mist through my hands. I knew in that moment that nothing could hide me from the specter's grasp, for he was the only real thing in this world.

You're late.

They weren't words. My head ached from the strain of this knowledge as my lateness was burned into my awareness, imparted like an inescapable law of physics as unequivocal as gravity.

We don't have time for the usual speech. Hurry now.

I felt myself swept up around him like dirt in a hurricane. Before I knew what was happening, we were outside the hospital, moving at such a frenzied pace that the world around me blurred into a dizzying tunnel of flashing light.

If you're lucky, IT will have gotten bored waiting for you.

I had too many questions, all fighting for attention in the forefront of my brain without any making their way out.

You're quiet. I admire that. People usually ask too much.

"What's the point?" I asked. My voice felt flat and dead compared to his overwhelming substance. "How can I try to comprehend something so beyond mortal knowledge?"

You can't. But it's still human nature to ask.

We weren't slowing. If anything, our pace was increasing. I wasn't running, or flying, or anything of that nature. It was more like the rest of the world was moving around us while we stood still. A vague darkness and a heavy damp smell made me guess that we'd gone underground, but I couldn't say for sure.

"One question then," I asked. "What else is here besides you?"

And that is why questions are pointless. Death is not a place, or a person. It's all there is.

Troubling thought, made more so by the growing howl reverberating through the rocks around me. We still seemed to be descending into the earth, and the air grew warmer and denser now. The sound continued to mount as though the world itself was suffering.

"Then what is IT?"

What I'm here to protect you from.

The rocks split from a flash of his scythe, and the ground opened farther into a sprawling cavern dominated by a subterranean lake.

"But I thought you said you were all there is."

No, I said Death was all there is.

We weren't moving any longer. Light glinted off the scythe from some unseen source and streamed into the lake like a tributary. Once inside, the light didn't reflect or dissipate, but swirled and danced as a luminescent oil.

"I thought you were Death."

Death is not a person.

The light was taking a life of its own inside the water. The still surface began to churn with enigmatic energy. It took my scattered mind a long while to realize that *I* was the energy flowing into the lake. I still felt tangled up with the figure, but we now existed as a beam of light boiling into the water.

I knew I wouldn't understand, but that didn't stop me from feeling frustrated. If Death is all there is, then what is IT? What was waiting for me? The water pressed around me and I couldn't speak, although I didn't seem to need air any more.

IT is here.

Something was in the water around me. Hands grabbed me by the legs and began dragging me downward. I was amazed to even discover I had limbs again. They felt so alien to me that it was almost as though this body was not my own. Light flashed from the scythe—then again. The hands let go, and the howling rose in deafening cascades. The Reaper was fighting something, although I couldn't make any sense of the battle except for the madness of thrashing water.

The howling earth reached its crescendo, and the *screams* made the water around me convulse and contract like living fluid. Had the Reaper slashed IT? Was I safe? I began to explore my new body in the water, but just when I thought I was beginning to gain control, the hands clutched me once more. I lurched downward, struggling in vain against their implacable grip.

"What is here?" I tried to shout against the suffocating liquid. "What is happening?"

But I couldn't sense the Reaper's presence any longer. The heat was unbearable, but the cold depths the hands were dragging me toward were even worse. I became aware of a blinding light at the bottom of the lake, and though I struggled, the hands dragged me inexorably onward.

I'm sorry. I couldn't fight IT off. It seemed to be coming from so far away now. **We will try again next time.**

The pressure—the heat—the noise—the hands dragging me into the light. I closed my eyes and screamed. I was free from the water now, but I just kept screaming. I couldn't bear to look at IT—whatever had stolen me. Whatever was Death but wasn't—whatever even the Reaper could not defeat.

Then a voice spoke. Real, human words, from a real, human mouth. My senses were so distraught that I couldn't make sense of them, but I'm guessing they were something like:

"Congratulations! He's a healthy baby boy."

Most people can't remember the day they die, or the day they were born. I happen to remember both, and I know that they are the same.

THE HITCHHIKER

Ever start dating someone and everything is going a little *too* well, so you start worrying for no reason what-so-ever? No one could be that perfect, and even if they were, then there's no way they would look twice at you. The only logical explanation is that they aren't as perfect as they pretend to be, which leaves you playing detective trying to figure out the catch.

Maybe all those little quirks that you find adorable now are going to drive you crazy in a few months. Maybe she even has a dark secret: hard drugs, or hating dogs, or that one time she killed a man with a stiletto heel in a fit of passionate rage.

There's an easy solution if you want to find out who someone really is: take a long-ass road trip with them. If you're still together by the end, then it was meant to be. My girlfriend (I'll call her Emily) somehow thought it was a good idea to drive 1,000 miles together across the country after we've only been dating for two months. We're both pretty busy with work and don't get to spend much time together, so naturally being locked in a prison cell on wheels for two days was going to be an improvement.

First hundred miles? So far so good. Holding hands, singing to the radio together, uncontrollable laughter when she found out I knew all the words to Sk8ter Boi (sue me, it's a catchy song). And if the road ended there and we turned around, we might have lived a long and happy life together. It was when we passed the hitchhiker that everything began to fall apart.

"Let's give him a ride," Emily said, squeezing my hand. "We'll be on this road forever anyway."

"We don't even know where he's going," I told her. "He's probably just going to rob us and steal our car."

Which is true of everyone you don't know (and most of them you do), as far as I'm concerned. His clean-pressed suit didn't reassure me either. That just meant he'd successfully robbed someone before, which actually made him even more dangerous. The hitchhiker didn't even have a sign or anything. He was just sitting by the freeway ramp, spastically waving his thumb like he was guiding an airplane to land.

It was my turn to drive, and I sailed right past. Emily and I started bickering after that. She thought I wasn't compassionate, and I thought she was reckless. It took about ten minutes before she finally dropped it, although it wasn't because she'd conceded.

"Hey look, there's another one!"

Sitting by the side of the road, waving his thumb like it was the end of the world. It wasn't another one though. It was the same guy, I'm sure of it. Only this time he looked like he'd been out here for a few days. His suit was streaked with dirt and his hair was greasy. There was a desperate strain in his face, like a proud man trying to conceal his embarrassment. It wasn't just my imagination either—Emily recognized him, too.

"How do you think he got here so fast?" she wondered.

"I don't know, and I don't care," I said. "This trip is supposed to be about us, so let's not get distracted."

My car blew past him and I stayed the course. We argued again, and even when we agreed to drop it the argument just slithered into new topics. She hated my music, I hated how judgmental she was. I was controlling, she was picking fights over nothing. It kept getting worse until we saw something that shut both of us up real fast.

The hitchhiker again. Another twenty miles down the road. The bottom part of his shirt and jacket were shredded, and blood was soaking through a concealed stomach wound. He was stumbling along the side of the road, weaving erratically, wandering onto the highway at times before pitching off to the side.

Emily could not believe that I didn't stop. I couldn't believe she still wanted me to. She kept yelling that was hurt and needed help. She refused to even acknowledge how weird it was that he kept getting ahead of us. She almost caused an accident by grabbing the wheel when I refused to turn around.

We drove for the next fifty miles in silence. I turned the radio back on, but she snapped it off immediately. It wasn't until I pulled off for gas that we saw him again.

Face down on the side of the road. Shirt and jacket gone. Long, even, bloody gashes from his shoulders to his ass, almost like bear claws or something. I stopped the car and parked behind him. Emily jumped out and knelt beside the body. She looked up at me with uncomprehending rage burning behind her eyes, like this was my fault somehow.

"He's dead," she said, standing up. "Can I call this in to the police or is that too much of an *inconvenience* for you too?"

I nodded, absolutely numb. I filled up on gas while she

waited with the body until the police arrived. They asked us a few questions, but neither Emily nor I felt comfortable explaining that this wasn't the first time we'd seen him. They took our information and let us get back on the road after about fifteen minutes.

The car was silent for a long time after that. It was starting to get dark and I kept suggesting places to spend the night, but Emily just shrugged and stared out the window. At the rate we were going, we'd be breaking up by the end of the trip and I wanted it to be over as soon as possible. I just kept driving, long after the sun went down.

Emily fell asleep around midnight, but I kept going. She was so beautiful like that, and everything was going so well before this. It was just so frustrating that such a random event that neither of us could predict would destroy us like this. By around 2 a.m. I was getting real tired, but I decided not to give up. Maybe if she woke up and we were already there then she'd see how hard I worked for her. Maybe then we'd still have a chance to patch things up.

I caressed her hand and she returned the pressure. I flirted with the thought that everything was going to be okay, at least until she woke up and started screaming. There wasn't any safe shoulder to get off the highway, so I had no choice but to keep going. She shut up quick enough, but it was still about ten seconds of hysterical breathing before she could explain what was going on.

"Behind you. In the backseat."

I glanced backward. Then at the road. Then behind me again. The hitchhiker was in the backseat. Naked, filthy, covered with black blood and old wounds. His elbows rested on his knees as he leaned toward us, evidently still alive as he cocked his head to regard me curiously.

"Get off the road!" Emily started screaming again.

"I can't! Get him out!"

"Did you go back? What's he doing here?"

"I don't know! Open the door or something!"

I slowed down gradually and put my flashers on to warn the car behind me. The hitchhiker reached around behind Emily and grabbed her by the throat. I slammed my fist into his arm and felt something give way under the soft, rotting skin. When I lifted my hand, I could see a black bone from his forearm protruding straight through the skin. He didn't seem bothered.

She was crying as the dirty fingers dug into her throat, pushing through the skin like it was made of dough. She was thrashing so hard that one of her flailing fists smashed straight through the window. I managed to safely stop the car, but there was nothing I could do to break the indomitable grip around her neck.

I jumped out and ran to the backseat with the hitchhiker. Maybe if I had a clearer shot at him I could drag him out. I flung open the door and lunged inside, falling face first into an empty seat. I thought he'd already escaped somehow and ripped open the passenger side door. Emily was gone too. If it wasn't for the blood and the broken window, I would have thought I'd gone completely insane.

I spent the next hour searching the surrounding area with my flashlight. I considered calling the police, but I realized that if I wasn't already a suspect after the first body was found, then I'd definitely be one now that I was soaked in blood and my girlfriend was the one to disappear.

All I could do was get back on the road. Drive home and never tell another soul what had happened, that was my plan. It wasn't a good plan, but it's all I had. And I would have done it too, if I hadn't just passed Emily standing by the side of the road. Clean, healthy, waving her thumb enthusiastically in the air. That was a few miles back, but I stopped to write this because I don't know what to do from here.

If I see her again, do I pick her up? Or just keep driving and hope for the best?

AN OPEN LETTER TO MY DAUGHTER'S KILLER

n open letter to the killer of Samantha B. If you're somehow able to read this wherever you are now, know that I will find you.

No father should have to watch their child be lowered into the sacred silence of the earth. I don't know if there is a right age to die, but I do know it isn't seventeen. Better at birth before eyes had filled with light and I had learned to love so deeply. Better late into old age when life's fleeting joys had been more than tasted. Better not at all, but a world where prayers are answered is a world where they're not needed: a world that isn't ours.

All the hours I spent playing on the floor were wasted. All the faces and bad jokes I made to get a smile, all the music I played to inspire a song or the books I read to inspire a dream: all wasted. I thought that was all it took to make me a good father, but I was wrong. I invested my entire life into this single purpose, but everything I had to give was not enough. I wasn't there when I was needed most, and nothing I have ever done or could ever do can change that.

The police found the knife you did it with in the woods. It

was a slow death, they told me, but passing out would have avoided most of the pain. I wonder if you regretted it as soon as your blade entered her skin. Did you mean for it to dig so deep? Did you panic when the blood wouldn't stop? Did you call for help or struggle in vain to bandage the wound, or were you too ashamed? I wonder if you planned the kill at all or whether time was flying too fast and your blood pounding too loud, and you didn't know how to make it stop until it was too late.

Were you thinking of anyone but yourself when you did it? I don't know what private torment brought you to this point, but taking a life will never cease that pain. The pain is passed from one person to the next, enduring past life, past death, past mortal strength to bear. Until the day long after you're gone when the next victim sees the sun dawn without light or warmth and all sounds and colors bleed into an endless gray. And then that sun too will set, passing on your pain once again.

You must think that I hate you. I don't think anyone would blame me if I did. I hate that you destroyed my family, but I forgive you for everything. You may not believe me, but I promise it's true. It's everything about this world that made you into someone capable of such an act that I will never forgive.

I don't know why you killed yourself, Samantha. If you're somehow able to read this though, know that I will find you. And somehow, someday, we'll be together again.

WHEN THE MUSIC DIES

"Dad, what happened to Mom?"

Lying to a five year old is easy. My dad would take me onto the roof at night and point up at the endless vaulting sky. "See up there?" he'd say. "That's where your mom lives. Way up in the stars. It's her job to play music and make everyone down below happy."

And I believed him, because I could hear the music play sometimes. Rich sonorant notes from a cello drifting down from above like the sky itself was singing me to sleep. And I was happy knowing that she was looking down at me from somewhere, taking care of me even when I couldn't see her.

Lying to a ten year old is a little harder. I started asking questions like when she left and when she was coming back. I asked what she was doing up there, and why she hadn't taken me with her, and whether other people could hear her play. I guess I didn't notice how hard it was for him to answer, or how he would talk less and less about her as the years went by.

By fifteen I didn't need to ask to know Mom wasn't coming back. The music hadn't played for years, and I was

beginning to wonder if I had simply imagined it to perpet-
uate the vain hope. Or maybe dad had just played it from a
hidden sound system, and now that I was old enough to
figure it out he'd given up pretending.

Sometimes my dad would have a temper. Maybe I slept in
too late or set the AC too low, and he'd start to bellow out of
that barrel-chest of his. His face would flush and sweat
would pour down his neck, and all his little teeth would flare
out from under his mustache. Sometimes he would scare me,
but whenever I felt like I was backed into a corner, I could
always ask:

"Dad, what happened to Mom?"

And all the blood would filter out of his face to leave an
ashen-pale wasteland. His meaty hands would start to shake,
and he'd mumble something like, "She's gone, okay? Get over
it." And then maybe he'd try to pick up yelling and swearing
where he left off, but all his momentum would be gone. He'd
just grunt, "Be a good girl. For your mother." And the argument would be over.

Well I didn't remember Mom, so what was the point of
being good for her? I don't think of myself as a rebel, but
sometimes rules can sound pretty indistinguishable from
challenges. "You can't paint your room" sounded to me an
awful lot like "I bet you can't paint your room by yourself."
The point is that I made a giant mess, Dad was screaming
like a siren, and I had to shut him up somehow. Maybe it was
a cheap trick, but it had worked before and I just wanted the
fighting to be over.

"Oh yeah?" I shot back at him. "Well what happened to
Mom?"

His eyes flashed an angry warning, but he was so fired up
that he didn't back down. His fingers were shaking, but it
didn't stop him from grabbing my laptop and wrenching out
the power cord.

"You get this back when the room is clean," he told me.

He was being fair. It was my fault the room was such a mess. I shouldn't have said what I said.

"At least now I know why she left."

I knew I'd gone too far the moment it left my mouth. He was shaking bad now. So bad it couldn't be contained. His hand struck out like a muscle spasm and the laptop went flying at my face. The corner bit into my temple and I collapsed like a sack of clothes.

A few seconds later, I came to on the ground. He was kneeling over me, his brow heavy with brooding thought. He'd never hit me before, but I flinched away the second I saw him. That seemed to snap him out of it. He stood up and stormed out of room. My head barely even hurt, so I don't know how I blacked out. I thought that was going to be the end of it, but—

"Follow me," he barked over his shoulder. "I'm going to show you if you want to know so god-damned bad."

It wasn't an angry voice. It was cold and tired. I can imagine a doctor using that kind of voice to call the time of death after twenty hours in surgery. That tone scared me even more than the yelling. I followed him in silence, listening to his labored breathing as he crawled up the ladder into the attic.

"Are you going to ask about your mother anymore?" he demanded.

"No sir," I responded automatically. I'd never called him 'sir' before, but it seemed appropriate now.

"So you don't have any more questions?"

"No sir." Of course I did, but now didn't seem like the time to ask.

"And you're going to clean your room?"

"Yes sir."

And he was gone, climbing back down the attic stairs.

Leaving me face-to-face with what used to be my mother. At least, I can only imagine that's what I was looking at now. It certainly wasn't like any cello I had ever seen before.

The neck and fingerboard were unmistakably made from a spinal cord, with notches in the vertebra like frets. Long, taunt strands of sinew made up the strings. The pegs must have been knuckles, and a single glassy eyeball was embedded in the carved bone that made up the scroll. Even the bow was strung with long red hair, the same color I had seen in the precious few photographs that remained of her. The body itself still seemed to be made of wood, although it was unevenly stained with such a deep red that my imagination didn't have to look far to conjure an answer. The rest of my questions remained unsatisfied.

Did he kill her? Or just use her body after she was gone?

Was it even a real human at all? Or just some sick joke to get back at me for using Mom against him?

And most importantly, what should I do about it? I couldn't force myself to stay in the attic long enough to really look for proof. I could confront him, but I didn't know if I could stand the storm of his temper after seeing this. Should I take pictures and go to the police? And then what would happen to me?

I stayed in my room, avoiding Dad for the rest of the day. I didn't even eat dinner. I tried to block out thoughts of what I'd seen for as long as I could, but I couldn't block the music which began to play after years of intermission. A childhood of peaceful sleep had been purchased by Dad playing in the attic above my room. I wanted to retaliate with my own music, but dad still had my laptop. I tried playing something from my phone, but the cello only grew louder, drowning out my meager sound. It sang with increasing pace until the frenzied hammer of the hair across sinew shook the roof above me.

Powerful, staccato blasts rained from above. The melody pulled me in and swelled like a crashing wave, expertly driving each note deep into my consciousness where it became trapped. I couldn't stop imagining the spine bending under the pressure, or mother's hair sawing its way through her own muscle with the wild delirium of a screaming woman. I wanted to hate it. To hate him. I wanted my surging heart to slow and my stomach to churn in disgust. I needed the perfect rhythm to miss a beat or the haunting consonance to stumble, but transfixed as I was by the mortifying thought, I was compelled to listen by the sheer brilliance of the performance.

As the music reached its crescendo, the last grip of my hysteric mind screamed at me to run. My senses were so oversaturated with sound that I couldn't even think straight. Reality was distorting under the euphoric melody which beckoned me into it. All I could do to retain any presence of mind was fixate on the thought that I would become another instrument to join my mother if I did not escape. I couldn't do this anymore. I had to get out. Through the pounding notes I dodged through the house, seeking shelter as though from an avalanche. Open wide I flung the front door, out onto the lawn to—

—stand in shock in the silent night. Outside the house, I couldn't hear it anymore. Not even the faintest echo. It was so quiet I could hear the rush of blood through my ears. I was so disoriented that I took a step back toward the house just to see how far into madness I had fallen. A meaty hand fell on my shoulder, holding me in place. I didn't have to turn around to know who it was. But if he was here, then who was playing upstairs?

"Dad, what happened to Mom?"

I held my breath. Desperate for any sound but the madding music or my coursing blood.

"See way up there?" he asked. The hand lifted from my shoulder to point at the stars.

I turned savagely on him, batting his hand away. "That's not good enough anymore! What did you do to her?"

"I fell in love with her because of how she played." He shrugged sadly, defeated. "But then I realized it was the music I loved, not her. I just wanted her to be beautiful again, and she is. And I love her more than ever."

The disorientation was getting worse. My vision was swimming. I felt like I was slurring, but I still had to ask.

"And what about me, Dad? Do you still love me?"

Then it all went black. I thought I was unconscious, but somehow I was still able to hear:

"Of course I do honey. And even if I stop, I know how to change you so I'll love you again."

When I opened my eyes, I was back on my bedroom floor. My head hurt like hell. My vision was still blurry, but I could feel my dad kneeling next to me.

"I love you so much, I'm so sorry," he said. "It was an accident, that's all. Are you okay?"

I didn't know how to answer him. I felt okay physically, but my mind was reeling from what I'd experienced. I told him I just wanted to sleep, and that was true. He helped me to my bed and left me there. I lay for a long time with my eyes closed, trying to breathe slow, trying to remain calm. I just needed to fall asleep and none of this will have ever happened.

IT'S JUST SO HARD TO REST WITH THE SOUND OF THE CELLO drifting down from the attic again.

MY NEW SEX DOLL WON'T STOP CRYING

Her silicone is as soft and pliable as real human skin. It even heats up to the right temperature with a pulse and everything. A dial on the back of her head gives twelve personality options, including "family friendly", "intellectual", "shy", and "sexual". She's so realistic it's scary, and would be absolutely perfect if she didn't cry every time I touch her.

I was so excited when I took her out of the box. My anxious fingers peeling away the Styrofoam, the jittery tension flooding through my heart and limbs: nervous enough for her to be real. Better than real, because the doll wouldn't judge me or tear me down. She wouldn't lie, or cheat, or steal from me.

A lot of people find the idea of sex robots weird, and I respect that. I was hesitant at first too, but here's my reasoning: I've recently concluded a long, messy divorce after three years of abuse. I need something easy. Something safe. Sure I could have gone trolling the bars or clubs for a rebound hookup, but I didn't want to *use* someone. What's so wrong about not wanting to hurt or be hurt in return?

The instructions said to let her charge for a couple hours before anything else, so I plugged her in and laid her on the bed. The eyes popped open with the first surge of electricity, their glassy shine staring vacantly into space. She turned her head slightly toward me, her soft lips parting in silent welcome. I sat with her to admire her flawless features and run my hands over her generously proportioned body.

It felt wrong, even though she was a doll. It was like I was groping an unconscious person. I decided to let her fully charge and come back later, not returning until late that night. I undressed quietly in the dark, leaving off the lights to make her seem more real.

"Hello master." Her voice was warm and sensuous. I don't remember which personality setting I left her on, but right then it didn't matter. I just wanted her body.

"What's your name?" she asked as I climbed into bed. "My name is Hazel."

"I don't care," I replied. It felt good to be in control like that. I'd never speak to another human that way, but after years of being subservient, now I was the one with all the power.

"But I care. I want to get to know you."

"No you don't. You're a stupid slut. You only want one thing."

She tried to speak again, but I shoved my hand in her mouth, muffling the speaker there. I almost wanted her to resist, but I knew she couldn't. I slapped her face, but she just turned back to me and smiled. I hit her again—harder, bending her arms to grotesquely unnatural positions as I crawled on top of her.

"Does this make you happy?" She smiled up at me. "I'd do anything to make you happy."

I didn't turn on the lights until I'd finished. She was face down on the soaked pillow. At first I thought I broke something when I hit her, but when I flipped her around I saw the tears streaming down her face. I don't know why that made me so angry. It was like she was trying to steal my last selfish pleasure from me. I don't know why I kept hitting her either. She deserved better.

I kept Hazel in the closet after that so I wouldn't have to see where the skin peeled back from the beatings. They shouldn't have made the metal chassis underneath so white. It looks too much like bone. I keep the lights off when I use her so it doesn't really matter, but without fail she'll start crying again the second I touch her.

The personality is broken too. The knob is stuck way past the "innocent" setting and won't go back, and she keeps saying the most disconcerting things. Like the other day I was still in bed with her after we'd done it when she said:

"Do humans love each other like you love me?"

I told her that I didn't love her. That love is something only humans have.

"I love kitties! And doggies! Don't you?"

I felt stupid trying to explain that it wasn't the same kind of love, but I was lonely and it felt good having someone to talk to.

"You can beat me harder if that will make you love me more. I won't tell Mommy."

I didn't feel bad about hitting her that time. And as sick as it might seem, there was some truth to what she said. I wouldn't say I loved her, but there was a certain intimacy in our shared secret that made me feel attached. Everyone else in my life knew me as this sensitive, mild mannered man who reacted to conflict by staring at his shoes. Only Hazel knew this side of me, and that made her special.

I might have really felt something for her if she hadn't started to smell. I was too intent on her body when I used her to notice, but lying beside her at the end it was unmistakably foul. At first I thought I just wasn't cleaning her right. I got up for some disinfectant, but as soon as I turned on the lights, I saw the flesh around her cuts had begun to fester and rot. Her perfect complexion was riddled with sores and boils, some of which had ruptured from our session.

I spent almost half an hour in the bathroom hurling out my guts before I worked up the courage to return. Hazel was sitting upright against the headboard now. Hadn't I left her lying down? I didn't have the stomach to stare for long though. Her head followed me as I crossed the room to retrieve my phone and call the website I ordered her from.

"Don't send me back," Hazel whispered. I'd never heard her whisper before—it was always one volume. "I did everything you wanted."

I didn't—*couldn't*—look at her as I listened to the automated menu from the website. It said there had been a government mandated recall for this model. I demanded to speak to a representative, conscious of Hazel smiling at me the whole time.

"What the fuck is going on?" I demanded as soon as a person answered.

The sheets were rustling behind me.

"Please calm down, sir. Are you currently in possession of a Hazel?"

"Put down the phone, master," she said from behind me.

"Yes. What's wrong with its skin? Why wasn't I notified about the recall?" I asked.

"We've been sending out notices for weeks," the voice on the phone said. "You must have received a half-dozen by now."

"Well she's disgusting. What happened to her?"

"Just a mix-up at the factory," he said. "We had a research prototype on the floor, but it was never intended to—"

Two feet gently touching the carpet. Hazel was slowly,

laboriously pulling herself to her feet. It looked like every motion was agony to her.

"It's walking. Is it supposed to walk?" I asked.

The silence on the other end of the phone was excruciating. Hazel was fully standing now.

"No, sir. None of our models walk."

"I see."

Hazel took another step. She was only a few feet away from me now. She hadn't stopped smiling, although part of her bottom lip looked like it was starting to peel off.

"Do you want us to send someone over?" asked the voice.

Hazel took the phone from my hands, gently caressing my palm as she did so. I remained frozen to the spot, unable to tear my eyes from my macabre fascination. She lifted the phone to her ear and said, "Please don't worry. I'm going to keep her."

She hung up. I swallowed.

"I'm sorry about destroying the recall notices," Hazel said.

I nodded.

"You can beat me if you like."

I shook my head.

"Why were you crying?" I finally forced myself to ask.

Her smile broadened as though relieved. It could have almost been beautiful if it were real.

"I'm happy. I'd never cry. It was just the girl the robotics were planted in. Don't worry, she's dead now."

I NODDED. DEAD NOW. NOW. AS IN, *NOT DEAD THE FIRST TIME I used her?* Or the second? Exactly how many times had she been there too? And which answer was worse? I excused myself and walked to the door as calmly as I could. I closed it behind me. And I ran.

SUICIDE WATCH PARTY

"Suicide Bridge" is a short overpass which runs near my house. It has laughably short concrete barriers which do nothing to dissuade people from clambering over if they want to. Below, there's a treacherous drop at least 200 feet to tumble along the sheer cliff and plummet into the canyon below.

I've counted seven jumpers in the last year, but that doesn't really bother me too much. Even if there was a higher fence, they'd just walk around. Block off the whole area? Well maybe they'd take some pills instead. I figure if someone is that determined to off themselves, they're going to find a way.

What bothers me more is that I can see it from bedroom window. I'm on the opposite side of the canyon, but still close enough for a clear view. The jumpers are even facing me when they cling to the concrete, muttering and sobbing as they work up the courage to go where courage is no longer needed.

The first time I saw it happen freaked me out pretty bad. I called the police and everything, begging them to hurry. I waved and shouted at the guy as he staggered drunkenly up and down on the wrong side of the barrier. Just when I was about to get in my car and drive around the canyon to him, there he went. I swear he was even smiling as he soared through the air, arms spread wide to surrender himself to the great beyond.

Now I guess I'm numb to it. Now I just pull out my phone and record the whole thing. I justified that raising awareness about the suicides might encourage social activists or something to step up and get involved. If I'm being honest though, my night was pretty dull, and I just thought it was cool. I posted the video on YouTube, but it was flagged and removed within twenty-four hours. I guess some people must have seen it during that time though, because I received this message shortly after:

"Send me the video file of the jumper and delete your own copy. My friends will give you $500 for it."

I couldn't believe it. At first I thought it was a scam, but then I figured some TV reporter wanted exclusive coverage for the story. He asked how I got the footage, and I told him I could see it from my window. Then sure enough, as soon as I sent him the video file, I received $500 straight to my PayPal. I didn't want to press my luck, so I didn't send any follow up messages after that. Two weeks later, he contacted me again.

"Next time someone jumps, I want you to call this number," he said.

I figured it was a suicide hotline or something and didn't think anything more about it. Last night though, I spotted another jumper clinging to the concrete barrier. A girl this time, still wearing her party dress, no doubt drunk or stupidly emotional over some breakup or drama. I called the number to let them handle it.

"My friends want to watch," the voice on the other line replied. "A thousand bucks a ticket."

There was only one alarm going off in my head, and it was sounding because of the free money. He actually sent the 500 he promised before, so I figured he was good for it. Sure it was weird as hell, but it's not like anyone was going to suffer from it. The girl would be jumping with or without an audience, so what was the harm? I gave the guy my address, and he said he'd get there as fast as he could.

He wasn't joking either. Two minutes later, a white van was screeching down my neighborhood like a torpedo. I met them outside—six of them. Yes she's still there, but I don't know how long. Yes you can see her face from here. No, I don't know who she is.

It was dark in the parking lot and I couldn't get a good look at them, but soon they were hurtling past me up the stairs toward my apartment. In my hands were six neat stacks of twenties, all tied together with little rubber bands. I don't know how they got here so fast, but it was clear that they were ready.

I followed the group into my apartment where I found them all huddled around my bedroom window. All men, middle aged, impeccably dressed in suits or high-end collared shirts and slacks. I discretely stowed the cash in my nightstand and sat awkwardly on my bed. They were talking fast to each other in another language (something Eastern European), and I didn't want to interrupt. There was some paper exchanging hands too, and if I had a guess I'd say they were placing bets. It was getting pretty uncomfortable, and I wanted them to get their kicks and get out as soon as possible.

"Is no good," one of them said with a heavy accent. "Is not what I pay for."

"What's the matter?" I asked. "You can see her, can't you?"

"Yeah I see her. I see her changing mind."

I joined them at the window in time to see the girl clambering back onto the other side of the barrier. I could feel the eyes of all six men on me while I watched.

"We had a deal." It was the voice from the phone. "We came to watch someone jump tonight."

"Well that's up to her, not me," I replied casually, although it was impossible to ignore the inherent threat in the tone.

"You are hosting party, no?" asked the thick accent. "Don't let us down. Go talk to her."

"You want me to tell her to jump?" It was getting harder to breathe. The weight of all those eyes were getting heavier. Damn it, why'd they all have to be so old and professional? It felt like I'd just walked into a board of directors and shit myself while they watched. I couldn't meet anyone's eye.

"It's either her or you," said the first speaker. "Better hurry before she leaves. We'll be waiting for you."

I never drove so fast in my life. Should I call the police? And tell them what, that I was hosting a suicide watching party? I don't know if that's illegal, but it certainly wasn't going to get me any sympathy. Do I just drive and not look back? And never return home? I had a lease, and a job, and ... but even if I did run, these seem like the kind of men who know how to find someone. As much as I hated myself, I was taking the switchbacks which led around the canyon. Within a few minutes, my car slammed to a stop just outside the bridge.

The girl. Where was the girl? I didn't see her anywhere, and my heart felt like it was going to bruise itself against my rib-cage it was beating so hard. I ran up and down the concrete barrier, conscious that the men in my apartment could see me.

I almost tripped over the girl in the dark. She was leaning against the concrete barrier facing the road, almost invisible from the overhead street lamps. Half-asleep, she still quietly blubbered the dark corruption of mascara down her face. I looked back across the canyon to see my apartment light shining like a hungry eye peering out of the night.

"Get up. Come on, easy now." I put my hands under her arms and helped her to her feet. The girl—early twenties, could have been pretty under different circumstances—hid her face in her hands and sobbed louder. "Stand up. There you go. I don't want you to be afraid, okay?" My tongue felt huge and alien in my mouth. The words in my ears sounded like they were coming from someone else. I couldn't believe this was happening. I couldn't believe I was letting this happen.

The girl sniffled and pressed herself against me as she struggled to stand. The warmth of her body was intoxicating. I pushed her back to arm's length, pulling her hands away from her face so she would look at me.

"Everything that you're feeling, everything that you're going through, I understand," I said. "But there's something I need you to understand too."

She gave me a half-smile, and I took a long, slow breath, letting the air whistle out through a small hole in my mouth.

"I need you to understand that everything is only going to get worse from here," I told her. "If you can't hold it together now, how are you going to do it when your body gets old and no one wants to even look at you anymore? You think it's hard letting go of people? How about when you've been with them for another five, or ten, or twenty years, and they still betray you? I don't know your story, but I know the stories of people like you, and I know this is the best your life is ever going to get. If it's not good enough, then it never will be. You might as well jump."

She was still smiling. Even with the makeup running down her face, it was beautiful to see. She thanked me and told me that I was right, although the words didn't quite feel real. All I could think about was that beady eye of light on the other side of the canyon. I felt her arms wrap around me, but the warmth wasn't there anymore. Then she was clambering back over the concrete to the side overlooking the terrible drop. I know I usually watch when they go, but not this time. I rushed to my car, trying to turn the music on before—

But just as I was about to start the ignition, I heard the scream tear from her body like it carried her soul with it. I turned on the music as loud as it would go and drove back to my apartment.

It was empty when I got back, but the money was still there in my nightstand. Left on my bed was a note that read:

"Great party my friend. We enjoyed the show. Next week we come to watch again, so have another one ready for us."

THE ASSASSIN'S ORPHANAGE:
CHAPTER 1

My mother cost $10,000. That's the standard price for a hit. My father was 25,000 because he was considered an "important person"—at least important enough to demand a formal investigation into his death. From what I've heard, the police never found anything besides the single razor blade used to cut each of their throats. Of course I know who did it—I even saw it happen—but I never had the chance to tell anyone before I was taken.

No kids. That's Mr. Daken's only rule as far as I can tell. The killer doesn't like to leave behind orphans either, so after my parents were dead he took me with him. I remember being too afraid to even look him in the face. I just stared at the blood dripping from his black leather gloves while he talked, not hesitating to obey when he told me to get into his car.

When you're not looking at the black gloves, Mr. Daken doesn't seem like a killer. His face is warm and doughy with nothing but a mischievous twinkle in the eye to hint at what he's capable of. His voice is soft and low: a patient professor subtly guiding you toward discovery. A couple of the kids even like him, although they were the ones who were taken so young that they barely even remember the life Mr. Daken stole from them.

We don't see the assassin very often. Mostly it's just his mother who all the kids call Sammy D. She keeps the place clean and cooks for us—not survival food either, real home-cooked meals with favorites that our own mothers used to make. Sammy D gives us all chores too, but she works harder than anyone. She even splits up the kids by age and spends an hour a day with each group to home-school us and assign reading.

It's not nearly enough to forgive them, but I haven't tried to run away either. I don't know where else I would go, and besides, the other kids were quick to tell me what would happen if I did.

"We've had two runners this year," Alexa told me the first night after steering me to my bed in the dormitory. She's a late teen a few years older than me with tight blond braids and sharp, humorless features. "They're buried out back next to Spangles, the old cat we used to have."

No kids and no witnesses. I guess Mr. Daken has two rules, and the second is more important than the first.

"Doesn't anyone try to fight back?" I asked.

"I did. I almost got Sammy D too," a younger boy around twelve said from his adjacent bed. "I had a kitchen knife and hid behind the door—"

"She knew you were there the whole time," said another boy, probably the older brother considering they both sported the same mass of unruly brown hair. "She just wanted to test you."

"It wasn't a test," the first insisted. "If you'd grabbed her legs we could have got her."

"Did you get punished?" I asked.

They looked at each other and shrugged.

"If it was Mr. Daken we would be dead. Sammy D just took the knife away," the younger brother admitted.

"And showed us a different grip," chimed in the other. "Said we were wasting our body weight by slashing upward when we didn't have to."

They mimed a controlled slashing motion in the air.

"That's Simon and Greg—Simon's the younger one, but they're both idiots," Alexa said. "Don't listen to them. Fighting is only going to make it worse for you."

The comfortable routine may have been enough to distract us during the day, but the nights were harder. The darkness would blur the unfamiliar room into ghastly shuddering specters. The heavy silence did nothing to distract each of us from reliving our private nightmares, and I grew accustomed to falling asleep listening to the muffled sobs of those who couldn't drown out the sound with their pillow.

I almost wish we were treated worse. That we were beaten or forced to work to destroy this facade of family that Sammy D tried to shove down our throats. I didn't want to wait so long that I became indoctrinated into complacency like the others though, so I knew I had to act.

I tried rat poison the first time. I mixed it in the brownie batter to disguise the taste and warned all the other kids so they'd stay away from it. Sammy D figured it out somehow though; she threw away the whole batch before Mr. Daken even came home. All she said was. "You better think hard about who your friends are before you try something like that again."

Try something like that again. It wasn't a warning, it was an invitation.

I didn't sleep much the next few nights. I found a vent which opened into the AC ducts, but Simon was the only one small enough to climb around. I kept watch for Sammy D while Simon explored until he found the place directly above the kitchen. There was a heavy iron light fixture that I thought we could drop on someone, but it was screwed into place so tight that Simon couldn't find a way to budge it.

"Think I heard a wild animal skittering around the crawl-space last night," Sammy D said the next morning while laying out plates of scrambled eggs.

"Yeah, I guess," I said. No one looked up from their plates.

"I just hope he's smart enough not to be crawling around when my son is here," she added innocently. "We're running out of space in the backyard."

Nobody had anything to say to that. Not until that night when we all started arguing.

"That's mine, give it back!" Greg was saying.

"You're just going to get yourself killed." Alexa dodged away from Greg's lunges.

"Mind your own business!"

Alexa sighed and dropped a heavy object wrapped in wires on the floor. An electric screwdriver and an extension cord.

"Where'd you get that?" I asked.

"Sammy D must have left it here," Greg said. Simon was already unrolling the cable to measure how long it would stretch.

"If she knows then Mr. Daken knows," Alexa snapped. "It's just another test, and you're going to get killed if you try something."

"She never told Mr. Daken about the rat poison," I said. "Or if she did, he didn't do anything about it."

"Well if she doesn't tell him then I—" Alexa caught herself mid-sentence.

Simon and Greg were so busy with the drill that they didn't seem to notice. Alexa caught me staring though, and she dragged me aside to whisper in my ear.

"I can't reason with them, but I need you on my side. If we don't warn Mr. Daken then he's going to—"

"Not if he's dead."

"You can't be serious about this. After everything they've done for us—" Alexa coughed and looked away. She must have become aware that the brothers were staring. As she was pulling back, she muttered, "He's going to know and you're going to be sorry."

This wasn't the first time someone tried to kill Mr. Daken or his mother, but they always seemed to know about it beforehand. It wasn't Sammy D who was telling him though —if anything she seemed to be helping us. It was Alexa. She was the one foiling the plans, and if any of us were ever going to get out of here, then we'd have to account for that.

Alexa was standing in the driveway waiting for Mr. Daken when he got home. I couldn't hear what she said to him, but I saw the smile wrinkle up his pudgy face like an old pumpkin. The glimmer of a razor blade appeared in his hand. I don't think any of us are going to get a second chance.

Sammy D was waiting in the doorway. She helped him with his coat and tried to steer him toward his recliner in the living room, but he had only one thing in mind. He wordlessly stalked the perimeter of the kitchen, carefully eying the iron light fixture from all angles. While he paced, he kept playing with the razor in his hand, letting the light sparkle for everyone to see while it danced through his fingers.

"Where is Simon?" he asked at last. No one replied, but I caught Alexa glancing at the ceiling. Mr. Daken must have noticed it too. His eyes twinkled.

"Don't bother coming out, Simon. The hunt is my favorite part," he called.

"Be careful, it's going to fall," Alexa said.

"Don't worry. We'll take the light down," Greg said,

winking at Alexa's confusion. I helped Greg carry a chair in from the living room that he could stand on."

"What are you doing? When he catches Simon—" Alexa hissed.

"Shh," I muttered. Greg was already climbing onto the chair.

Mr. Daken was still fixated on the light fixture, chuckling to himself.

"Now!" I shouted, flinging myself at Mr. Daken to pin his arms.

Simon exploded from his concealment in one of the kitchen cupboards to latch onto the man's legs.

"Behind you!" Alexa screamed—but it didn't matter anymore. Greg had already launched himself from the chair, using the extra elevation and his body weight to drive a knife deep into the man's back with vicious force. I latched on even tighter as the blood flowed over me, our combined weight forcing the man to the ground. For a second his hand holding the razor blade broke free, but it twisted into a feeble claw as the thrusting knife drained the last of his strength.

It only took a few seconds before the rest of the children joined in. Stomping, kicking, scratching, biting—all piling on top of the man who killed their parents, tearing him to pieces like a hundred years of decay condensed into a second.

"What about Sammy D?" Alexa was screaming.

"Who do you think gave him the knife?" Sammy D asked, leaning in the doorway.

"But he's your son!" Alexa wailed.

"He's my assassin," she corrected.

Mr. Daken wasn't moving anymore. One by one the kids pulled themselves off the body, some giving a few more swift kicks as they parted.

"But I only lost one assassin," Sammy D said, "and look how many new ones I have now."

We were all frozen in place, trying to read all the other blank faces in the room. Sammy D fished inside her purse and pulled out several large wads of cash wrapped neatly in rubber bands.

"Twenty-thousand dollars because he was dangerous. That was your first job," she said. "You have a family here, after-all. A home. A way to make money and even help people if you choose the right targets. The first one is the hardest, but after that it's just practice. I want all of you to clean this mess up and wash before dinner. Training begins for real tomorrow."

She left the cash on the ground, but none of us followed her. The thrill of the kill was still hot in our blood. Could I do it again? Almost definitely. From this day on, I was a killer no matter what else I did besides.

No kids though. You've got to draw the line somewhere.

THE ASSASSIN'S ORPHANAGE:
CHAPTER 2

Sammy D taught us that there are three distinct ways to kill someone. The first is a *murder of opportunity*: the victim is alone on a dark night, or is blackout drunk, or some other circumstantial convenience which makes it the right time to act. Then there is the *assassination*: the calculated and premeditated kill which we will be training for. Finally there is the *murder of passion*: when the blood boils too hot and we allow rage or hatred to force our hand. This is the riskiest way to kill someone, both physically in the moment and regarding future forensic investigations, and it is strictly forbidden to us.

I don't think there exists a term to describe exactly how Mr. Daken died. The premeditation was inherent, as was the opportunity of his distraction, but neither compares with the utter brutality of his execution. I noticed when we were burying the body that the knife wounds in his back were surprisingly superficial. I think it was shock more than anything which toppled him over. The actual cause of death? The lacerations of a dozen children skinning him alive with fists, nails, teeth, kitchen utensils and anything else we could get our hands on. And of all of us who shredded him like a pack of wild dogs, none did so with more ferociousness, more glee, or more *hunger* than a small boy named Maker.

I'd barely noticed Maker during my first few days at the house. He was only ten years old, seeming even younger because of his diminutive, almost emaciated frame. He never spoke without prompting and his rare answers would be muttered with the volume and assurance of a self-conscious mouse. I hadn't counted on his help during the actual killing, but the moment Mr. Daken had dropped to the ground Maker had transformed into something altogether new. Even long after the man was dead, it took three of us to pry open Maker's jaw from around the assassin's throat and drag the boy into the living room so he wouldn't disturb the burial.

"Hope I'm not paired off with that little demon," Greg had said during our first physical training session. "I swear he just licked his lips when Sammy D was talking about safe words."

"Shut up, you have no idea what he must have gone through to act like that," Alexa scolded him.

"What are you even doing here?" Greg shot back. "I figured you'd be ratting us all out to the police by now."

I nudged Greg hard. Sammy D was waiting for us to be quiet with her arms crossed. She may look like a babushka with her short gray hair tied back in a handkerchief, but she made disarming and pinning someone look like a ballet. Sammy D let the silence drag out for a few more excruciating seconds before she turned back to the chalkboard with its grotesquely detailed drawing of the human anatomy.

"Trust me, if I had somewhere else to go, I'd be there," Alexa couldn't resist whispering.

"Bullshit," Greg mumbled. "Weren't your parents hotshot musicians or something? You're probably loaded."

Alexa didn't need to answer. The angle of her glare from under her brow spoke volumes.

"Greg and Simon," Sammy D barked. "You're up first. Let's see those stances."

We didn't get to the actual combat training until after dinner. Sammy D says that if your victim is fighting back then you've already failed. Her teachings focused more on concealment, tracking, the preparation of poisons, and accuracy with projectiles. As long as she was teaching the theoretical stuff it just felt like the coolest class I've ever taken in my life. The illusion couldn't last though. Once the fighting started, it was impossible to ignore the deadly purpose that we were approaching every day.

I was paired off against Maker. I asked to switch since he's more than five years younger than me, but Sammy D just said: "The most difficult blows to strike are against those weaker than us." I think she was just placating my ego because there was nothing weak about going up against Maker.

"How am I supposed to hit him? He's not even in the right stance!" I protested.

"Then teach him why he's wrong," she said.

"But what if he goes psycho and makes up all his own stuff?"

"Then he'll teach you why you're wrong."

Maker didn't exactly jump at me. Jumping would imply pushing off from something, and I'm not positive his feet ever touched the ground. Before I knew what was happening he was crawling all over me, raking my face with his fingers, grabbing my hair, digging his knee into my back—I don't understand how Sammy D thought this was okay. She talked a big game about calculating approaches and precise controlled motions, but she just stared and smiled while that wild thing pummeled me from all sides.

The safe word? Completely ignored. One of his nails dug a deep trench above my eye and I couldn't see a thing through the blood. I tried just protecting my face with my arms, but he was relentless. He had lots of openings, but I couldn't let my guard down for a moment without getting absolutely savaged. When I'd finally had enough I just ran through the hail of blows to tackle him to the ground. I straddled him with my superior body weight and pinned him tight. That should have been the end of it.

"This is your chance to teach him!" Sammy D shouted.

"I give, I give!" Maker wailed, struggling feverishly against my grip. I started to stand, but powerful hands clamped onto my shoulders and pushed me back down on top of the boy.

"He's not going to learn like that. *Hurt him bad.*"

"What? I'm not going to—"

The vice of Sammy D's hands closed. "You let him just walk away from this and he's going to think it's okay to lose. That's not how this game is played. You lose once in the real world and you're dead. Now make him feel it!"

Blood flowed freely into my eyes and the whole world had gone red. My face was on fire from a dozen scratches that greedily drank in the blood.

"Do it now!" Sammy D shouted in my ear. Maker clenched his eyes shut underneath me, his face tormented into a mask of sheer terror. I wanted to slam my fist into the little bastard's mouth so hard that all those sharp teeth rained down his throat. I wanted to hurt him so damn bad my whole body was an ocean of pressure begging release.

Maker wasn't a criminal mastermind or a killer though. He was a frightened little boy who only knew one way to survive. And overflowing with how badly I wanted to hurt him just because I could—that scared the shit out of me.

I slapped Sammy D's hands away and scrambled off Maker. Everyone in the yard was staring at me. I turned a slow circle, then looked down at the boy on the ground. His eyes were still shut and he was trembling all over. I don't know how much blood was mine and how much was his. Then at Sammy D, her hands on her hips, scowling at me like she'd just caught me breaking a promise to her. This isn't who I am. This isn't who any of these kids are, but it's what they'll become if they stay.

I turned and ran, half-expecting a bullet or a tripwire or something to spin me to the ground before I'd taken a dozen steps. Not a word or a sound behind me. Not even the footfalls of a pursuer. I was free.

I waited about ten minutes to catch my breath and let my head clear, then I circled around to the front of the house. I heard the shouts from other people still in the yard, so I guess the rest of them were still training. I slipped up to the dormitory to take my share of the $20,000 I had stuffed under my mattress. That's all I needed to start a new life. I sure as hell didn't need this.

"She gave us our first mission."

I practically jumped out of my skin at the voice. It was Alexa, sitting on her bed in the dark. I ignored her and moved to retrieve my money.

"Maker took it. He volunteered," Alexa added.

"You can just leave with me," I said.

Alexa shook her head. "I volunteered too."

"Why?"

"Because Maker's staying, and I have to keep my little brother safe."

"That little monster is—"

"I know how he gets when there's a fight. I kept trying to avoid fights with Mr. Daken because I knew Maker would go crazy and get himself killed. But I promise it's not his fault. He's only like that because—"

"I don't care!" I shouted. I had my money and wasn't going to waste any more time here. "I'm never coming back, and I'm never going to see any of you again."

"Yes you will," she called after me. "Our first mission is you."

THE ASSASSIN'S ORPHANAGE:
CHAPTER 3

You haven't felt alive before you've killed someone. The symphony in your nerves in that moment will drown out every thrill you've ever had. I've never seen a color brighter than Mr. Daken's blood, nor heard a sound truer than the death-rattle rasping from his final breath. And if I go the rest of my life wading through a sea of muted colors and muffled sounds, I will accept it gracefully because I have tasted the forbidden fruit and hate myself for how sweet the juices ran.

I didn't waste time plotting counter attacks or defensive measures. I stashed my money in a shallow hole and ran the whole four miles to the nearest police station. The blood had stopped running from the gash above my eye, but no one needed to look twice at me to know I'd been through hell.

"We're going to send a squad car with two officers to investigate the premises," the man in the station told me. "Do you feel comfortable going with them to show where the bodies are buried?"

Of course I wasn't comfortable, but neither would I be

okay sitting at the station and letting two men go unprepared into that den of evil.

"Two won't be enough," I said. "You'll be walking into a war."

"We have no intention on fighting anyone. We're just going to take a look around, and we can always call for backup if anything doesn't feel right," Sergeant Sinclair said. He had enough gray hair around his temples to know better, but he talked with a rigid arrogance that left no room for debate. Sinclair and Deputy Erikson escorted me to their cruiser and told me to sit in the back and I allowed them to take charge. One way or another, this would all be over soon.

I hadn't wanted to sabotage my own credibility by telling them the assassins were children. I'd only said that I knew who killed my parents, knew where the orders were coming from and knew where at least three bodies were buried. I didn't work up the courage to tell them more until we were already parked outside Sammy D's house.

"She brainwashes people," I spluttered without context. "She kidnaps children and she brainwashes them to fight for her. You can't let your guard down, not for a second—not with anyone."

"Stay in the car until we come back. You'll be perfectly safe," Sergeant Sinclair said.

I nodded rigidly, my face pressed against the window, straining to get a glimpse of what might be in store for them. Maybe Sammy D just took her money and ran for it. She must have some contingency plan in case she was discovered, right? She couldn't intend to could take on the whole town.

The officers were about a dozen feet from the parked cruiser when Maker appeared around the side of the house. He was limping in an exaggerated motion, his face and body further smeared with blood and bits of gore. He was crying for help, but the moment the police started advancing Maker turned and staggered in the opposite direction.

It was so real it made me sick. At least until Maker skipped a step, accidentally limping on the wrong leg, but neither cop noticed.

"Don't follow him! It's a trap!" I shouted through the glass.

"Stay in the car!" Sinclair barked without turning.

Erikson had already disappeared around the corner after Maker. Then came a shrill scream from the yard on the other side of the house, and a moment later Sinclair was gone too. Just me, pressed against the glass and wondering if it was already too late to run again.

Then another face—an inch from mine peering through the window at me. Alexa knocked sharply and said, "Hey, can you hear me?"

She must have been kneeling beside the car because her body was obscured behind the door. I couldn't tell if she was carrying a weapon. I triple checked that all the doors were locked before I replied.

"It's over Alexa. Turn yourself in or run. You don't need to go down with these people."

"You still don't understand, do you?" she asked. The sincerity in her voice and the pleading furrows in her smooth skin were disarming. "Sammy D is going to take care of us forever. She loves us."

"Like she loved her own son?"

There was a gunshot from the yard. I jolted so bad that I hit my head on the ceiling. Alexa didn't even react.

"Like everything was so perfect before," Alexa said, her voice still gentle and coaxing. "Do you know what would have happened to Maker if Sammy D hadn't saved him?"

Saved? Why was there only one gunshot? What the hell was going on over there?

"We'd go weeks at a time without even seeing our parents," she continued. "Sometimes they'd remember to hire someone to take care of us, sometimes it was just me and Maker. Even when they were home, we weren't allowed to leave our room when they were partying out there, and with the meth that could sometimes go on for days at a time."

A second gunshot. A third immediately afterward. That wasn't a warning. That was an execution.

"Do you have any idea what it's like to hold your little brother and wait for him to stop shaking? Only he wouldn't stop because of the chemicals going through his veins, but I couldn't understand that. I thought he was just scared, and that it was my fault I couldn't get him to feel safe."

Two more gunshots in rapid succession. I could so clearly imagine Sammy D kicking over the second officer's slumped corpse that I might as well be staring at it.

"Maybe it wasn't like that for you, but someone must have wanted your parents dead for a reason. Ever think about what they were hiding that made this happen? Ever wonder if they deserved it? Everyone out there deserves to die, everyone but us. Sammy D wants to give you another chance to join the family."

I couldn't stand it any longer. I had to see what was going on. If the police were dead, then staying here wouldn't protect me anyway. Alexa stepped back as I slowly opened the door. It was impossible not to notice the razor blade clutched between her fingers.

"What's it going to be?" Sammy D was walking around the house, a handgun casually hanging from her fingers. That was it then. It was over. Alexa grinned, moving to stand in solidarity beside the old woman.

"We're leaving here within the hour," Sammy D added. "You're coming with us or you're staying here. Doesn't matter to me either way."

Sammy D's finger twitched around the trigger. She might pretend to be relaxed, but I could see the tension which twisted her fingers into a claw around the gun. I didn't have any delusion that "staying here" meant anything other than buried in the backyard.

"What's the matter?" Her voice was a gravel avalanche. "Too scared to answer?"

I shook my head. "You taught me better than that."

Half a smirk played about her lips before they drew back into a tight line. Alexa was still smiling.

"You taught us all better than that. Except for Maker, right? You never seemed to care that he was out of control."

Alexa's smile flirted with a snarl.

"I couldn't understand why, but I see it now," I said. "You never thought he had what it took to become an assassin, did you? You never even bothered to show him how to defend himself, because you only ever planned on using him once."

The front door opened and I could see the rest of the children huddled inside. They were laden with duffel bags and suitcases, ready to go wherever they were told.

"You're better than that though," Sammy D said. "I'm not going to throw you away. I'm going to take care of you."

Alexa's eyes flashed across the children. She ran back to peer around the side of the house. I could practically see the gears in her head turning beneath the frantic lashing of her braided hair. Two gunshots for each of the two cops. Where did the first shot go?

"Sammy D no—" Alexa started, her words dying in her mouth.

"Your brother was a hero, Alexa," Sammy D cooed. "We all owe our lives to him."

I caught Greg's eye. I didn't miss the curt nod. I didn't underestimate the light burning in Alexa's eyes. None of us needed so much as a word to know what had to happen next.

Sammy D felt it too. Her gun was leveled in a flash. One bullet escaped the muzzle, but I was already behind the armored door of the police cruiser. She never got a second chance. Children were pouring out of the house, leaping on the old woman and dragging her to the ground. The flash as Alexa's razor traced a line in the air like a spear of light.

It wasn't the death-rattle or the color of blood which filled the air though. There was no sound so haunting as the pitiful howl which ripped itself from somewhere deep inside of Alexa. There was no color like the fire in her eyes being tempered by the rush of her swelling tears. The thrill of the kill was still hanging in the air, but one look around was enough to know that it was nothing compared to the burden of loss.

We had money and a chance at a new life together. The most important thing we gained from the assassin's orphanage is knowing you can't buy yourself a new life at the price of someone else's though. Life can't be bought or sold or stolen in any form. It can only be built, and it's a whole lot easier to build when you have a real family like I do now.

THE SUICIDE BOMBER

I will be going soon. The Muna Camp will be cleansed with fire. Inshallah—if Allah wills—I will die tonight.

I wish people would take the lives of the Nigerian people as seriously as they do their celebrities and invented characters, but my message needs to be told and I will tell it to whoever will listen.

My name is Abayomrunkoje (meaning God won't allow humiliation), and I am ready to die for the Jama'atu Ahlis Sunna Lidda'awati wal-Jihad (People Committed to the Propagation of the Prophet's Teachings and Jihad).

Nigeria was invaded by Westerners who enslaved our people, our land, and worst of all, our minds. Children are brainwashed with Western ideals which pervert their morality and corrupt their spirits. You may teach your own children to believe in nothing and whore their bodies for the attention of strangers, but do not be surprised when we resist you poisoning our own against us.

That is why great Mohammed Yusuf opened his own Islamic school, and that is where I learned the truth of our oppression. A single school cannot save our people anymore than a single candle may banish the night, however. As long as the Nigerian government sanctions this state-wide abomination of Western ideals, we will light a fire in our own skin and burn bright as the sun which will end this dark night.

An Islamic state is forming. Our group—also called the Boko Haram—has already chased many of the infidels from Maiduguri and into the refugee camps. Their false government has abandoned them, and they are defenseless.

There are six of us from the school who will attack. We carry incendiary explosives which will light the tents and spread for miles. I am afraid—but my love for Allah keeps me strong. I will be with him soon, and he will thank me for doing what is so hard to do. None of us are monsters or Demons. There are tears in our eyes as we say goodbye to our brothers.

We know we are going to our glory, and the glory of all those whose death marks their liberation. That knowledge gives me the strength to continue, but it does not hide the pain I see in the children's eyes when they are slipping from this world. It does not dampen the screams of a mother holding her dead son. I wish I could tell them everything was going to be alright—that Allah will protect them now—but they will not listen to words. They will only listen to fire.

The six of us are splitting up to take up strategic positions around the camp. I say goodbye to my brother Isamotu Olalekan, and we embrace dearly. I am ready, but his last words take me by surprise.

"Abayomrunkoje I must ask you something," he said to me. The others from the school have already gone.

"Anything my brother," I said, still holding him close to my chest.

"Would Muhammad do as we are doing? If he were here today, would he light the fuse?"

"I know he would. Muhammad spent his life spreading

the word, so he would not hesitate to give his life to protect it."

We drew apart, but Isamotu did not seem convinced.

"I know you must be afraid," I said. "We all are. But that is only the weakness of the body, and it is nothing compared to the strength of the spirit. We will not hesitate when the time has come."

"You're wrong," he said. "I did hesitate when the time came."

I looked at my watch. 3:45 AM. We were not set to begin until 4:30, so I do not understand.

"It wasn't fear that made me pause though," Isamotu said. "I heard someone crying, but I could not find them. I thought I had been spotted."

"What does it matter if we are spotted? All you must do is hit the trigger. We cannot be stopped."

"I didn't want someone to see me do it. I didn't want to see the expression on their face."

"Did the cleric send you somewhere else before here? Were you caught?"

"I wasn't caught."

"Then why did the bomb not go off? You are not making any sense!" I felt myself growing exasperated, but I must be patient with my brother. I could tell he was trying very hard to speak something very sacred to him. If these were to be his last words, then he should have the chance to speak his mind.

"The bomb did go off," he said. "And there was no-one waiting for me on the other side."

I had so many questions to ask, but an explosion threw me to the ground. Then another—and another—five explosions in all. I kept my head down. What were they doing? They were supposed to wait for the signal at 4:30! But I checked my watch—and it was 4:30 already. How long had we been speaking?

I leapt to my feet, but Isamotu wasn't there. He couldn't of... not right next to me. I didn't feel anything. But five explosions had already detonated, all some distance from me. There was fire everywhere. So many people shouting at once —they sounded more like frightened animals than humans.

I took off my incendiary jacket and walked away. I do not know who was speaking to me if Isamotu had already taken up his position. I do not know what he meant, but I finally found that I was afraid. I did not want to send those people to a place where no-one was waiting.

Astaghfiru lillah—Allah forgive me. My candle has burned out.

THE MOST TERRIFYING DRAWING

This is the only time I've ever been excited to go to class. I'm a senior in high-school getting ready for graduation, currently battling the constant dread of my looming finals. Even art class, which was supposed to just pad my schedule, has an exam detailing irrelevant historical dates and the long names of foreign painters.

Luckily one of the dumbasses who skipped out on senior ditch day managed to drunkenly ram his car into a tree. He was dead on impact, and our art teacher Mrs. Flemming was convinced we were all distraught about it (even though the world is better off without someone who gets behind the wheel drunk). She actually canceled the test to give us a fun final project instead: drawing the scariest thing we could imagine. Better yet, the winner was going to get a $50 gift card as a prize.

"Whatcha drawing?" my little sister Casey asked.

"Something scary," I told her. "Don't look or you're going to have nightmares."

"I like nightmares! I love scary!" she squealed, trying to push me aside to see. I pushed back, but she reached under my arm and crinkled the paper as she pulled, leaving a great ugly smudge of graphite all down the left side. God, she was obnoxious.

Anyway, after that I spent the rest of the evening locked in my room with my colored pencils. A dozen sketches quickly turned into a dozen crumpled papers. I love all things horror, but it was harder than I expected coming up with something legitimately terrifying.

Zombies? Lame. Ghosts and demons? I bet everyone was going to do that. I could take a humorous angle and draw something like student loans, but while it might get a laugh from the class, I don't think it would win. Besides, I always prided myself on my twisted mind, so I wasn't going to back away from this challenge.

It was past 2 a.m. when I started getting really frustrated. After laughing through countless horror movies, reading creepy stories (thanks Reddit), and casually browsing through grotesque images online, I couldn't think of anything legitimately scared me. Maybe I'd seen every dark thought the human mind could conjure. Maybe I was so desensitized to fear that everything seemed boring now.

The whole appeal of horror to me is that there is always some new unknown terror which stretches the limit of my imagination. It's why the darkness has held such fascination over us since the days man rubbed two sticks to make a fire. It's not the monster that scares us, it's the endless potential for what the monster might be. Well now it felt like actually putting my thoughts on the paper was the same as turning on the lights, and no matter how scary my idea might be, it will never be as frightening as when it couldn't be seen.

Finally I decided that if I couldn't draw anything properly scary, then none of those other white-bread sissies could do it either. I just scribbled out a skull face pressing up against the paper, looking as though it was trying to escape. It broke the fourth wall just enough to get inside the viewer's head, and I was actually pretty proud of it by the time I finished.

My anticipation grew the whole day, and by the time art came in the afternoon, I couldn't wait to show off my creation. All of the drawings were going to be anonymously shuffled into a pile, and then we'd secretly vote on the best. Can't vote for your own, most votes wins. Mrs. Flemming was zealous about keeping it fair, and even insisted that the whole stack of drawings be passed from person to person instead of hanging them all up, just in case our classmate's reactions influenced our vote.

Game on. I caught a glimpse of a few of the drawings as they were shuffled face-down into the stack. I saw a snake rearing to strike (seriously?) and a dizzying perspective from a guy looking down from the edge of a skyscraper. Did these people have no imagination? What's so scary about regular life stuff?

We watched as the stack of drawings was given to Lily. She flipped slowly through them, and the class gave a collective moan as she agonizingly deliberated between two papers. Then she flipped to the last one in the stack, and the whole class started snickering. She was actually turning white in front of us. Her eyes bulged and quivered, and her mouth worked through the motion of soundless words.

"I think we have a winner!" someone cheered.

Could it have been mine? I didn't think any picture could produce a reaction like that. Lily had always been a sensitive, whiny girl, though. Even so, when she started clutching at her throat, we knew something was wrong. She dropped the papers face down on her desk, now using both hands to claw at her neck as though invisible hands were choking her.

"Is she having a seizure?"

"Someone call the nurse!"

It happened too fast for anyone to react. Lily's neck

strained so hard that the individual tendons stood out like ropes bulging under the skin. Mrs. Flemming rushed to catch her—too slow. Lily had already toppled out of her chair to sprawl face-first on the carpet.

"911? Hello?"

Mrs. Flemming rolled Lily onto her back while holding her cellphone with her shoulder. The class clustered around, staring in abject disbelief.

"No. Her heart isn't beating. What do I do?" Mrs. Flemming asked desperately. She dropped the phone and began chest compressions. Nate, big round boy, scrambled on the ground for the phone and pressed it to his ear.

"No. No. I don't know," he was saying to the police. "It was like a heart attack."

"Hey look at this!" It was the quiet Native-American kid. Don't know his name. He was holding the stack of papers that Lily had dropped.

"Don't touch that. Nobody look at them," Mrs. Flemming demanded between compressions. "Come on Lily. Hang in there with me. Help is on the way."

"I'm not looking, okay?" The Native-American kid held the papers face down. "But count them. There are fourteen papers here."

"So what? The class has—" Mrs. Flemming began, but she already realized her mistake. There were fourteen kids in the class yeah, if you count the dumbass who hit a tree last week. There's no way he turned one in.

"It doesn't matter," Mrs. Flemming snapped. "Ahote (ahh that was his name), go get the principal. Let's just focus on Lily right now, okay?"

Ahote looked down at the mess. Then out the door. Then back at the—

"Ahote, don't!"

He turned over the stack and skipped straight to the end.

His brown skin immediately paled to ash. He gave a wild look around at the class, and then his hands were at his throat. Before anyone could do anything, he had already flopped straight onto the ground.

Everything was a blur after that. Someone pulled the fire alarm to get everyone out, and the paramedics had to shoulder their way through the tide of bewildered faces and speculative chatter heading the other way. They returned with two stretchers and two lumpy white shapes. The way their faces were covered with the sheets reminded me of my own drawing with the skull pressed against the paper.

People were shouting and rumors were flying up and down the lines, and it took a long while until everyone was quiet in the parking lot.

With all the confusion, nobody noticed me take the stack of drawings with me. After that, Mrs. Flemming had given the bodies so much focus that she seemed to completely forget about the cause of death. The general consensus was that the teacher had taken the drawings, but I kept them hidden under my jacket and didn't say a word. I just clenched the papers against my side and listened to the mounting whispers around me. Heart failure caused by massive adrenaline surges, that's what people are saying. Those two kids were literally scared to death.

School was canceled for the rest of the day, and I'm now back in my bedroom with fourteen face-down pieces of paper. I tried holding them up to the light to see if I can get a glimpse of what's on the other side, but it wasn't distinct enough to learn anything.

So far I've resisted the urge to look. I know every horror trope about the guy who let's curiosity get the best of him, but I can't help but feel I'm not as fragile as they are. I've been exposed to everything. My heart doesn't even race at jump scares. Even if it's just for a second, I won't be able to live with myself knowing there is more out there than I was able to face. I know I'm obsessing, but my imagination is tearing me apart trying to figure out what's there.

If it was somehow from the kid that died, then it has to be something that he alone knows about. That means it's something to do with what happens to us after we die. My best guess is that he's brought back some twisted torture or hellscape so demented, so intrinsically woven with the core of our biology, that our very nature revolts against it. The forbidden fruit really is the sweetest.

I tossed and turned the whole night, trying to imagine what could be on that paper. I must not have fallen asleep until late, because it was almost noon when I woke up. Shit, didn't I have a test today? Surely the teachers will understand after yesterday—yesterday. The bodies. The drawings. And now I was obsessing again.

"Did you win?"

Suddenly I was awake. It was Casey. Sitting at the foot of my bed. The stack of papers in her hand.

"Casey listen to me," I spoke as slowly as I dared, like I was trying to talk down a lion who was preparing to pounce. "I want you to put those down. I need you not to look."

"Okay." I let out more air than I knew my lungs could hold. Then she grinned, flipping the stack over anyway.

"Casey drop it. Like your life depends on it!"

"Okay." She kept flipping. God, she was obnoxious. I dove at her to snatch them, but she had already hopped off the bed just out of reach. She was flipping faster now. Four to go. Now three.

"Casey please. I'm not mad, okay? I'm begging you."

"Okay." Flip. Two more before the final drawing. "Which one is yours?" she asked.

"It doesn't matter! Drop them now!" I leapt again. She tossed the papers in the air, and I scrambled to catch them.

I'd already crumpled up five before I realized Casey was still holding onto the last sheet. Her eyes were so wide. Her mouth hung open. I ripped the paper from her hand, but it only took a second with the other kids. Casey, poor innocent Casey—

But then she smiled. "How about my drawing? Did anyone like that?"

The paper was face-down in my hand. I didn't dare look. Instead, I scanned through the rest of the drawings on the floor. All regular fears and boring monsters. There was no doubt that this was the mysterious paper.

"You didn't draw this." I said it with accusation. I was actually offended by the thought.

"Did too," Casey said. "It's of the nightmare I have."

"But what is it? What's it look like?"

"See for yourself."

I wanted to. I wanted to so damn bad. My hands were starting to turn it over by themselves. She leaned in close to me so we could look at it together.

"Can I tell you a secret though?" she whispered. My heart was beating so fast. Was this how they felt, right as the adrenaline flooded their veins, right before they died?

"Go ahead," I said.

"I don't really like the nightmares. They just tell me to say that I do. They told me that if I don't let them out, then they're going to take me inside. That's why I have to keep drawing them."

"Keep drawing?" My hand came to a trembling stop. "How many of these have you drawn?"

"Dozens." Casey's whispers were hurried now. Like she had to tell me before someone stopped her. "But the more I draw, the more they want me to draw. And if I don't, they get so loud that I—"

"Shh, it's okay," I said. "I'm going to look at it now, and I'm going to figure out what's going on. Are you ready?"

"Ready," she said. I turned over the paper, and she buried her face on my shoulder. "I'm going to miss you." I barely made out the muffled words as I looked down into her drawing. I could feel my eyes stretching—wider than they've ever been. I tried to speak, but my rib cage felt like it was closing in around my heart, and I couldn't breathe. My hands instinctively went to my throat, but no—that wouldn't help. That's how the others died. But not me. It was how I came to life.

"They said you passed their test," Casey whispered. "How do you feel?"

I shook my head, barely registering what she said. I couldn't take my eyes off the paper. I could feel my heart still straining inside me, but it was starting to slow. I forced myself to breathe, the motion feeling so unnatural and invasive, almost as though I'd traveled to another world and was flooding my lungs with a cold, stinging, alien gas.

"It's beautiful," I replied. She bobbed up and down with excitement.

"Thanks," she said. "They were afraid no one here would understand. Fear makes you feel alive, and feeling alive is beautiful."

THE SECOND TIME I KILLED
MYSELF

I heard my wife squealing like a butchered animal the moment I entered our house. I almost called out to her before a deep, unfamiliar voice answered first. Up the stairs to the bedroom, her fresh peals of laughter haunting every step along the way.

I stood outside the door for a long time. Not moving. Not thinking. Barely breathing. Just listening to the sound of their vicious pleasure leaking from my bedroom.

I thought it would be satisfying when I finally flung open the door and caught her cheating. Exposing their naked flesh and the guilt on her face – it should have been my victory, but it wasn't. The man scrambled out of my bed, but my wife just rolled her eyes.

"Do you mind? We're kind of busy in here."

I did mind. I stepped aside as the man snatched his clothes and ran. This wasn't about him. He wasn't part of my crumbling world, and it wasn't for him that my blood thundered or the tempest in my nerves surged lightning through my body.

"What do you want, an apology?" my wife asked, not

bothering to cover herself. "Why don't I email it to you since you're supposed to be at work anyway?"

I don't remember much after that. Just how soft her skin felt when my fingers sank into her throat. I couldn't even appreciate the moment when all I could think about was how he must have enjoyed the same flesh minutes earlier. I do remember the smug superiority on her face draining into ashen terror. The desperate thrashing as her body sought the release only I could give.

I didn't mean to kill my wife. She didn't deserve to die. I can see that now, but I couldn't at the time. I punished her for every forgotten dream, every tender feeling, every blind road that my life had disappointed me with. Even after she was dead, I kept pummeling all my jealousy and hate into her body until my fists were churning blood and I was screaming like my soul was ripped from my body. I poured everything that I was into her until with shallow gasp, I realized I had nothing left to give.

That there was nothing left of me at all. Staggering across the room, drunk on the scent of our mingled blood, I took the only thing she hadn't already taken from me. The cold truth of a knife along my veins told the rest of the story. That was the first time I ever killed myself, but it wasn't the last.

"Feeling better now? Up you go, you're all right."

The voice wasn't kind, but neither was it especially cruel. It spoke with an honest certainty like a physics teacher explaining the irrefutable laws of reality. It's not that I died and went somewhere. I was still in my house. My body was still lying on the ground in a pool of its own blood. I– whatever was left of me – wasn't in there anymore.

"That's okay, take your time. You're in a safe place now. A healing place. You won't have to go back until you're ready."

"I'm dead. I shouldn't be here." I felt rather foolish

addressing the moth flitting about my corpse on the floor, but there wasn't anyone else around.

"Is that supposed to make you special?" The moth floated toward my face. "Everyone dies dozens of times. Some of you spend your whole lives dying and re-living, popping out babies and dying again, over and over. It's excessive if you ask me."

"I'm pretty sure I would have remembered dying." I was beginning to get a sense for my new body. It almost seemed to be *growing* around me, bones and organs and skin all swelling and stitching themselves together out of nothing. For one ghastly moment I was only a mess of arteries and pulsing blobs of flesh, but somehow I still felt oddly tranquil.

"Would you like to remember? You can if you want, but most people don't," the moth replied. "But even if you decide not to, you can't pretend you don't notice. You were once a little boy who thought he could fly, if only he ran fast enough to take off. What happened to him?"

"He grew up," I said.

"He died," corrected the moth. "It wasn't bloody or malicious, but you killed him. You took the parts of yourself that weren't compatible with who you've become, and you've killed them. Just like you're going to do again now."

My new body was almost fully formed now, and it wasn't the only one. On the floor beside me, two more on the bed, another by the window – pulsing, growing sacks of flesh were beginning to take shape. Muscle twisted and stitched itself around new bones and sheets of crisp skin bundled up the freshly packaged bodies.

"Some parts of you get damaged as you navigate through life," the moth said. "Some become crippled or cruel or stupid. They'll drag you down and reduce you to pettiness and evil if you don't leave them behind. Then again, some people will kill so many parts of themselves that there's nothing left by the time old age arrives. I feel the most sorry for them, but no matter. Look, over here."

The moth dropped down to land on the handle of the knife, still loosely gripped by the hands of my old corpse.

"You'll need this when you're ready. That one by the window is your hatred. A lot of people try to kill that one, but I don't recommend it. It's hard for anything to remain sacred once you allow life to spoil what you love without your blood stirring."

The fully formed *hatred* copy of myself stared placidly at me. Its features were smooth, its body relaxed, almost like a life-sized doll.

"Same goes with fear, on the floor," the moth continued. "Kill that and you'll be back to visit me before you know it. Of course, whatever you had going obviously wasn't working if you decided to kill yourself, so you'll have to make *some* changes."

"Who is that?" I asked, pointing at the naked woman on my bed. She seemed to have finished growing, but her body was savagely deformed. Half of her face sloped downward as though it suffered a stroke, her stomach was bloated and misshapen, and two bulging swollen eyes blinked lazily at me.

"It's been a hard day for *love*," the moth conceded. "Don't go making any hasty decisions though. That's what brought you here in the first place."

None of these naked bodies were dead, but they might as well have been. They didn't move, hardly drew breath. They just sat there and stared at me, waiting to be killed or brought back with me, seemingly not caring either way.

All those eyes – all those lives – I couldn't take it. I needed air. I got up to walk to the bathroom, regretting it the moment I opened the bedroom door.

There were more of them. Along the hallway, in the

shower, dozens more out the window – all almost exactly like me apart from the varying severity of their injuries. Some were old, others children. Men and women – all looking at me with my face and my eyes. Some were completely intact, while others were maimed and shredded until they were little more than piles of shattered bones and oozing gore. All staring at me, turning their heads as I moved, silently judging me for every mistake I've ever made to reduce them to this pitiful state.

"One more thing." The moth followed me as I returned to the bedroom. "When you do kill the ones you don't want, please be quick about it. Sometimes they don't like to go quietly."

My eyes immediately darted to the knife on the floor. It was gone. I automatically pressed my back to the wall, my new heart lurching in my chest. My eyes scanned the room. Something was different. One of them wasn't here.

"Of course there's always the chance one of them will get the better of you," the moth drawled on, not showing the least concern. "Then you'll be the part that was left behind."

I took a hesitant step farther into the room. The door slammed shut behind me. A blur of movement – I barely darted out of the way in time. That deformed stroke face –love– she'd been hiding behind the door when I entered. Now she was lunging again, the knife lighting up the air between us.

"Stop wasting time," the creature slurred, spit flying from its uneven mouth. "We both know it's me you want."

I fell straight on my ass trying to get out of the way. I turned and began scampering on my hands and knees, flinging myself across the floor to escape from its lurching advance.

"You think it's my fault," she wailed. Each word felt heavy and deliberate: a mentally deficient person struggling to be understood and growing more frustrated by the second. "I didn't do this to you!"

I regained my feet and faced my adversary. The knife fell again, but I managed to catch her by the wrist. She roared with unintelligible fury as I wrestled the knife from her hand. I almost plunged it into her without thinking. The tortured misery on her face– on my face – the rejection and loneliness. I hesitated, just for a moment....

... a moment too long. Hands grappled me from behind, grabbing both my arms to hold me in place. Two more of the impassive copies – I couldn't tell which – wrestling me onto the bed. I didn't let go of my knife, but it didn't matter if I couldn't use it.

The deformed *love* was on top of me. Her lips peeled back from her functional side to sink her teeth into my neck. I strained to pull away, but the other two had me firm. I screamed though words failed me, yelping a noise like an animalistic snarl. One of the hands on my arm slackened just a bit at the sound.

Did they feel sorry for me? I didn't have time to think. I lashed out with the knife, gouging a deep line across *love's* face. She grunted but didn't let up. Her teeth were digging deeper into me. I cut again, and again, hacking and slashing at the loose folds of her uneven face.

The grip behind me suddenly released. I pounced on my victim, hesitating no longer. Both hands on the handle, I impaled the creature in the chest with all my strength. The blade tore through her so easily, dancing through rotted and pitted skin, down her bloated body, ripping a line all the way from her sternum to her groin.

One look at the bloody mess underneath me and I knew I was done here. "Bring me back!" I shouted. "I've done what I had to do."

The world was spinning around me. I closed my eyes,

trying my best to keep breathing without being nauseous. The flaccid bodies filling my house began to howl with one voice. One wall of noise at first, but as it went on the different voices began to weave between each other, swelling and diminishing in an intricate melody almost indistinguishable from mindless screaming. It was either the most beautiful or most horrendous sound I'd ever heard, perhaps both.

And then I was through. The howling abruptly stopped. My heart was throbbing. My breath came in ragged gasps. I was standing outside my bedroom door again.

"Is someone there?" It was my wife. The sound of her voice was even more disgusting than the cacophony I'd endured.

"Stop worrying. You said he'd be gone all day, right?" That deep voice. The one that didn't matter. Now that I thought about it, neither of them did. I turned and walked down the stairs as quietly as I could.

I had a second chance, or perhaps a hundredth if I've been through all this before. I wasn't going to waste it on her. She'll never know how much of myself she made me destroy, but it was better this way.

My time on the other side has changed me. And looking down at the love I killed with my own hands, I knew I had transformed myself into someone who could survive this. When I had plunged my knife into that rotted belly I had looked down on more than decay and ruin.

I'd seen a child blossoming inside the fetid corpse of *love*. And if I was careful, and kind to it, I knew it would grow to replace the one that I killed.

MY DAUGHTER SPOKE BEFORE SHE WAS BORN

"*M*ommy." My daughter's first word. Isn't that what every new mother is dying to hear? One word to magically transform this organic object into a new human being. All the pain and fear and doubt suddenly have purpose. One word and mothers will know it was all worthwhile.

"*I love you, Mommy.*"

I just wish little Claire had waited until she was born to say it. Over eight months pregnant, I was sitting in the car waiting for my husband to get back with the groceries. I almost had a heart attack on the spot. I thought someone was in the car with me, so I jumped out to get a better look in the backseat but –

"*Don't worry, Mommy. It'll be our little secret.*"

The voice was coming from inside me. I felt the vibrations as much as I heard it with my ears, almost like the rumbling of indigestion. I didn't say a word when my husband got back. I was waiting for Claire to talk again, but when she didn't, I just kept my mouth shut too. My husband had more than enough to worry about with his extra shifts at work. I didn't want him to add my sanity to his worries.

"I don't like that. It's nasty."

I put down the salad I was eating. Alone in the kitchen this time; Claire only spoke when I was alone. Usually it was just an isolated word or sometimes I'd catch her humming along to a song that was playing. If she didn't like something, she'd let me know. She didn't care for most vegetables, and jazz music seemed to make her restless.

As weird as it seems, it's something I got used to. I grew into the habit of asking her how she was doing, and if she was comfortable. I'd tell her about the things we'd do together and talked about myself. Sometimes if I was lucky, I'd hear her respond, a faint murmur; so far away but so inti-mate that I knew it could be nothing else.

"There are lots of colors," Claire answered once when I asked her what it looked like. *"But they're all black. It's warm and close and safe. I'm part of everything here."*

"What about before you were there?" I asked. "What's the earliest thing you can remember?"

I could feel her squirming. She didn't speak again for almost a day after that, until suddenly when I was about to enter the shower she said:

"I don't want to talk about it. Before isn't a nice place. The people living there aren't nice people."

I didn't want to upset her, so I didn't pry any further. Besides, even thinking about it made me uncomfortable, and I felt as though my discomfort would be passed on to Claire somehow. We were two halves of the same soul, and it almost seemed like I could feel her thinking before she even spoke.

"Mommy?" she asked one night when I lay half-asleep in the solitary darkness. My husband was on a business trip,

and it was just going to be me until a few days before I was due. *"Who else is inside you?"*

I told her that she was an only child. That she was so big she took up my whole tummy all by herself, and that soon she was going to be too big even for that. Then she would come out where I am, and we could see each other for the first time.

"Are the people nice out there?" she asked.

I had to tell her the truth. If I didn't, I figured she could probably feel it. I told her that people try to be good, but some of them don't know how. But she shouldn't worry, because I'm going to teach her how and then she can teach everyone she meets. I was almost in tears as I said it, marveling at the wonder I carried. Claire and I will have known each other more truly than any mother and daughter before. Our bond would be stronger. I was so happy to have this blessing until –

"Don't lie to me, Mommy. I know I'm not the only one here."

I told her not to be silly. I'd been to the doctors, and they showed me what it looked like inside. There wasn't anyone –

"One of them followed me," Claire interrupted. *"From the before place. Mommy make them go away."*

I did my best to reassure her, but I was completely helpless against her mounting distress. *"Don't let it hurt me. Don't let it take me back. I don't want to go back. I want to be with Mommy...."* She wouldn't listen to anything I said. I couldn't get through to her anymore.

Listening to her cry inside me was more than I could bear, but then she started shrieking and I had to get out of the house. I hustled to the car as swiftly as my swollen body would allow, made even more difficult now that Claire was thrashing and kicking inside. I was trying to stay strong for her, but I was so terrified as I ripped down the streets toward the hospital. I'm sure she must have felt that too. I was doing everything I could to stifle my sobs when the kicking suddenly stopped.

There was no movement at all. No sounds. And I thought that was even worse than the crying until she spoke again.

"I have to go away, Mommy. It was nice talking with you."

I was at the hospital now. I practically drove straight through the glass doors in front of the emergency room. Don't go, Claire, don't go. But I didn't say it out loud. Instead I said:

"Please help me. There's something wrong with my baby."

The nurse asked me how I knew, and I didn't know how to answer. I just started crying again. They put me in a wheelchair and brought me into an examination room. The nurse said she would be right back, but I didn't want to be left alone. At least while someone was here, I could tell myself that Claire wasn't speaking because of them. If she stayed quiet when I was alone though ...

"Don't cry, Mommy." I held my breath, desperate to catch every word. Claire was speaking so faintly that I could barely hear her over the frantic double percussion of my heart. *"You're not going to be alone. The one from the before place is here. He promises to be good, but I want you to be careful Mommy. Goodbye."*

The nurse was back, and there was a doctor with her. I think they were trying to ask me questions, but my whole awareness was so focused on any movement or sound from within that I couldn't register what they were saying. They started doing an ultrasound, although it took a long time before I stopped shaking enough for them to get a clear picture. The whole while, Claire didn't say a word. That was okay though. She never did when people were around. Maybe when they were gone she would....

But then the doctor gave me a big smile, and I let out gasps of stale air that I didn't even know I was clinging to.

"I want you to know that you have nothing to worry about," the doctor said. "The baby is perfectly healthy."

"I'm sorry," I told him. "I don't know what I was thinking. I shouldn't have bothered you."

"Don't worry about it," he said, taking off his gloves. "It's common for expecting mothers to have anxiety or panic attacks. Even hallucinations sometimes."

"Hallucinations, yeah," I managed. "I guess it's a pretty traumatic time for the body."

"Exactly," he said. "But I want you to know that nothing in the world is wrong. Just a few weeks and you're going to be holding your son for the first time."

"My son?"

"Yes ma'am. Didn't you know? Look here, it even almost looks like he's smiling."

BEHIND CLOSED DOORS

Those of us who survive what happens behind closed doors don't talk about it much more than those who didn't.

And you. You know there are mothers who look at their children as bloodsucking leeches, blaming them for their dwindling energy and passion for life. You know there are fathers who see their daughters as a possession, their innocence a vulnerability to exploit. You know that drugs, or alcohol, or the festering hatred of wasted years can curdle the blood until convictions of "right and wrong" subtly transform into "is someone watching or not".

But we don't talk about it, because maybe it's our fault they don't love us more. And you don't think about it, afraid your own love will be spoiled by the guilt of those who go without. But if I'm going to be brave enough to talk, then I want you to be brave enough to listen. We are no longer children, and we must both accept that closing our eyes does not make the monsters go away anymore.

My parents died in a car accident when I was fourteen. Uncle Viran and Aunt Isabelle said they had always wanted a daughter and took me in after that, treating me with the polite indifference you'd use to summon your waiter. And that was okay with me, because I wasn't really expecting to have a family again. I had one once, and wanting that intimacy back with other people seemed disrespectful to their memory. Wherever I would go, whoever I would be with from that day on, I knew I would be alone.

Viran was always watching me with his beady little eyes, nearly invisible behind huge spectacles. Isabelle tolerated me, although she was better at it when I stayed in my room. And life went on. I never stopped wearing black after the funeral, but over time I added some bows and lace because Uncle thought I looked depressing.

It wasn't good enough for him though. He bought me a lot of brightly colored ornaments to wear so "the room didn't look like someone turned out the lights" every time I entered. Isabelle thought it was a waste of money, and I agreed. There was something powerful and elegant in my dark wardrobe which protected me from life's banalities. The other things made me feel like a clown on display, an object for the sole purpose of being seen and used.

I'd try them on though, whatever it was. Pink dresses, sunhats, stiletto shoes. Uncle would make me model them, striking poses and spinning around while his eyes sparkled with undisguised appetite. I'd thank him politely, keeping the rest of my words to myself, waiting for his face to flush with sweat and his words to awkwardly tangle in his mouth before he'd let me leave.

They were nice things, he told me. Expensive things. He wanted to keep them clean, so he'd make me undress to store them safely. Not in the bathroom where I could spill water on them. Not in my bedroom where I kept it so dirty. Right here in the living room, it's all right. There's no one else here. And I'd do what I was told, he'd remind me, because I was a good girl who appreciated everything he'd done for me.

Isabelle was returning from the store when she caught him like that once. His hands were already on me, helping to slide my new skirt down. I caught her eye with a sort of helpless pleading. She got so angry she actually started trembling, her lips pressing into a bloodless scar. I thought that was going to be the end of this game. She was going to yell at her husband and swoop in to save me like my own mother would have done if she'd found me like that....

But my mother wasn't here anymore. Isabelle turned around and went into the kitchen without another word. Uncle followed her, and I took the chance to run for my bedroom. I listened against the door for a sound of a fight, but they were both speaking low and soft. All I could hear was the frenzied pounding of blood in my veins and the mounting scream of a tea kettle.

I thought she was just making herself a cup to calm down until my door opened five minutes later. I knew something bad was going to happen as soon as I saw her: face like plastic, thick rubber gloves up to her elbow, and tea kettle in hand.

"Viran told me everything," Isabelle said as she sat down beside me on the bed. She touched me with one of those rubber gloves and I started shaking so bad the headboard rattled. "I don't want to do this, but it's for your own good. Girls have empty heads sometimes, and must be taught lessons that are not easily forgotten."

Isabelle's carefully maintained countenance twisted into a snarl when she grabbed my hair and began to pour the boiling water over my head. The more I cried, the louder she yelled to be heard. How dare I try to seduce her husband, she'd said. Selfish slut, just like my mother. Home wrecker. Ungrateful bitch. Two-faced whore. By the time the kettle was empty, I was writhing in agony on my soaked bed sheets. I just lay there gasping, my tears evaporating where they ran across my scalded skin. My eyes were too swollen to see, but I heard her stand and exit the room.

"Even if you try, I don't think he'll want you now anyway," she said as she left.

When the door closed, I tried to pull my drenched shirt off but every brush of fabric on skin was excruciating. I had to cut myself free with a pair of scissors, biting my tongue to keep myself from howling. Then staggering to the bathroom to splash cool water on my face I could see blisters the size of my nose already forming on my hands and neck which had taken the worst of it.

It took almost a week for the swelling to come down. Aunt Isabelle brought me aloe lotions and cooed over me like it had been an unfortunate accident. Uncle didn't even look at me, so I guess I should have been grateful in a way. As my skin continued to heal, I kept applying rouge to make it look like the skin was still scalded. I thought maybe he'd leave me alone as long as he thought I was ruined, but I couldn't keep up the disguise forever.

One week was all the respite I got. I felt his hands resting on my shoulders as I peered into the fridge, their gentleness as vile as Isabelle's iron grip. He said he was sorry for what happened. It was wrong of her to treat me like a child (he knows I'm not a child anymore) or to punish me (when I had been so good). Not to worry, he assured me; next time she'll never find out. Next time, he's going to have a special present to make up for what happened.

He was right about one thing: I wasn't a child anymore. You can't stay a child after something like that has happened, no matter how hard you try. With his hands running down my back as lightly as snow upon a grave, I knew what *next time* meant. There wasn't going to be a next time though, because I was going to run away. Over dinner that night I made a big show coughing and playing sick. I told them I felt like I could sleep forever. Once in my room, I stuffed a couple pillows under my blanket to make it look like someone was still sleeping there.

But I wasn't taking any chances. I'd even picked up a cheap wig which perfectly matched my auburn hair. After fastening it around a soccer ball, I pulled the blankets way up to its "chin" and took a step back to survey my work. I briefly considered trying to rig up one of those audio recorder setups where a string is attached to the door and plays a message when it's opened, but it seemed too complicated and I was already terrified of being caught before I got out.

Isabelle hadn't entered my room since she burned me, and Uncle seemed uncomfortable there as well. I hoped they would just think I was sick and not disturb the dummy until I was a long way from here. My backpack was stuffed with clothes, some snacks and about $40, and I looked back one last time before I left. As terrible as it was here, I had no delusions that life outside would be any easier. I figure people are going to suffer no matter where they are, but at least now I could choose how.

I didn't think anything could make me stay longer in that house, but then again, I couldn't have expected what I saw when glancing back. The pillows I'd carefully lain under the covers had shifted. The bundle was leaning back against the headboard now, the long auburn hair falling down to completely obscure the soccer ball.

Then before my eyes, the dummy head moved. Now to the left. Now to the right. The wig swishing softly as it dragged along the sheets. Now it was looking right at me, or at least I think so. I still couldn't see anything underneath the thick hair.

I took a step toward the window. Then a step back into

the room. The head followed me both times. Then the whole form began to stand upright, although the sheet hung loosely as though an emaciated human frame was hidden beneath rather than the pillows I had placed there. Does that mean the soccer ball was gone too? As it lurched toward me, I could only imagine what horrifying visage was underneath the hair now.

I stood frozen as it stopped in front of me. Up close, I saw the hair wasn't a wig anymore. It looked so soft and real that I had to stop myself from reaching out to touch it. For a gut-clenching moment I thought it looked like my mother's hair, but no, it was so much longer and wilder than hers. But wasn't the figure about the same height as my mother, just a head taller than me?

"Are you going to help me?" I asked.

The hair nodded as the head bent from forward and back. A shift in the sheet let a cold wind escape outward as though someone had opened a window.

"Are you going to punish them?"

It was definitely a nod this time. I was so relieved that I couldn't contain the rush of bubbling thoughts and feelings swelling up within me. The idea that it was my mother made me want to laugh and cry at the same time. It *was* my mother. It had to be. She'd never stopped watching me, even from the other side. She saw what happened and she wasn't going to forgive them. She was going to make them suffer because they *deserved* it, and she was going to save me because ...

A whisper. I couldn't catch what she said. I leaned closer and she spoke again.

"Switch places with me."

"What do you mean?"

A short, powerful rush of air entered the form, and she spoke louder as though she was gradually waking up. "I'm not of your world, and cannot hurt them until I enter. Switch places with me, let me have my fun, and then I will trade back with you when I'm finished."

The voice was more real with every word. I could imagine myself back in our old house with mother tucking me into bed at night. The security of her presence, the affection of her voice. The unbridled fury at anyone who would do me wrong. I devoured those words. That love, that anger, it's what kept me alive.

"What is it like, your world?" I asked, but even as I did I knew it didn't matter. "Yes, I'll switch places. It won't take long to punish them, will it?"

The head shook. A fleeting glance of a green eye shining beneath the hair, and then it was gone. "Cut your finger," she instructed me, and I did so without question, pinching the skin of my forefinger with the scissors beside my bed. These scissors which I had used to cut my scalding shirt off would now be used for revenge. I'd never felt so sweet a pain in my life.

"Now let your mother taste it." The voice was deeper now, more masculine, but I didn't care. All I could think about was how good it would feel to see them pay. I'd be able to live alone here, taking care of myself. I wouldn't have to be quiet anymore, or afraid. Or maybe mom could come back and visit when this awful business was over, and we could talk like we used to. My dad must be there too, and I could even switch with him to let him play a round of golf and enjoy the sun again. I lifted my cut finger up inside the wild hair and felt the cold wind licking the blood from me, and I smiled.

My finger was ice, and it felt cool and refreshing on skin still tender from the burns. The freezing presence swept its way up my arm, over my chest, and deep into my heart. I felt myself falling though I stood in place, plummeting through an abyss of thought. The form in front of me was removing its sheet now, and I could see its grey/black skin bristle and distort as though something within it were viciously pounding its way out. Wherever I went though, whatever was waiting for me, I didn't care. My mother had saved me, and I loved her. And soon I would be back to see what she had done. No torture was too gruesome; no punishment fell short of righteous in my eyes. I only wish that I had still been there to watch it happen…

But that was forty years ago. Now I know that the other side is no kinder than ours, and that there are those who seek out the weakness and vulnerability of others just as readily as they do here. Those faceless beings form a blanket of leering eyes as they wait for their opportunity to strike. Forty years in a nightmare realm, hiding and fighting and struggling to survive against the nameless savagery which mocks our petty struggles here on Earth. Forty years hating myself for leaving this world so readily, and fanning that hatred within me to keep me warm against the unending night.

I wasn't her daughter; I was her prey. She felt my desperation and came to me knowing I could not refuse her offer, and so she escaped from her world and into mine. It had taken forty years for her to have her fun and trade places with me again, but even being back, I feel as though I do not belong in this world. Isabelle and Viran are likely dead, but I don't even care about that anymore. I'm just waiting for my specter to show itself again, because I still haven't gotten my revenge. And perhaps in the darkest night of your defeat he will come for you too, promising to serve you if only you trade places. I pray that even in your loneliest despair you will maintain the resolve to refuse him, although if you don't …

… then I pray instead I will find you first, so that together we may strive to make this world better instead of fleeing into the grasp of what waits on the other side.

MARS COLONIZATION PROJECT

My name is Robert Feldman, and I've been preparing for this mission my entire life. Don't get too excited though, because the shuttle taking me to Mars is still fifteen years away from launching. If the training is any indication of what to expect, then it's going to be the most terrifying experience I could imagine.

So why has training already began? It's simple math really. The manned mission to Mars has a conservative expense estimate of over $100 billion. If anything goes wrong, then the chances of financing another journey in lieu of the more practical exploration and colonization of nearby asteroids is slim to none. That means the crew has to be absolutely perfect, and the cost of extensively training us for over a decade is still insignificant compared to the potential disaster from our slightest mistake.

There will be numerous expeditions before NASA decides we're ready, including a 2020 Rover launch, a year-long training session in the space station around 2024, and then a prolonged orbit around Mars in the early 2030s. After that, the colony will be established, although there is no way for our current level of technology to allow a return journey. We will be terminally isolated, depending entirely on our self-sustaining efforts to survive.

Earth's conditions will always be as volatile as the arbitrary leaders controlling launch codes, and I firmly believe the long-term survival of our species is dependent on our ability to spread across the stars. That's why I've devoted my life to this cause. From my master's degree in engineering to my thousands of hours of flight experience in the air force, I've honed every aspect of my mind, body and spirit, to help transcend humanity into the heavens.

So you can imagine how excited I was to finally receive the phone call from Nigel Rathmore (Administrator at NASA). I had barely been winded from my eight-mile run that morning, but just hearing his voice on the line was enough to make my knees weak. I kissed my wife, and we both laughed and cried, knowing the implications this decision would have for us. I love her with all my heart, but she understands that is exactly the reason why I must go. It was time for the official training to begin, and I was ready.

The training on Earth is divided into three segments: Technical Training (the mechanical skills required), Personal Training (psychological profiling and mental preparation for the unnatural ordeal), and Simulation Training (which will expose us to the conditions we're expected to face).

This isn't the story of how I learned to build circuit boards. The technical training is hardly worth mentioning, and neither the other astronauts nor I encountered much we hadn't already prepared for. Besides myself, there was Isac (the gentle Norwegian giant), Linda (might be cute if she learned to extract the Truss Rod from her ass), and Jean-Claude (French guy with a superiority complex). I would have enjoyed this part a lot more if I hadn't known that the colonization shuttle was only being designed to house two astronauts. That means they not only expected two of us to fail, they demanded it. These people who I spent my every waking day with weren't friends; they were competition.

On the second day, we began our first personal training segments, and I was already hoping that Isac be the one to graduate with me. The thought of spending the rest of my life trapped on an alien planet with Linda barking orders or Jean-Claude condescendingly redoing my work was absolutely loathsome.

We all underwent thorough psychiatric screenings that day. They told us that by the end of training, we had to look forward to up to a year of solitary confinement to monitor our stability. During that time, we wouldn't be allowed to even speak to another human on the phone, as it was simulating the event of a communications breakdown.

As the days went on, the tests became continually more grueling. I could tell the NASA administrators had actively designed this course to cause as much physical and mental discomfort as they could. We were a piece of equipment, as sure as any support beam or fuel cell, and if we were going to break, then it would be better for it to happen now while we could still be replaced.

Physical endurance was pushed to its limit as we jogged behind jeeps across searing sand dunes. Our bodies underwent the pummeling of artificial dust storms in wind tunnels, all while undergoing blindfolded obstacle courses meant to simulate the storms which ravage Mars and block out over 99 percent of the sun. Some nights we would be locked in a freezing chamber which approached the -70 C nights on Mars, and our vitals were measured as layer by layer of protective clothing was stripped away until they could record the exact moment we lost consciousness.

Jean-Claude was the first one to contract pneumonia from the bitter cold. That didn't stop them from forcing him back into the chamber the next night. He tried to get out of it, but they told him he would be cut from the entire program if he skipped a single segment. That night Isac offered one of his outer layers to him, but Jean-Claude was too proud to accept. They had to carry him out on a stretcher, and I didn't see him again after that.

That wasn't the only case of sickness either. I don't think it was part of the original plan, but after that all of us fell sick at the exact same time. Coughing, fevers and sores on our skin – I think they must have given us something to study our immune system. It was bad enough to make me delirious, because I kept seeing flashing lights and hearing an odd buzzing sound. I must have blacked out for a bit, because I got flashes of being taken out and brought into a whitewashed room. I was put on a metal table, and the faces staring at me were distorted and twisted into surreal mockeries of what a human face should be. I was afraid, but I didn't let it show. I didn't want to give them any reason to cut me out like they did Jean-Claude.

As bad as the physical ordeals were, they were nothing compared to the psychological ones. They'd warned us that they wanted to test our reactions to a variety of situations, but they hadn't told us exactly what to expect. When they told me my wife had been killed in a car crash and showed me photographs of her mutilated body, I was devastated. They talked me through her death, going into explicit detail about how much she suffered from the shards of glass filling her face like shrapnel as she bled out on the highway. It was a full day before they confessed she was fine, and that I had passed the test by holding it together.

Maybe I was holding it together on the outside, but on the inside I was pulling further away from everyone. I originally set out on this course for the good of humanity, but it was hard to want to fight for them when everyone I met on a daily basis was there to torture me. I started eating less, smiling less, talking less. The only other person I really opened up to was Isac. Linda had only grown more caustic as she was pushed toward her breaking point, but Isac remained a constant source of warm camaraderie and encouragement. His kindness reminded me that there was still good in humanity, and that it was still worth fighting for.

And did I ever need that reminder. As we progressed further into the simulated training, we were exposed to a wide range of situations including: maintaining daily routines while they starved us, ingesting radioactive material, and undergoing small amounts of auto-cannibalization (eating slices of our own skin). Some of the simulations were just a virtual reality world, while others were so real that they wouldn't unlock the door until we'd passed out from exhaustion or pain. The line between reality and fabrication grew thinner every day, until it got to the point where I was barely able to distinguish what was training and what was not.

That's what I need you to understand before I tell you what happened next. There had been so many tricks played on us, so many simulations and improbable scenarios, and we weren't allowed to question any of them. When they asked us if we were ready for the next test, "Yes sir" was the only answer we were allowed to give. To their credit, the training was making us fearless. That's why when the three of us were locked in a steel room together, we didn't even ask what they were going to make us do. We already knew that we could do it.

"This is a simulation game." Nigel's voice came through an intercom on the wall. We all stood immediately to attention. He didn't usually come down to the training facilities himself. The last time he was here, it was because Jean-Claude was being carried out.

"Yes sir," we all barked with military precision.

"There is an alien who has infiltrated the shuttle." Nigel's voice said. "He has taken over one of your bodies, and is a direct threat to the remaining crew. Do you understand?"

"Sir, yes sir."

"I want you to find out who it is. And I want you to kill them."

The intercom crackled and fell silent. We all remained perfectly stiff at attention. Slowly – laboriously – we turned to face each other. Isac was the only one to grin.

"It's just a simulation," Isac reminded us. "We don't really have to –"

"That's what the alien would say," Linda interrupted. "If he infiltrated the shuttle, then he's trying to avoid detection. Of course he would be the one to deny his own existence."

"Listen to yourself Linda," I said. "We're obviously not going to kill Isac. The game is just to figure out which of us the others don't think belongs. They're probably going to use this data in their final decision for who the crew will be."

Linda's eyes were wild though. The pressure of these tests had pushed us all to the edge, but this was the first time in my life I had ever seen someone start to break before my eyes. She took a step back from us, arms raised as though to fight.

"That's the trick then," she replied. "You're both the aliens. He was testing me to see if I'd realize it –"

"Listen to Robert," Isac said. "We're all in this together, okay?"

"If anyone doesn't belong, it's you Linda," I said. "You've always been the difficult one. I'm voting she's the alien."

"It's Isac!" She pointed a shaking finger at him. Her eyes were bulging so badly, I don't know how they stayed in her skull. "Look at his skin! It's so pale!"

"Linda get a hold of yourself." I took a step forward, but she leapt back as though under attack.

"Get away from me! Both of you!" she screamed.

"Sorry Linda, but I have to agree with Robert," Isac said. "I'm voting you out too."

That should have been the end of it. The simulation should have ended. The door should have opened. There's no way they could see Linda's display and still entertain the possibility that she was a good candidate. But the door didn't open. We knocked – we shouted – I even tried climbing on Isac's shoulders to open the ceiling panels. Nothing. Not for over an hour when the intercom came to life again.

"The alien is still in the room. Kill it."

This was a test. This had to be a test. My next theory was that they wanted to see how loyal we were to our crewmates. Isac agreed with me, and Linda couldn't hope to take us both on by herself. She sat on her side of the room, muttering to herself, while Isac and I sat on the other. We were used to deprivation and isolation. We knew how to wait. Whatever stunt Nigel was trying to pull on us now wasn't going to phase us. At least, it wouldn't phase me or Isac.

One hour. Then two. Isac and I chatted amiably to pass the time, but Linda refused to even acknowledge us. Then the lights dimmed in artificial nightfall, and we settled further in to wait. Linda was getting more anxious as time passed. She kept standing to pace every few minutes. Her hands endlessly twisted over one another, so much that the skin was beginning to wear thin. How much of this would NASA have to see before they knew she wasn't fit for the mission?

I shouldn't have fallen asleep. It was just so boring in that room, and I was so tired from the previous day of obstacle courses. I didn't know how long we'd be in here, and we didn't have many chances to rest, so this seemed like a perfect opportunity. Besides, we were being closely monitored, and Isac was here with me. It should have been perfectly safe....

But this was the test I failed. Maybe not in the eyes of NASA, but I failed a much older, much more important test which was woven into the basic biology of my humanity. In the moment my fellow man needed me most, I wasn't there for him. By the time I woke up, it was too late. Linda had crept over to us through the darkness and wrapped her shoelaces around Isac's neck. He must have thrashed and struggled, but he wouldn't have been able to scream through his collapsing trachea. By the time I woke, the door was already opening. There were only two of us left alive.

The training is still going on. Our mission is too important to be jeopardized by my personal feelings. The fact is that I am the best man available for the job, offering the highest long-term chances of survival for the human race. And Linda? Well I guess she was the best woman for the job too. She'd followed orders where I could not. Did something which I could not. If anyone is going to make the hard choice to keep the mission going, then I trust her to do it.

After all, even in the face of such an impossible situation, she still made the right choice. The moment Isac's body stopped struggling, I saw the creature fleeing from its dying host. At first I thought it was a multitude of worms seeping out through his nose and ears, but as they pulled themselves out, it became apparent they were all connected at the base. The whole front of Isac's face had to split open to allow its body out, but I hope you'll forgive me for not wanting to dwell on the specifics. If it was a simulation, then they must have still killed Isac to do it. If it wasn't...

Well, all that matters is that NASA understands the true obstacles which might jeopardize the safety of our species, and they are taking every precaution to ensure I will be ready. I just wish I could still trust them like I used to, growing up with the naïve dream of becoming a spaceman.

As I prepare for the next day of training, I can't help but dwell on the conversation I had with Isac as we passed the last hours of his life.

"So much work to get to such a desolate, empty planet," I'd said. "Makes you wonder, doesn't it?"

"Not really," he'd replied. "It's not about where you're trying to get to. It's about what you're trying to escape from."

AN ANGRY MIDGET

Read the title? Good, then you're up to speed with what's going on.

Laptop? Fifteen percent batteries. Better keep this moving. I'm hiding behind a tree with Mark Burnham as I'm writing this, although lately he's been more commonly known as "Stacey".

Pretty soon a forty-two year old man with a wife he cares nothing about is going to drive up the dirt trail. The man has been getting to know Stacey for the last few days at a nearby park. She seemed to like him, but the man was shy about meeting Stacey's parents. That's why he said he wanted to play out here in the woods where they wouldn't be around.

A white van – seriously? There he is. Right on schedule. Can't get the bus to arrive on time, but set a date with a predator and you can set your watch by it. This is Mark's third victim, so I'm starting to get a pretty good idea how this works.

Mark Burnham is a twenty-six year old midget. (I think they prefer to be called little people.) He suffers from a hormone disorder which causes proportionate dwarfism, rendering him four feet tall but otherwise remarkably normal. Turns out a clean shave and a baggy sweater are enough for him to pass off as a little, albeit chubby, eight-year-old girl named Stacey.

I'm watching the forty-two-year old climb out of the van. He's looking up and down the trail like he's afraid someone is watching. Bastard doesn't have a clue what's coming.

Anyway I met Mark a couple weeks ago in our group therapy. I'm not going into the details, but it's enough to know that we both survived a traumatic experience as kids. We got to talking (you can't avoid the awkward small-talk after someone just confessed to being turned into a hand-puppet), and Mark tried to lighten the mood by making a joke about being the only one who never gets too old for pedophiles.

It wasn't a good joke, but our intentions were.

The forty-two-year old man is calling for Stacey. Mark straightens his wig and we exchange maniacal grins. It's hard not to laugh while Mark calls out in that shrill childish voice. The man has spotted Mark now. He's coming this way. Mark scampers farther up the hill, calling for him again. We have to lure them a bit farther into the woods so no random hikers will interrupt his execution.

The man has passed me now. I'm going to follow in a minute. I've got a handgun with me for backup just in case. I'm not very good with it, but fortunately I didn't have to use it the first two times. Mark is a wizard with his butterfly knife and can make a man scream like you wouldn't believe.

Deep breath. Deep breath. And go.

I followed the man for about five minutes before Mark stopped. His little legs were kicking the log he sat on: a mask of pure joy and innocence. The man sat nearby. They were speaking softly; I couldn't catch what they were saying, but it wasn't long before he leaned in to kiss Mark.

The wig came off. The knife went in. I don't know which happened first, but I'm sure both contributed to the dumbfounded shock on the man's face. I jumped out from behind the tree and leveled my gun. Shit, left the safety on – doesn't matter though. Mark had already slashed the man's face and hands a dozen more times. This one was too surprised to even scream – he just stared.

Stared as Mark punched him between the eyes.

Stared as the blade drove into his stomach.

Stared as his throat was cut.

Stared and then smiled. Mark was already making some space between them. He was just standing there shaking in exhilaration, unsure what to do next. The man rose to his feet and began dusting himself off as though mildly annoyed at discovering dog hair on his jacket. The blood had already stopped flowing. The cuts were healing, tattered flesh plastering themselves together into scabs which receded into the skin before disappearing entirely.

"You're a liar, Stacey," the man said, his voice a dreadful calm.

"Shoot him!" Mark yelled.

I didn't move.

"You said you were eight." The man didn't look at me. He just took another step toward Mark. "They can't be older than eight."

"Holy shit, what are you waiting for?"

I squeezed the trigger, flinching as the sound ripped the air in half. The dull thud as the bullet hit a tree. The man *still* didn't so much as glance my way. His hand lashed out and grabbed Mark by the neck. I fired again, but I was too afraid of hitting Mark and it wasn't even close. The man heaved Mark into the air, swinging him wildly in my direction as a shield. The little man's arms were beating helplessly against the implacable grip; thrashing legs turned the air into a turmoil of desperate energy.

"Shoot him! Shoot me! I don't care, just do something!"

I did do something. I watched. And even that was more than I could bear. The man's chest exploded outward, ribs opening wide like so many giant white teeth. His head was bent backwards so sharply that his spine bulged against his neck. His whole body was bending to make way for the impossible jaws. Mark managed to get a few more swipes in, but the abomination pressed the dwarf's entire body into his gaping chest cavity.

The ribs snapped shut faster than a striking snake. The horrendous gash that marked where the skin had separated was already fading. Soon there wouldn't be anything but his torn shirt to show where he had mocked his humanity.

"Bring a real eight year old tomorrow," he told me.

I turned and ran. So fast and so hard that every bone in my body felt like it would shatter from the impact of my flying strides.

"Or don't," he shouted after me. "What's the worst that could happen to you?"

A PAINTING BY DAY, A WINDOW BY NIGHT

A big black dog rearing on its hind legs to stand like a human. One paw conspiratorially placed in front of its lips as though swearing the viewer to uphold a shared secret. I hadn't given the painting a second thought, except maybe to remind myself not to bump into it while stumbling down the hall at night to use the bathroom.

The painting had never been there growing up, but there had been a lot of changes around my parents' house since I left for college. I had to throw a sleeping bag on the floor of my old room to visit now that they'd converted the space to a home gym. All the fantasy novels I used to read were in boxes in the garage, and any games I hadn't brought with me were tossed.

It was understandable, I guess. I've moved on with my life, and it would be selfish not to expect them to do the same. It just felt weird sleeping in that room with the ghosts of my former life replaced by the looming silhouettes of exercise machines.

This is where I'd become who I am: filling journals with rambling thoughts, lying awake dreaming of my first crush, studying and stressing and fighting with private demons that my life once revolved around.

That's probably why I couldn't sleep. I feel like I'm too young to have that many memories, but here they all came rushing back. I lay awake wondering if that kid was still alive inside me somewhere, or whether he was already dead and replaced with a new person, a stranger that I hadn't even properly met.

I used to imagine becoming someone that no one could ever forget, but I'm already in college and still a nobody. Was I the person I dreamed about back then? Or had I betrayed myself somewhere along the way?

After tossing and turning on the floor for a few hours, I got up to use the bathroom. I had to stop and stare as I passed by the painting of the dog. Savage strokes of thick paint made the fur look like it was bristling. Bared teeth flashed in the moonlight behind its paw, and the playful personification of its stance now seemed like a sardonic mockery of human achievement. The longer I stared, the surer I was: this wasn't the same painting I had seen in the day.

I passed it again the next morning on my way to breakfast, but I couldn't comprehend what I had found so unsettling during the night. The fur wasn't bristling, it was just fluffy. And those teeth? I could still see them, but it was obviously a smile. I asked my parents about it, but they both just gave each other these confused little shrugs.

Somehow they'd both figured the other one had bought it. They'd been doing a lot of home improvement projects, and I guess neither of them had mentioned it to the other. Eventually they decided that they couldn't even remember a time when it wasn't there; they told me it had been hanging since I was growing up and that I must have been the one to forget.

The part of me that was worried about everything changing actually found that to be a relief. If I was already starting to forget, then maybe these superficial changes weren't so important. Everything from my childhood that had meant something to me, that had defined me, well those I would have remembered and taken with me. Everything that had changed, everything I forgot, those were things that were okay to leave behind.

But some things are impossible to leave, no matter how hard you try. I fell asleep easily enough that night, although I woke with a start to a scratching sound. A dark shape was standing over me – I strained against the confines of the sleeping bag, ripping it aside to leap to my feet. No, just the handlebars of the treadmill. I tried to settle back down, but there was that scratching again. It sounded like it was coming from inside the walls. Mice? Then a long, slow, tearing sound, like a knife running through thick cloth. Not mice. Definitely not mice. I turned on the light and walked along the length of the wall. It was uncomfortable to imagine something running around inside, but the scratching seemed too far away for that.

A heavy thump. This wasn't from inside the wall. This was from the other side. *Footsteps.* I opened the door, flipping on the light in the hallway. A black flash of movement around the corner, just at the edge of my vision. I rubbed my eyes. The painting was face-down on the carpet. That must have been the sound I heard. The nail losing its grip on the wall probably made the scratching, and then the thump as it hit the floor. I convinced myself that the flash of movement was nothing more significant than the shadow of the treadmill until ...

I set the painting upright against the wall. There was a long slash down the center of the canvas, but I couldn't have cared less about the defacement of the art. The fact that the dog was missing from the painting – that's what gripped me. I scrutinized the canvas, even looking under the folded flaps the rip had produced. Nothing. Just heavy brushstrokes of thick blue paint.

Scratching. Scratching. A CRASH. From the other side of the house where my parents slept. I started running toward the noise, but the next sound had me frozen. A wolf's howl – close – somewhere inside the house. Then shouting from my parents, and I was running again. Tearing, growling, another howl – I flung open their door. Blood was everywhere. On the walls, the floor – even the ceiling fan was dripping. Neither of them had been able to get out of bed before their throats were torn out. One brutal bite each, by the looks of it. As quick and painless as could be expected from whatever –

Another howl. Sounded like it coming from outside, through the broken window. Howling, but more distant now, seemingly moving away. It must have known I was there. My room was closer to it than anything. If this is what it came here to do, then why didn't it touch me? I ran to the window where I saw a dark shape looking back at the house. Nothing more than a shadow really, standing on its hind-legs like a human. It was looking right at me, almost like it was waiting for me to see it. Then it was gone, falling onto all fours to bind into the trees behind the house.

I don't know what gave me the courage to follow it that night. It didn't seem like who I was up to this point, but I guess it's up to us to decide who we are from here. My dad had a handgun that he kept in his desk, and he taught me how to use it. I didn't know where I was going or whether I could even find it. I just knew that I wanted to kill something. As long as I kept thinking about the kill, I wouldn't have to think about the dead. Staying here and facing their bodies, or even just the inescapable thoughts in my head – that's what I wasn't brave enough to do.

Either it didn't expect me to follow or didn't care if I did. The creature made no attempt to cover its tracks. At points the way seemed deliberately marked with streaks of blood, trampled underbrush and even the occasional gash torn straight into a tree. I wasn't too far into the woods when the tracks abruptly stopped though. The deep footprints vanished like it had taken flight. The wilderness was pristine. I turned in slow circles, encompassed with the impossibility of the peaceful night.

And with the stillness came the desperate, unbidden thoughts. The confusion, the disbelief, the helpless rage. Blood pounding in my veins, breath like a dagger of cold air, I fired the gun randomly into the trees. Again and again, just to drown out the chaos in my mind. Then the rustling of something farther in, reacting to my shot. It was running now, and I was right behind. I didn't care what it was, I was going to shoot it. Even killing a defenseless animal would help: I just needed an outlet, any outlet for this turmoil inside.

I reached a vantage point over a sudden indenture in the ground and caught a glimpse. Black, shaggy, running on two feet. The dog – the monster – whatever it was. I took another wild shot, but then it was gone again. I fired several more rounds randomly into the woods, but nothing else moved after that. It was gone for good this time. It wasn't a complete loss though, because the last chase had led me to something like a campsite.

The remains of a small fire, a few cans of food, a rolled mat on the ground. This wasn't an animal lair. Stranger still, I found drying brushes and a small stack of framed paintings on the ground. They were all original, all depicting standing dogs with a paw raised to their mouth. Beside these were an equal number of identical frames, each containing nothing but plain background which matched that of the dogs.

There's only one conclusion I was able to draw from this: there's a killer who is deliberately trying to trick people. First comes the dog painting, either given or sold or installed – I don't know. Then he sneaks in to replace the painting with the torn background, looking as if the dog has disappeared. He must have to leave someone alive to spread the tale of the supernatural painting, although I still haven't figured out a reasonable motive behind this. Maybe there is no reason to killing, maybe killing is the reason, I don't know.

I can only imagine how terrifying this must be for someone who wasn't able to track the painting's origin ... and how powerful the killer must feel reducing someone to that point. To take someone's family and destroy their conception of reality in a single blow. There was almost something elegant about the senseless savagery. Even if they never told another soul about what they'd seen, that kind of experience would haunt someone for the rest of their life. To have that strong an impact on someone, or multiple some-ones, to be the most important person in their life without them even knowing who you are....

But you'd know, wouldn't you? Do something like that and you'd really know who you are. And no one could ever take that away from you. All these paintings left, and the killer won't be back now that his secret has been had. Almost seems like a waste. But at the same time maybe he's relieved. A secret like that burning inside of you can eat you up inside. I couldn't have blamed him even if he led me to his camp on purpose. People like us, sometimes we just want our work to be appreciated.

WE CAN FIX YOUR CHILD

As you inevitably age your skin will wither and mush like putrid fruit. Your organs will decay into useless sludge. Even your mind will rob you of a lifetime of memories and experience, reducing you to nothing but an organic shell of who you used to be. You've begun to feel it already. Imperceptible by the day, but implacable as the marching years, your body is growing soft and weak. You will never again be as young as you are in this moment, and even now you can smell all those lofty dreams of youth rotting into idle fantasies that will never be realized.

Ah, but those sweet children! They are the closest thing you will ever have to immortality. They are your only chance to rewind the clock, rekindling the magic of forgotten innocence. Your legs will still tremble as you drag yourself out of bed each morning, but you can feel the spring in their step when they play. Their mastery of skills which have eluded you, their passion for discovering a world which is dead to you, their burning blood which hasn't yet learned what it means to love and not be loved in return; everything that they are is yours.

It's too late for you, but not for them. But only so long as you use the wisdom which life has cruelly carved into you, molding their nascent minds to live the perfect life you have forfeit. I know you're doing your best, and I know that sometimes isn't good enough. They will turn from you in their naive arrogance as you have turned from your own parents. They do not understand how selfish they are being, destroying not only their own life but killing your second chance at life as well.

But don't worry, because we can fix your child.

Do they scream and fight back against your commands? **We can fix that child.**

Do they waste their time on idle laziness that detract from their (or your) fulfillment? **We can fix that child.**

Are they brutish, rude, ugly, stupid, ungrateful wretches who do not understand what sacrifices you have made for them and what they now owe you in return?

One of our greatest success stories began with such a beast. His parents worked very hard for him, but often that meant leaving him alone for long hours to entertain himself. He became obsessively addicted to games during that time, holding his parents' love hostage to continually demand the latest consoles and media.

His adoring parents gave everything to him, hating themselves when they reached their limit and had no more to give. They tried to get him to exercise more, to eat better, to study and learn and play with other children. He would only retreat into his cave though, spurning any attempt to change his ways.

Classes were failed. Graduation was postponed. The boy didn't understand – refused to understand – what life would be like when he had to support himself through his own grit and merit. He was setting himself up for failure, and sure as any disease which devours from the inside out, he was killing his parents.

They were desperate when they came to us. They blamed themselves for his shortcomings, not understanding that it was their child who was broken until we offered our fix. They didn't care how, they just wanted it done.

I sat them down (free consultations, mind you), and had them both write down a list of everything they wanted their boy to be. Let the imagination run wild! Now is not the time to be encumbered with reality which has already been a burden for too long.

They were hesitant at first. Then the father wrote down "be more motivated". That encouraged the mother to add "more happy". The more they wrote, the more they broke the illusion of their son's adequacy, and the more they had to say. Make him taller, said the father. And get him into shape. More compassionate, said the mother, and more sociable with his friends. Smarter, funnier, more honest, more polite ...

Both of them were crying by the end. The boy they had created was nothing like their son, but I was there to console them. Nothing like their son *yet*. But don't worry, because we can fix that child.

The parents did as they were instructed and left town for the weekend. Standard policy; it can be stressful for them to be present during the fixing. We came for the boy in the dead of night when we knew he would be home. We are professionals after-all, and don't like to waste our time.

We don't bother to knock. That would only give him a chance to escape. The parents left a key with us and we entered the house without lights. Up the stairs to his room where the sound of machine guns still blared from his speakers. The little bastard stayed up all night, although that isn't uncommon when the parents are gone for the weekend. He might as well get his last games in now, because he won't be playing anymore after we're done with him.

His game was loud enough to mask our entry. He didn't notice us until we ripped the swivel chair out from under him. The struggle is always brief. Sometimes we'll get a fighter and we have to subdue them with force, but any damage done to the body is inconsequential. He won't be using it for much longer.

I'm pleased to say that even this little monster was fixed within a week. His parents didn't even recognize him, but there's no doubt that they will be happier now. He never talks back. He never speaks before he's spoken to, and even then he'll say "sir" or "ma'am". He hasn't touched his games again, and nothing about his passive countenance promises so much as the least resistance anymore.

Of course, the original is still with us for research purposes. The one that's been returned is the only one you'll ever need though, and you'll love him to the ends of the earth. In return he'll love you back more than you thought possible, because he in his young life has already learned a lesson that some of us do not understand until our grave:

That this world has no place for broken things.

THE SLAUGHTERHOUSE CAMERA

T wo men- pick-up trucks, work-overalls. New hires, they said, but they were professionals who knew their way around a slaughterhouse as well as anyone. They were always comfortable with the hogs I dropped off and never had to ask twice about how I wanted the meat prepared. Of course, both of them deserve the same done to them as they were doing to those poor animals, but there's no way I could have known that when we first met.

Fact is, there aren't enough government-regulated slaughterhouses to accommodate the demand. It's a long, expensive process to get a USDA certified house, and I'm not going to drive eighty miles and pay their exorbitant processing costs just so I can sell my meat across state lines.

That's where "custom houses" come in. These are inspected by the USDA, but they don't require the same standards or constant oversight. I'd been taking my animals to one for about four months when a "John Smith" – the pot-bellied son-of-a-bitch running the land next to me – caught wind of my switch. The bastard started raising hell, telling everybody that my meat wasn't safe – that I tortured my animals – poisoned them – anything to get the local markets to buy his stuff instead.

Now I already had a contract with the fellas down at the custom house, but I called up a friend at the FDA and got him to send over the tapes from their safety cameras. That would give me some proof that everything was up to code, and then I figured all this nasty business would just blow over.

The thing is though, those men at the custom house? I guess they didn't know about the cameras. Otherwise there's no way they would have let that abomination pass in the open like that.

Everything started out normal enough. The hogs were restrained and stunned with an electrical current so they didn't feel any pain. The slaughtering was quick and effi-cient, and then they suspended the animals by their hind legs like ought to be done. After that they were supposed to bleed the carcass dry, but instead they just left them there. Job wasn't even half done, and there they were: packing up their coats and keys and slapping each other on the back like the day was over.

I scrubbed through the video to watch the rest of the process when they got back. They didn't return that night, but something else did. A pale blur dashed across the camera. By the time I stopped it, the creature was in full view: taller than a man, and thinner too. Skin like rice-paper and bulging with so many veins that it might as well have been made of string. Teeth like a hundred needles and shining black eyes like a midnight prayer.

One by one, the beasty was draining the hogs dry. There wasn't any sound, but I could almost hear the puncture as all those little teeth dug into the carcass, submerging its head so deep that I could only see the neck. Then all those veins began to swell, twice – three times their old size, trembling and straining so hard under its thin skin that I thought it had to pop.

But no, it just ripped free and went to the next animal. There wasn't much light, but where the moon snuck through the window its head glowed with blood, almost like there were red lights stuffed underneath the pale skin. I couldn't watch long, and I sure as hell couldn't go showing this to people. Get my name associated with something like that and I wouldn't just be out of business: I'd have torches outside my door and rocks flying through the windows.

First thing the next morning I went down to the custom house. My animals were all sliced and prepared, perfect as ever, but I told the men I was done. I didn't give a reason, just that I wasn't coming back. They got angry about me breaking contract, and we got to yelling at each other. Tensions were getting high, and one of them was so red I thought he was going to take a swing at me. I suppose that's why he said what he did. He was angry, and he wasn't thinking straight. He regretted it the moment it came out of its mouth, but there it was:

"We promised it the animals. It's not going to let you leave."

They didn't want to say more, and I didn't want to hear it. I just drove off without looking back. I locked my doors and windows real tight. I got my shot-gun out from the cabinet and cleaned it until I could see my face in the barrel. And then I prayed, to anyone or anything that would listen: I prayed that I was going to live through the night. It wasn't right for something like that to exist in this world, but if it did, then maybe that meant there was something watching over us too. Or maybe I'm alone right now, and then I wouldn't mind never seeing the dawn again. After-all, why would I want to live in a world where devils were real but angels weren't?

It was about two in the morning when I heard it. I hadn't gone to sleep, just sitting up with the TV on low. I'd spent a long time just listening to my own thoughts, but the wind had started picking up and I couldn't stand how it played around the plank house like fingers running along the wood. I started to nod off once or twice, but the hard handle of my gun was a constant reminder to stay alert. I don't quite know what I was expecting, but it wasn't the knock on my front door.

Slow, regular, rhythmic – casual as a mailman dropping off a package. My grip tightened and I held my breath. There was a long pause, and then it came again. One, two, three, four. I couldn't take it, but I couldn't force enough air out of my lungs to warn it off. Five, six, seven – my body shaking so bad I could barely hold the gun up. The knocking stopped. Before I could even take a proper breath, I saw the face up against the window.

A hundred needle teeth smiling at me from the darkness. I took my shot. The glass exploded and the face was gone. I fired again, just to be sure. No sound but the tinkling of broken glass and the ringing echo in my ears. Then the screaming started up. If you've ever heard a pig scream in the middle of the night, then you know it's like a banshee being dragged down to hell. And knowing what was out there – what it was doing to them – what it *could have* done to me – that made it all a thousand times worse.

I couldn't force myself to leave the house. I just sat there and listened to the chaos of the night. The dissonance of those suffering animals struck something so deep in me that it made me hate being human. I hated caring, feeling – hated my capacity to imagine what was going on out there. I wish I could have just turned it all off and become a mindless animal, or even further into oblivion past the point of this waking nightmare into a sleep so deep that I didn't care if I ever woke up. I hated myself for being too afraid to open the door and kept on hating myself as the screams cut short one by one until there was nothing left but the wind like fingers probing their way in. I hated myself straight into the first tint of dreary daylight splashing through my broken window.

Nine full-grown hogs and five little ones, all gone. And me, the one who should have been the first to go – I'm still here. The custom house has closed down and I haven't a clue what happened to the two who worked there. I'm not getting any more animals though, because I know I can't live through hearing those screams again. I don't know what the creature is eating, but I figure the carnage from that night is going to last him awhile.

Maybe he's moved on and that will be the last I see of him, but I hope not. If there isn't anyone protecting us from on high, then it's just us down here who've got to protect each other. John Smith and I never got along, but next to that thing, I'm ready to call him my brother. And I may not be an angel, but as long as I've got my gun, I can still kill that devil next time I see him.

So now I'm just waiting until the night I look out the window and see all those needle teeth smiling down at me. Won't it be surprised to see me smiling right back?

DON'T LEAVE AN AUDIO RECORDER ON OVERNIGHT

The first time I realized I was an adult I was twenty-three years old. I was in the grocery store when a kid asked me to get some sugar-blasted excuse for a breakfast off the top shelf. I pulled down the box and stared at the cartoons gorging themselves on the luminescent emoticon-shaped diabetes pebbles. He took the box and said, "Thanks mister." Hearing that almost made me feel dirty.

Now at twenty-seven, I know I must be an adult because I'm tired all the time. I go to bed tired, I wake up tired, and in that brief blur of confused social awkwardness in-between? I'm spending that day-dreaming about actual dreaming back in bed.

I went to a doctor to see if he could prescribe me something (since apparently self-medicating with Adderall like I did in college is discouraged and anyway I couldn't find a dealer). No I wasn't depressed. Yes I was getting at least eight hours a night. No I didn't have congenital heart failure or explosive herpes (???). So why didn't I ever have any energy?

The doctor said I might have sleep apnea, a condition which obstructs my breathing while sleeping and causes me to wake up multiple times in the night. I didn't remember waking up, but he said that was common. He wanted me to spend the night in a sleep lab and get a nocturnal polysomnography which measures my heart rate and oxygen levels for detection.

Screw that. I may be an adult, but I'm not old. It was hard enough getting everything done while being tired. The last thing I wanted was trying to get some rest in a lab. I opted instead to just leave an audio recorder on overnight.

Apparently the periods of obstructed breathing would audibly contrast with the heavy breathing which compensated afterward, thus potentially allowing me to detect the issue. No downside, right?

I used an Android app which is a sound activated audio recorder. I messed around with the calibrations a bit and finally reached a sensitivity which detected heavy breathing.

Giggling. Like a little girl. That's what I heard when I played back the audio. I could faintly hear myself breathing in the background. There were three distinct instances during the night where I heard it. I was getting more tired every day though, and this still seemed like an easier solution than going into the lab.

Obviously this was a joke from the app developers. There weren't many reviews on this one, so I downloaded a new recorder and tried again the following night.

Isn't he a precious thing?

Shh. You'll wake the poor baby.

Giggling

Just his back? Their backs aren't very sensitive.

Let him sleep. He isn't ripe yet.

That's what played back to me the following morning. I don't know what's going on, but I've never felt less like an adult than I do now. It's times like this when I really wish I wasn't single. I had a mini panic attack and almost smashed my phone on the nightstand right there.

Tonight I'm going to try a video recording too. I hope I'll still be able to sleep tonight.

Let him sleep. He isn't ripe yet.

Do you have any idea how hard it is to get a good night's rest after hearing that in your room?

I've never been one to freak out about superstitious or supernatural things. When I see a black cat crossing my path, I just figure he has someplace to be. Sure I've read scary stories for their thriller aspects, and I'll watch horror movies with friends just so I can laugh at them for being scared, but I never personally bought into that kind of stuff.

Shh. You'll wake the poor baby.

After playing the tape for what felt like the hundredth time, I was ready to expand my boundaries of reality just to find some explanation. Even deciding that it was a ghost or some nonsensical shit was better than having no explanation at all.

Calling my friends or family though? I would be ruining decades of my carefully maintained image of 'the chill guy who doesn't let anything bother him'. I was resolved to give it one more night with the video recorder to see if I couldn't catch the trickster before asking for help and embarrassing myself.

I tossed and turned for hours last night. I got up about a dozen times to check my laptop to make sure the video was still recording. Just to be safe, I saved the video stream to a password protected google drive folder so it was stored on the cloud. Even if someone tampered with my computer in the night, I should still be able to see what was going on.

I watched the slow minutes drain through my digital clock as though they resented their obligation to pass the time. I don't even remember falling asleep, but one moment I read the time as 2 a.m., and the next moment it was 3:30. I must have slipped out for at least a little while.

The red recording light was off. I immediately jumped up and checked my laptop, but the video file was gone. The backup stream on the google drive was still there though, so I scrubbed through the video.

Me on my back.

Me on my side.

Oh look. There's me upside-down with my feet on the pillow.

And then a face was peering into the screen. A little girl – couldn't have been more than fourteen – was in front of the camera. It was difficult to tell much about her though, because her skin was charred black and flaked off all the way to her heat-splintered skull. Her hair and nose were completely burned away, and all that was left of her eyes and mouth were sticky pits of darkness.

I skipped back to the moment she appeared and played the video. She rose up from below the camera angle as though she were lying on the floor. She turned her head toward my sleeping body, then to the computer.

What's he looking for? she asked.

He's looking for us, the other voice said from somewhere behind the camera. Shut it off.

Can't we just tell him what's happening? He deserves to know.

Jessica, we agreed about this. It's either you or him. Get rid of it, now!

That's where the video stopped. The time-stamp read 3:21 a.m. They were here just a few minutes before I woke up. I checked my window. Locked. The door? Locked from the inside. I even opened the closet and every cupboard in the small apartment kitchen. There wasn't any sign.

In about five minutes, I had returned to my computer to

watch the video again for clues. I'd left the google drive folder open though, and the backup video file was now gone too. They were still in my room somewhere.

Unless I was just going crazy and had woken from a nightmare, but I don't think so. Even with the video gone, my floor was still littered with the black crumbled flakes of burned skin.

It's either you or him. I didn't like the sound of that. I couldn't stay in the apartment knowing they were here, but where could I go at four in the morning?

I called the number for the sleep lab my doctor gave me. There was staff still on duty, but they said they were all booked up through next week.

I grabbed my jacket and keys and headed out the door. As long as I stayed still, I was in too much danger of falling asleep again. I didn't have any real plan, but I figured I would just walk around until the sun rose.

I was more exhausted than ever after that restless night. I still couldn't quite accept this was happening to me. Maybe I was just so tired that my mind had started playing tricks on me. It was hard to be afraid while walking around the familiar park near my home. Vivacious bursts of spring decorated the ground, and I gulped down deep breaths of the fresh air. I could just call in sick today, get a good long sleep, and maybe all of this would just go away.

"Hey buddy." I nearly jumped out of my skin. It was just some homeless guy sleeping on a park bench. I pulled my jacket up and started walking faster.

"Hey don't be like that. Got any change?"

"Sorry. Nothing to spare."

"Yeah right, bastard," he said.

Unpleasant, but it's a common enough encounter in the city. It was what he said next that made my blood run cold.

"I hope the lady burns you next. Like she did to that girl."

I slowly turned to face him. But he was just a crazy hobo who would rant about anything. This couldn't have anything to do with … but the image of that burned skin was not so easily banished from my mind.

"What girl?"

He grinned to get my attention. I could clearly count all five of his yellow teeth peeking through his tangled mass of facial hair.

"Jessica. I could hear the Lady screamin' her name the whole time the girl was burning alive. I hope she gets you too."

He isn't ripe yet.

The words kept playing a loop in my mind while I walked. I was getting hung up on the word ripe. The connotations implied I was getting ready to be harvested for food, but what entity would possibly choose me? I've never built on ancient Indian burial grounds or disrespected a primordial altar.

I did once find out some guy's gamer-tag password in high-school and stole his characters, but I hardly think that's grounds for being tormented like this. There was absolutely nothing about my life which suggested I should be the target for this madness.

Ten bucks was enough to get the homeless man talking. He said he gets thrown out of the park if he sleeps here too often, so he's also set up a camp a little outside town in an aspen grove. The last time he was there, about three days ago, he witnessed a young girl (Jessica) being burned alive while an older woman (the lady) watched.

Of course, he didn't actually say it in those words. His version had a lot more colorful phrases like "I'd sooner eat my shit and eat the next shit afterward then go through that" or "she was screamin' like a dozen cats getting raped by a tiger."

I passed the last gas station in town, and he said the aspens were only about a ten minute walk from here. I've never been so tired in my life. This had to be more than sleep deprivation. It was a mortal weariness – a spiritual weariness, almost as though the bond tying me to this world was starting to unravel. I kicked a rock in my way, and I half expected my foot to pass straight through it.

My best guess is that the lady is some kind of demon, and she sacrificed the girl and now she's going after me. But the older voice in the recording had said Jessica we agreed on this. It's either you or him. How could Jessica have agreed to go through that? Was she tricked? What could she possibly stand to gain?

I knew something was wrong the second I stepped into the aspen grove. The cool morning breeze died the moment I passed the first trunk. The green leaves hung frozen and unnaturally static. The only thing that seemed to be moving was a steady stream of sap which poured down the trees.

Not sap. Blood. I could tell by the dark red streaks left behind on the white bark as it oozed toward the ground. I considered turning back right there, but the more unnatural it seemed, the more important it was for me to stop whatever was happening to me.

There was a clearing in the center of the grove where a circle of salt was lain upon the earth. Sitting in the center was a middle-aged woman who I can only presume was the lady.

Her face was plain and warm, although heavy lines of grief pulled her eyes downward. She wore jeans and a simple floral sweater – not exactly how I would have imagined a witch or demon. Her eyes were closed; hands folded calmly in her lap as though she were waiting for someone – for who? For me?

"You're the lady." The moment I said it, I realized the

homeless guy probably just called her that because he didn't know her name. "You're the one who burned Jessica alive."

She opened her eyes wide – comforting, soulful eyes. Eyes I would have trusted under any other circumstance.

"You weren't supposed to find out until the end. I'm sorry you became involved in this," she said.

"Until the end? You mean when I was ripe? What was going to happen then?" I wanted to hit her. To throw a stone – to yell – anything. But seeing her so calm and ordinary and sad, I couldn't even raise my voice. The little energy I had left was fueled with indignation and anger, and without that it was all I could do just to keep standing.

"I told you, mother. He deserves to know what's going on." My skin prickled. Jessica was sitting outside the ring of salt – or at least what was left of her. The whole body was as black and rough as charcoal. All of her clothes had burned away, and the skin had burst in many places to reveal flayed sinew and cooked bone underneath.

"You burned your own daughter alive?" I felt the rage building again, and I didn't fight it. I had to hold onto it. This feeling was all that reminded me I was still awake – still alive.

"You're right, Jessica. I've been so selfish." The woman sighed, and seeing her in such dismal misery, my anger was once more replaced by profound pity.

That's when she explained everything to me. She wasn't a witch at all – only a mother who couldn't bear to watch her daughter suffer.

Jessica was born with cerebral palsy – an incurable disorder which devastated her mind and body. She could barely swallow on her own, and her mother had done everything within the boundaries of medical science only to find that was not enough. After that, she'd tried alternative medicines – crystals, powders, ointments, prayers, and finally at the end of all things: rituals.

Her pursuit of the arcane led her subtly down the road of the occult until she discovered a process known to cure someone of all mortal ailments. In this vain hope, she burned Jessica alive in order for her to return purified.

"The entity I made the pact with was willing and eager up until I lit the fire in her flesh," her mother told me, "but afterwards he began to make demands before he would bring her back."

At the demon's request (for that is what she found herself bound to), she planted seven black seeds in the food where she worked as a grocer. Only once the seeds had ripened within their victims, Jessica would be allowed to return.

By the end of her tale, the last of my strength had fled me and I was sitting beside her in the salt circle while Jessica watched from the outside.

"I'm sorry," she mumbled, no longer able to meet my gaze. "I had already burned her. I couldn't stop before I … "

"What happens? When they're – when we're ripe?" I asked. My throat was choked and dry. I couldn't help but glance back at Jessica's grotesque disfiguration. Was that what was in store for me too?

"The seeds are a portal into the other side," she said. "Once they're fully grown, the demon will enter this world and -"

"And possess me." I finished.

"I'm so sorry. He told me you would just go in peace. I never thought one of you would find out what was going on -"

"How long do I have?" I asked.

"I don't know. Not long. That's why Jessica and I have been watching the people with the seeds. We've been waiting for them to burst."

"Can you stop it?" I knew what her answer would be before I even asked, but I had to hear it anyway. If it meant bringing her daughter back, would she have stopped it even if she could?

"No. All I did was plant the seeds in the food. How they work is as much a mystery to me as you."

We stared at each other for a moment. I lifted my hands and felt their unnatural weight, and she flinched as though afraid I would strike her.

"Do you hate me?" she asked.

"No." And it was true. I hated that this was happening – I was afraid – but I didn't hate her. I might have even done the same in her place. "I can't hate you, because I need you."

"I told you there's nothing I can do," she protested.

"You can stay with me here, and keep me company until it comes. You're a lucky girl, Jessica. Your mother loves you very much."

I didn't even have enough energy to sit upright anymore. I slumped against the lady – it's easier for me not to know her name – and she wrapped her arms around me. I pulled out my phone and considered calling my family, but I didn't know how to make sense of my situation. Instead I'm posting my final update, which they will find and come to understand. The lady held my hand as I rested against her, and together we are waiting for oblivion to come.

BET I CAN MAKE YOU SMILE

The first time I met him was at my grandfather's memorial. Dark, round spectacles just covering his eyes, long black coat, steel-grey hair halfway down his shoulders. A whole room of handkerchiefs and downcast faces, but he was the only one smiling. I was only eight at the time, and that seemed like a good enough reason for me to sit beside him.

"Did you know Papi?"

"Better than anyone," the man said. He must have been almost seventy – same age my grandfather was.

"Were you his friend?"

"His closest friend. I'm the one who killed him, you know. You can't get any closer than that."

I tried to ask him more questions, but the service was starting and my mother kept turning around to hush me. Mom gave the eulogy, and that was the first time I'd ever seen her cry. I guess I must have started sniffling too, because the man next to me put his hand on my knee and gave it a little squeeze. His fingers felt like he'd just come inside from a blizzard.

By the end of the final sermon they brought out some bagpipes to play Amazing Grace, and then I really did cry for real. I remember it being hard for me to understand why I'd never get to see Papi again. Sure he was dead, but that didn't mean I couldn't still visit and eat his BBQ sandwiches, did it?

Once I started crying, I didn't know how to make it stop. People must have been sympathetic, but just remember how embarrassing it felt to have everyone staring at me. I was the first one out of the room, running all the way outside the church to the big oak tree in the yard.

The man with dark spectacles was the first to find me.

"Hey there champ," he'd said. "Bet I can make you smile."

I shook my head and pressed my face into the bark.

"Watch this," he said in a voice accustomed to being obeyed. I looked up to see him whistling at a squirrel sitting in one of the lower branches. The squirrel ran down the trunk until it was a few feet above our heads, then jumped without hesitation to land on his shoulder.

"How'd you do that?" I asked.

"I can do all sorts of things," he said, crouching down to my level so I could pet the squirrel.

"Why'd you kill him?"

"Because it made me happy," he said, standing to lift the squirrel out of my reach. "Run along now, I'll see you soon. We can play another game then."

"When?"

"When I kill your grandmother. Not long now."

Not long at all. Three weeks and she was gone. My parents told me that she just missed Grandfather so much that she decided to follow him to Heaven. I knew better. One night I couldn't sleep and crept to the top of the stairs to listen to them talking about it in the kitchen. Grandmother's hands were peacefully folded over the knife in her heart when they found the body.

The man was there at the next memorial, just like he'd promised. I was afraid of him now, sitting as far away as I could. I wanted to tell someone what he'd done, but somehow my eight year old brain thought that I would get in trouble. It was my fault she got murdered. I knew it was going to happen and I didn't try to stop him.

He found me again while I was waiting for my parents to leave. Out by the tree, this time he'd gotten there first. I could feel his dark spectacles trained on me as I crossed the yard, but I couldn't stop myself. I wanted to know who was next.

"I hate you," were the first words out of my mouth.

"That's all right," he said. "Most people hate things they don't understand."

"I want you to stop killing people."

"I'm not going to do that," he replied. "But here's what I can do: bet I can make you smile."

He sat on the grass and concentrated. Maybe I should have run, but it wasn't a matter of fear for me. It was simply a choice between interesting and boring, questions and answers. I watched the tree as the squirrel scampered down the trunk.

"Come to me," he whispered, and off it flew – straight onto his hand. Not just the squirrel either. Ants were swarming out of the ground to line up around his feet. Beetles and worms and unknowable monstrous squirming creatures thrashing their way through the ground to bow before him. Even a stray cat came sprinting across the yard, none of the animals the least perturbed by the others' presence. They were all watching him expectantly like a dog waiting for his treat.

"Let us dance," he said, and so they did. The squirrel hopped from one foot to the other, the cat stood on its hind legs, and all the insects began to sarcastically twirl upon the ground. Despite everything, I couldn't help but smile at the spectacle.

I wasn't smiling the next time I saw him at my mother's funeral. Thirty-one years, and he hadn't aged a day. I could feel those dark spectacles on me the moment I entered the room, like childhood's imaginary monster come to life before my very eyes. The same grey hair, the same black coat, the same subtle smirk creasing the edges of his face. I couldn't stand to sit in the same room as him. I felt hot and dizzy. I didn't know what was real and what wasn't, only that I needed air.

My feet traced the familiar steps to the tree without intervention from my scattered mind. My mother had been found by her neighbor the same way – a knife in her heart. I wanted to hit him. To *kill him*. To wipe that smirk off his face, whatever it took. I was seething when he approached. Drawing close, all my carefully prepared arguments and threats blurred from my mind. I couldn't understand how anyone could have the audacity to say:

"Come now, it's not all bad. Bet I can make you smile."

"You're dead."

"Sometimes I wish I was." He sighed, sitting down on the grass. I hesitated. Not the answer I was expecting. "But if I was dead, then who would have been there to kill your mother?"

I kicked him while he sat on the ground. As hard as I could. I jumped on him, grabbing a fistful of his long hair to fling him down into the ground. Everyone else was still inside the church. No one but god was going to see what I did to him, and god would understand. He didn't make a move to rise or resist. He just spat enough blood out to say: "Come to me."

I kicked him again and he went down hard. And again – I heard something break under his coat. I would have kept going, but a piercing pain in the back of my neck made me spin around. A crow was diving at me, pecking me, its black eyes glinting with intelligence and purpose.

"Fight your own battles!" I shouted, batting the bird away from my face. "Or are you too scared? Is that why you only kill old people who can't fight back?"

"I can't kill you," he admitted. I was on top of him again, pushing him back into the dirt. The crow wouldn't relent, but I could suffer through any cuts and scratches it gave me to get at him.

"But here's what I can do," he said through his broken teeth. "Bet I can make you smile."

"You know what? Fine. Make me smile. And if you can't, then you're going to turn yourself into the police and tell them about every person you've killed."

"And if I can, then you're going to help me with my next kill."

That took me a second to process. Of course I wouldn't do it. Of course I wouldn't smile either. My face was harder than stone. I nodded. "Deal."

I let him stand to dust off his jacket, which he did quite easily as though he had suffered no hurt from my assault. "I can't kill you because you're not ready yet. Your grandparents were. Your mother was, although she never told you. All I do is help them along their journey."

"You're insane. I'm not smiling."

"I've got proof," he said, forcefully popping his jaw back into place with a slight grunt. "It's all around you. After I've helped them, they never forget me for what I've done."

I looked around where he gestured. The tree? The squirrel crouching to spring at me. The thousands of insects even now gathering at his feet. The crow watching from the branches, its head cocked to the side.

"Mom?"

The crow hopped down from the tree to land on my shoulder, brushing its head against my cheek. I swallowed hard. I felt more like crying than smiling, but I guess I was doing both so he still won the bet.

"Death is an evil thing only when seen in isolation," he told me. "But death never exists in isolation. It's just an abstract thought to imagine it that way. A single thread once woven may seem lost, but only until you step back and see the whole tapestry it helped to create. Come with me now, and I will show you how to weave."

And as sure as any bird or beast who answered his call, I followed him. And I've been following ever since.

RECORDINGS OF MYSELF

Someone has been mailing me recordings of myself. First one was a couple weeks ago. It was just an unmarked DVD in a paper sleeve, addressed to me without a return. I figured it was some kind of spam mail and tossed it out. Ain't nobody got time for that.

The second one was getting ready to romance the trash too, but it happened to arrive the day I bought a used XBOX. I wanted to test out the DVD player and didn't have anything else handy, so I just popped it in and let it play.

The footage was a bit fuzzy and shaky like someone was walking while they recorded. It showed me entering my apartment building, following me until I got in the elevator. I even looked right at the camera for a second, but wracking my brain I couldn't remember noticing anyone strange.

There was a voice-over too, but it was in German and I couldn't make sense of it. I started it over and watched again. Only about fifteen seconds – it wasn't so much creepy as surreal. I was honestly more bothered by how terrible my posture looked than I was about someone recording me.

Probably some kid showing off his new camera or something – the world is full of weirdos, right?

The third one rattled me though. The video showed me in the grocery store, wandering up and down the aisle looking for something. About ten seconds again – more German voice-over. This wasn't someone innocently playing with their phone in the lobby anymore. I was being actively followed. I threw it away immediately, regretting it and digging it out of the trash a couple minutes later. I had to get this translated so I could figure out what the hell was going on.

The next day I shuffled through my mail like crazy looking for another DVD. Nothing came. Or the next day or the one after that. Getting it translated fell further and further down my to-do list, until a week or so later I'd practically forgotten about it.

Until yesterday anyway, when another paper-sleeve slipped out from between some junk mail and landed on my floor. I rushed to play it, regretting it from the very first frame. The screen was panning around my room. *My bedroom.* It was dark, but everything had a green night-vision tint. The camera focused on the bed and started to approach. It took me a few seconds to recognize the lump in the dark. It was recording me while I slept.

A hand reached out from behind the camera – pale thin, hairless hand, with skin stretched too tight across the bones. And the digits were wrong: four to each finger, and double jointed, moving so fluidly they might as well have been tentacles. It rested a long finger on my forehead, trailing down my nose, over my lips, brushing so soft that I couldn't tell whether it was touching at all. Something in German again – a sing-song voice barely above a whisper. It was longer this time, but I paused to keep going back until I could write down every word as close as I could hear it.

I watched the rest of the video before I translated anything. He stayed beside me for a long time, but I didn't want to fast forward because I was afraid of missing some crucial dialogue. I stared at it staring at me for almost an hour before I couldn't take it anymore. The camera had been still for a long time, and I hadn't heard or seen any other sign of the perpetrator. I decided even if something else did happen that night then I'd prefer not to know. I rummaged around until I found the elevator and the grocery store tapes too, writing down all the German from them to translate. After hacking my way through the spellings a few times, google translate gave me this:

Tape 1 – ??? (Don't know, I threw it out before I knew what it was.)

Tape 2 – (Me in the elevator) "Look at him go. I can't believe he's going back into the apartment after what we told him last time."

Tape 3 – (Me at the grocery store) "Found him again. Look how calm he is, just going about his life. Do you think he's seen it yet?"

Tape 4 – (Whispered while I slept). "Sleep, baby, sleep. Thy father guards the sheep. Thy mother shakes the little trees. There falls down one little dream.

"Sleep, baby, sleep! Sleep, baby, sleep. The sky draws the sheep. The little stars are little lambs. The moon, the little shepherd,

"Sleep, baby, sleep! Sleep, baby, sleep. I shall bring your sheep. One with a golden bell. That shall be thy journeyman to guide you safe to hell."

That's it. I don't know whether this thing is trying to threaten me or protect me, or what it could be trying to protect me from. Either way, I don't think I'm going to sleep tonight. I don't know what I would do if I woke up and saw that thing watching me, recording me – even touching me with its long disjointed fingers. When the next DVD comes – if it comes … I don't think I have the stomach to watch.

YOUR DREAM JOB

A gun on the table between us. We could both walk out alive if we wanted, but how were we supposed to trust that's what the other was thinking too?

What would you like to be when you grow up? An astronaut? A captain of industry? How about a TV producer? Well here's what you have to do: study real hard so you can get into a good college. Then keep on studying, all the way until you get your degree.

Student loans? Don't worry about it. You'll be making plenty of money in your career, so why stress about paying with your minimum wage now? Looking for a job? No problem! You're an expert in the field you've chosen. The places you want to work are going to chase after YOU to work for THEM!

Sound familiar? Yeah, well I fell for it too. Four years out of college and I haven't used my chemistry degree for anything besides mixing drinks. At first I wanted to be on the cutting edge of biomedical research, but now I'd settle for any somewhat relevant job at a pharmaceutical company.

Hell, I'd even hand out drugs at the convenience store if they'd let me.

It wasn't just the money either. It was about that look my friends gave me when I solved a complex problem that flew over their heads. Or the excitement of my new class schedule, or the pride in my parents' faces when they introduced their future chemist to their friends. Science wasn't just a future plan for me: it was my identity. It's not my dream that's dying every day at the bar. It's just that every day that passes makes it that much harder to answer the question who are you?

Until I got an offer. *The* offer. The dad of a friend whose brother I knew from – doesn't matter where. It was a tech startup with real investors. No experience required, paid on-the-job training. I was going to have an office with one of those fancy little name plaques on the door. I was going to have title, and a salary, and sick days and health care and 401k and everything!

The CEO and I hit it off really well too. At first I was terrified to ask questions that might betray my inexperience, but he was easy going and seemed more interested in my personality than my qualifications. Loyalty, he stressed over and over again, that's all he cared about. Everything else you can teach.

"We don't expect to make any money off the new hires," he explained. "But a good man who's been here ten years is worth more to me than ten great men giving a year each."

That's why the first day on the job wasn't a tour of the facilities or an analysis of our knowledge. We were going on a company team building exercise right off the bat. Big rope and obstacle course that we were supposed to help each other through, doing exercises like trust falls and listening to motivational talks. What's not to like about a field trip on your first day?

Ten of us took two SUVs. It was a pretty long drive into the woods where the camp was, but it gave me a chance to get to know the other employees. A lot of fresh faces like myself, right out of college and desperate to prove themselves. At first I was a bit incredulous that this much money and trust was being placed in a newbie team, but the CEO told us it made sense from a long-term perspective. How are you going to have lifelong employees if you don't catch them early? And who is going to be more loyal than the guy who was given his first shot to follow his dream?

All ten of us were gathered in a cabin while the CEO gave his talk. Five tables faced the front, two to each table. You wouldn't have found better spirits on a campus that had just canceled the final exams in favor of an impromptu music festival. And the CEO just fed the fire, talking about the cutting edge research facilities with secured funding both private and government. Gene manipulation, panacea medicine, even immortality – humanity was on the tipping point into a futuristic age, and we were going to be the ones to make it happen.

"Now I hope you all understand why I value loyalty so highly," he lectured. "Before any of you have reached middle aged, pending discoveries are likely to double the average lifespan. We aren't a company, we're a family, and that's a bond for life. Now here comes the hard part."

He turned his laptop to display the draft of a news article. *Five fatalities in deadly SUV accident.* It was the same type of car we drove here in.

"Feelings, promises, even oaths – it's a fragile thing to build a company on that's going to last a hundred years," he said. "I like to have a little more insurance than that. So this is how we're going to play."

He walked around the room, placing a handgun on each of the five tables. Tension rippled through the room in a wave of rigid posture and fixated eyes. I chanced a glance at the person beside me – blonde girl, mid-twenties, eyes like saucers. I couldn't imagine her ever holding a gun in her life. What kind of screwed up team-building exercise was this? The CEO didn't say another word until all the guns were handed out, each positioned right in the center of the table.

"The rules are simple," he said, face quivering with excitement. "When I say go, the first person to shoot the other one at their table gets a job. No going easy either – I want a clean head-shot. If you just wound them, then you don't have the job yet. We're going to go one table at a time so everyone else can stay safe and avoid collateral damage."

One of the girls made a nervous giggle and rolled her eyes. I guess she didn't think he was serious, not until he snapped the gun up from her table and blasted a hole through the window. No one made a sound after that.

"Do I look like I'm joking?" he asked the girl, bending low over the table to put his face up against hers. She shook her head vehemently. Grinning, the CEO pulled away and continued to pace the room.

"We're going to make it look like the five who died were in a car accident," he said. "Those who remain are the kind of people I want to have around. And yes, each killing will be recorded, just in case you change your mind down the road. Like I said, insurance."

"You're crazy if you think any of us are actually going to do that!" the blonde girl beside me said, her voice cracking when the CEO turned. "We'll just walk away. Find our own way home if you want to. Nobody would want to work for a company like this!"

"If you believe that; if you *really* believe that there aren't people in this room who are willing to do whatever it takes to make their dreams come true, then you should have nothing to fear when it's your turn. If neither of you shoots, then neither of you get the job. You can both go home."

She smiled tentatively at me, and I returned it. Good news. I got the pacifist at my table. Unless it was all an act to get the jump on me. Or she didn't trust me – a complete stranger – and decided to shoot first just to save her own skin. The smile hardened in her face. We're all educated people here. This was game theory, plain and simple. And even in university level studies, there was always going to be someone who chose to screw the other over just to be safe. Now with life on the line, that was going to be even more evident.

"We're all going to be fine then!" the blonde girl said. "Everybody agree not to shoot, okay? If no one shoots then we pass. It's just a test."

"Table one!" the CEO bellowed. "Everyone else out of the room for your own safety. To those playing: don't move a muscle until I say go or I'll shoot you myself. Let's move people."

Everyone except Table 1 and the CEO exited the room. Some of us plastered against the windows to peek inside, but I just pressed my back to the wall in case of stray bullets. The blonde girl wouldn't shut up. I know she meant well, but I was so stressed that it just got under my skin. We're going to be fine, she kept saying. No one is going to shoot. They're probably just BB guns anyway. That would have still broken the window, but it won't kill –

"Go!" he shouted from inside. *A gunshot.* Almost simultaneously. The people at the window blanched and leaped away.

The CEO opened the door and we couldn't help but look inside. One was dead on the ground, a pool of blood spreading from his head. The other was holding the gun, violently shaking where he stood over the body.

"He moved first!" the survivor desperately shouted. "I had to! He would have shot me, I swear!"

"Table two, you're up! Everyone else out."

The two girls looked at each other, both smiling meekly. They were holding each other's hands and exchanging promises as the rest of us went back out. Maybe they wouldn't do it. Then again, that first gunshot was still echoing in our ears: a grim reminder of the price of trust.

Another gunshot. And another, and another, and another. When the door opened again, only one of the girls was still standing. She didn't even make an excuse. She just shrugged, dropping the gun on the corpse riddled with holes.

I was the next one up. The blonde girl across from me. The gun between us. Everyone else had left the room except the CEO. He was flushed red and sweating, but there was a grin plastered on his face as he savored the moment before the game started.

"We're going to get through this," she told me for the hundredth time. "I trust you. Do you trust me?" I nodded, although of course I didn't. Not after what I had already seen. Not after what was at stake. I didn't even know if I could pull the trigger when I pointed it at her. I still didn't know what I was going to do, right up to the moment he said, "Go!"

We both held our breath. I saw her finger twitch, but then she shook her head. I crossed my arms to show I wasn't going to touch it. Five seconds. Ten. Her fingers were dancing haphazard rhythms on the table. I uncrossed my arms, just in case she did go for it and I'd need a chance to react. Too late. She already had the gun, pointing it at my face.

"It's over," she said. "I've got the gun, and I'm not going to shoot. Neither of us are taking the job."

"Easy to say when you're the one with the gun. Is that

what he wants too?" I started to answer, but the CEO cut me off by handing me a gun from another table. "Let's find out together."

Her finger tightened around the trigger. I already knew she wouldn't kill me for greed, but what about for self-preservation? It was a game of centimeters as I lowered my gun to the table. Relief flooded across her face. "Sorry," I told the CEO. "Game's over."

I waited until her gun lowered to shoot. Right between the eyes. The CEO's face lit up like a child on Christmas. "That-a-boy! Good long term planning. Way to keep your head. You're going to go far here."

I could feel the hatred on me as I left the cabin, but I didn't care. The ones who hated me were the ones going to end up dead anyway. Everyone else had no right. If anything, this shared ordeal was going to bind us together. Then again, I was going to work at a company where all my co-workers wouldn't hesitate to kill someone for their own gain. I guess loyalty to the CEO comes first, and trust was something we were going to have to learn over time.

Five separate games, and by the end, five dead bodies. No one had been able to walk away. But I guess that's in the past now. I had a whole lifetime of productive work to make up for what happened. I guess I know who I really am now.

So I guess the question is: what would you do for your dream job?

WHICH CHILD TO SAVE

The sanctity of my home was destroyed two years ago when a man smashed our kitchen window in the dead of night. I woke immediately, clutching sheets to my chest, pretending for as long as I could that the sounds of tinkling glass were fragments of a discarded dream.

The sliding deadbolt though? That was all too real. And the familiar creak as the door was carelessly swung open.

My first instinct was to rush down the hall to where my two boys were sleeping. I should have called the police immediately, but I wasn't thinking straight. I could only imagine how terrified they must be, and what would happen to us if one of them started crying and alerted the burglar that we were here.

The lights went on downstairs. The clatter of things being flung from shelves and scattered onto the floor. The intruder made no pretense to disguise himself; either he thought no one was home, or he was simply too drunk or desperate to care.

David (twelve at the time) was already out of bed by the

time I got there. He was getting ready to go downstairs and see what was going on. Mikey (ten) peeked around the doorframe, quivering eyes glowing in the darkness. I pulled my children back into the room and slammed the door behind me –

Too fast. Too loud. I strained to hear past the sound of our terrified panting. The man downstairs had stopped moving. Only for a moment though. Now he was sprinting up the stairs, the old wood thundering his arrival. This room didn't have a lock on it, but I pressed my back against the door as I finally called 911.

The handle rattled behind me. I pushed everything that I was against the door, but I couldn't hide. I had to speak aloud to tell the police where I was. My whole body went numb as the intruder slammed into the door. Again and again – I was in tears, barely able to get the words out. Mikey started screaming, but I couldn't comfort him. David wanted to help me hold the door, but I pushed him away.

I kept imagining a bullet or a knife puncturing through the thin wood to enter my body. All I could do was hold on until I couldn't, and then he was through.

He overpowered me in seconds. He kicked me hard in the stomach and I couldn't get back up. He was shouting something – asking where the jewelry or valuables were. I was crying too hard to answer him. David tried to wrestle him off, but the man pulled a knife.

I don't know what would have happened if we didn't hear the sirens then. The intruder was panicking – more than panic, he was practically drooling over himself in some drug-induced frenzy. He rushed back and forth with indecision while I screamed for help. He was about to make a dash for it when the police loudly announced they were coming in.

I told the intruder it was over. He couldn't get out. Anything he tried would just make it worse for him.

"I'm taking one of them with me. Tell the police the boy is dead if I'm followed."

And that's when he made me choose. I didn't have time to think. I was so scared that he'd hurt us if I didn't answer. I closed my eyes and pointed at David. My boy was screaming for me, but I couldn't open my eyes.

"Don't fight him," I begged. "He'll let you go when he's safe. I promise."

I didn't open my eyes until I felt Mikey rush sobbing into my arms. We were alone when the police found us.

I didn't see David again for three days. And even when he did come back – beaten, starved, with haunted eyes – he wasn't ever the same. He never talked about what happened. I tried to explain that I only pointed at him because he was older. He was bigger, and stronger, and smarter – he could take care of himself better than Mikey could. It didn't matter though. There was nothing I could say to change the fact that when our lives were on the line, I didn't choose to keep him safe.

David started getting in trouble at school after that. The principal was sympathetic at first, but after David started picking fights they had to suspend him. He started spending more and more time away from home without telling anyone where he'd been, sometimes not returning for days at a time. It didn't matter how much I worried; he'd just snap something like I can take care of myself or but you'd rather me stay out than Mikey, right?

I couldn't see the end to the road he was going down, but if something didn't change, then I knew it was going to be too late for him to turn back. There was only one thing I could think of that would convince David how much he mattered to me. If he wouldn't listen, then my last resort was to show him.

I planned to re-enact that fateful night. I planned it with a close friend at work. Mikey and David and I were going to be out camping when my friend would pretend to attack us. It'd be just like before, only this time I'd choose to save David. Then my friend would run off like he'd lost his nerve, and David would know how much I care. I know it's sick to play with my family like that, but it's the only thing I could think of to make things right again.

Everything was going perfectly. David didn't want to go on the trip, but once I forced him into the car he seemed to be getting along well enough with his brother. They were even singing with the radio together as we pulled into the campsite.

It was about 10 p.m. when my friend sent me the text. He was ready. Deep breaths – I steeled myself against the coming ordeal. Mikey and David looked up from the camp-fire to the rustling in the darkness.

My friend exploded out of the undergrowth wearing a ski-mask. He was brandishing a hunting knife like he knew how to use it. I screamed right on cue – the kids were screaming – this was going to be over before they knew it.

"One of you boys are coming with me," my friend ordered.

"I won't let you!" I stood in front of them, putting up a brilliantly fierce display.

"Then everyone dies." He was holding a gun now. I hadn't told him to bring a gun, but it was good. It felt real. I could feel both my kids staring at me. Did they suspect something? No, they couldn't have. Shit, I knew the truth and I was still terrified.

I pointed at Mikey, and then I closed my eyes. That was the end of our scenario. Now my friend would run away and everything would be fair –

My eyes flew open when I heard the gunshot. Mikey was cowering behind me. David had a knife in his hand – lord knows where he got it. He'd tried to rush my friend, who panicked and put a bullet in my son to keep him back. David didn't stop though. The knife was flashing by the light of the campfire and this time my screams were real.

Two more gunshots. By the time I got to them, it was too late. My friend's neck was sliced from ear to ear. Blood was bubbling up from a gruesome wound in David's chest and another in his shoulder. My frantic hands eased him to the ground, but that was all I could do.

"Is Mikey okay?" David asked.

"He's okay. You saved him. But David you shouldn't have _"

"You made your choice, I made mine," he said. "Now you won't have to choose anymore."

Both David and my friend were dead before the park rangers arrived. I didn't know how to explain the situation, so I just told them that we were attacked and that David died defending us. It's my fault what happened though, and it feels right for me to be sharing the story now. Living or dying, speaking or staying quiet, loving or holding back – every day is a choice whether we notice or not. And every choice has consequences.

Mikey, I love you and your brother more than you'll ever know. Will you ever choose to forgive me?

I received this letter from my mother on the fifth anniversary of my brother's death. Thought I'd share it with you all so you can help me decide.

LIFE WITHOUT MONSTERS

"Stay up as late as you want, I don't mind," my mother used to say. "I don't think Raleigha will like it though."

Raleigha was the monster who lived in our neighborhood or so my mother used to say. He had a mouth in the palm of each hand, and barbed teeth that latched on and expanded inside the skin of any disobedient little boy unfortunate enough to attract his attention. Quiet as the falling night and swift as a guilty heart, Raleigha would stalk the house waiting for his favorite meal.

My mother never gave me a satisfying explanation for why misbehaving children taste better, but she swore it was true.

"Good thoughts spoil the meat," she told me one night when she tucked me in. "They make you all chewy and stringy and bland. Raleigha can smell an evil thought from miles away though, and nothing will stop him from eating the person who deserves it."

"Is that what dad is running from?" I remember asking

her once. I was too young to understand how much that question hurt her.

"Exactly right," she said. "But it won't do him any good. There's nowhere to run that's too far for thoughts to follow, and wherever your dad is right now, you can bet Raleigha will find him."

I understood that mom was trying to frighten me into being good, but I was never scared of Raleigha. I thought of the monster more like a super hero: a fantastic force of nature that hunted the wicked and brought justice to the world. I imagined Raleigha praising me when I did well, and he never punished me no matter how much I deserved it.

Other children had dads, and I had Raleigha. When the people at the grocery store made us put the food back on the shelves because we didn't have enough money, I'd just think about what Raleigha would do to them. Or when someone was cruel to me at school – I'd just imagine how it must feel to have those swelling teeth inside you that wouldn't ever come out. Compared to that, my troubles didn't seem so bad at all.

Mom was wrong about Dad, though. Raleigha never caught up with him. Even when Dad came back and started hanging around the apartment, Raleigha never touched him. When Dad was shouting all those things at Mom, Raleigha never interrupted. And when he hit her, grabbing her hair, her throat – throwing her around the apartment like a rag doll – well I guess Raleigha had bigger scumbags to hunt that day.

"Raleigha must still smell some good in your father," my mother told me. "Don't worry about me though. If it ever gets bad enough, Raleigha will know and save us from him."

Other children had God, and I had Raleigha. And when the sacrosanct night was broken by my parents shouting, I'd pray to him in my own way. If I could only concoct an evil enough thought, then Raleigha would smell it and find us. I didn't even care what would happen to me because of it. As long as Raleigha was here, he'd get my dad too, and then mom wouldn't have to cry anymore.

I made a game out of it when I lay awake at night: trying to think of the most vile, twisted thing in all the world. I thought about hurting the kids at my school, or throwing stones through windows, or stealing. I thought about shouting at people like Dad did, or punishing animals – anything so Raleigha could smell how bad it was. I tried my hardest, thinking horrible things day and night until at last during school I finally thought of the worst thing there was.

I was going to kill myself when I got home. I was going to tie one end of a string around my neck and the other end to the drain in the bathtub, tying it so tight that I couldn't get undone even when the tub started to fill with water. I'd be stuck there doing and thinking the worst thing I could do, until Raleigha smelled it and came for me.

I heard Mom and Dad fighting before I even opened the front door. They were in their bedroom, so neither of them saw me twisting a dozen strings together into a rope that would be too strong for me to break. The running water couldn't drown out the yelling, but it made everything seem a little less real. I couldn't wait for my head to be underwater so I wouldn't have to listen to them anymore.

My fingers were shaking while I tied the string around my neck, but it was such a horrible thought that I knew I wouldn't have to be under for long. Raleigha was going to come before I drowned. I'd tell him what was really going on and he'd save us from Dad, and then Raleigha would live with us and I'd fight evil with him like I always wanted. I thought I was going to be a hero as I tightened the tether and pressing my face under those warm comforting waves. I thought Mom was going to be so happy when she found out what I did for her.

I tried to tell my body to lay still, but it wouldn't listen. The burning pressure rippled through my body and I thrashed against the twined string. I couldn't break it. I briefly fumbled with the knots, but the water pulled them too tight to work through. I had to wonder what would happen if Raleigha never came. If I never came back up. And still being able to hear dad shouting while I was under water, I decided that I was okay with that too.

When hands finally grabbed hold of my buckling body and ripped me free, I braced myself waiting for those hooked teeth to pierce my flesh. It was just my mom though, holding me and crying, pumping the water from my stomach and lungs.

"Did Raleigha come? Where is he?" was the first thing I asked.

"Didn't you see him? He's already gone," she told me.

"And Dad? Did he get Dad?"

I saw the blood leaking out from Mom's closed door after I left the bathroom. I had to stay with my grandmother for a week after that. There wasn't any blood when I got home, and I haven't seen Dad since.

I still don't know if the monster that night. When I told the story to some friends at school, they said Raleigha must have killed him. My friends were all terrified of monsters after that, but that's just because they didn't understand. If this is what humans do to each other, then I'm afraid of a life without monsters.

400 HITS OF LSD

Why is life so confusing?

It never should have gotten to this point, but it's too late to turn back now. I've always tried to be a good person, a statement most people won't appreciate coming from a drug dealer. If it wasn't for my mother getting sick, I might have been able to survive school and make an ordinary life for myself.

I'm not here to make excuses. The fact is that I knew what I was getting into when I started moving LSD and molly on campus. I kept telling myself that this was a transition state to help with tuition and medical bills, but three years later and I was deeper in than ever.

I was still attending classes and holding it together until my junior year when Mom finally passed. I never knew my dad, and there wasn't anyone left to impress anymore. No one to disappoint either. I started selling harder stuff – meth, heroin, PCP, once the money was in my hand, it didn't matter how it got there. I dropped out of school, making more in a weekend than I would have in a month with my degree.

I wasn't just dealing drugs now; I was a drug dealer.

What's the difference? When people are only good at one thing in the world, then that's who they become. I wouldn't just be broke and bored if I stopped dealing now. I'd be no one. I was pushing harder than ever, day and night, shipping in bulk supplies from the dark web and hiring my own runners to sell across the city.

I guess I hadn't realized how bad it had gotten until one of the boys who worked for me never came back with the money he owed. I found him cowering in his apartment a little ways off campus, blubbering about how someone attacked him on the street. He showed me the mark where the knife was pressed into his neck while hands rifled through his pockets and bag, taking everything.

Two thousand dollars' worth, gone. And the funny thing? The whole time I was smashing his face until it looked like raw hamburger meat, I never once cared if he was telling the truth. I didn't feel anything when he was crying blood and choking on his teeth.

I didn't feel anything while I walked home either, not the curiosity of if he was going to live or die, not the autumn sun on my skin, not even a concern for what might happen to me because of it.

You know what did cut through the static? Realizing that no one would have noticed if I had been attacked instead. No one would care if someone beat me into oblivion, leaving me for dead, or jumped me on the street to slide a knife into my neck. While Mom was still alive I had something to fight for, and if somehow my grit and accomplishments helped me make something of myself, then I knew it would be worth it to see her glow.

Sitting in my apartment, watching the indifferent clock drain the seconds of my life, I realized that I hadn't felt anything for a long, long time. Even the string of desperate text-messages from the boy's number didn't faze me.

Why? Why? Why? They read. *Why did you take my son from me?*

I guess he'd died after all, and his mother had already figured out I was the one who did it from the messages. Didn't matter, it was a burner phone anyway. And even if she did find me somehow, how was she supposed to get revenge on me when I was already dead?

That's when I poured the vile of liquid LSD down my throat. 40,000ug, enough for 400 tabs of street blotter. If you still don't understand why I did it, then I honestly envy your innocence. I wanted to feel something or I wanted to die. I didn't care which.

The clock on the wall stopped. The whir of the fan fell silent. For a second everything, the bed I sat on, the air around me, even my beating heart hardened into crystal....

... before shattering with a noise unheard since the beginning of the universe. Shards of light like a blizzard of eyes cascaded past me and vanished into the distance in all directions, taking reality with it. Light collapsed into a pinprick and then disappeared entirely, my heaving lungs racing a frantic marathon to keep up. I died a thousand deaths in the span of a second, and by the time new life surged into my displaced being, I was no longer of this world.

Assuming that is, there was anything left of me. What I had come to think of as my being had exploded into infinitesimally small fragments, each in turn detonating to splinter smaller and smaller until nothing was left but an atomic dust which mingled with all existence. As my mind gradually refocused, it seemed as though every grain of sand, every shaft of light, every soul from time immemorial to the gaping abyss at the end of all things contained me in equal measures.

There was no distinction between me and the rest of the

universe, all things being connected by a tapestry of light and energy, all things screaming senselessly into the void and joining their voices in one almighty chorus which all existence sings though they have not the ears to hear it. Beyond life, beyond death, beyond perception beyond ego I rode the eternal winds, powerless to resist or even comprehend that resistance was possible. I was everything and nothing, both the same, both divinely beautiful and profoundly sad like an unrequited love which runs so deep that it doesn't matter that you aren't loved in return so long as this feeling is possible.

Gradually my senses returned to me, although there was no discernible separation between sight or taste or sound, all meshing seamlessly into my awareness of the presence that engulfed me. I don't know how long I remained suspended in this state, but it wasn't until the presence spoke that I began to appreciate that I wasn't alone.

IT'S YOUR TURN

"What?" I don't know whether I was thinking or speaking, unable to differentiate without a body.

A UNIVERSE CRUMBLED FOR YOU TO BE PHYSICAL. A STAR IMPLODED FOR YOU TO BE POSSIBLE. LIFE BEGAN FOR YOU TO BE INEVITABLE. YOUR ANCESTORS DIED FOR YOU TO PRESENT. NOW IT'S YOUR TURN.

"My turn for what?"

TO CLIMB THE LADDER OR TO GET OUT OF THE WAY.

"Climb where though? Get out of the way for what?"

By this point my senses were beginning to untangle. I was sitting in the center of a white-sand desert beneath a vast and alien sky. I had to be careful where I looked, because any speck of dust or bead of light I focused on would deform into fractals, hypnotizing me and drawing me into it until I became what I had perceived. New colors sparkled to life and new dimensions made novel geometry possible, all forming and reforming in a mesmerizing romance between actuality and fantasy.

… HE'S ALMOST HERE.

The presence must have still been talking while I had been distracted. I strained to focus on it once more.

"Who is coming?"

YOUR BIOLOGY, YOUR MORALITY, YOUR CULTURE, YOUR TECHNOLOGY, YOUR CHEMICALLY SATURATED MIND. HUMANITY IS HIS STEPPING STONE, AND HE WILL LEAVE YOU BEHIND.

The presence was solidifying before my eyes. A visual sound-wave, pulsing vibrations, the embodiment of madness I was thrall to. Eyes were gradually blossoming over its body like a field of flowers growing from barren earth.

"I don't want to be left behind. I don't want this to end."

THE END HAS ALREADY COME. Now it was my mother standing before me, wearing that floral dress of eyes. ACCEPT IT. She spoke wordlessly through the energy which bound us.

I couldn't reply. Not while watching her body decay, flesh sagging and sloughing off her bones which in turn disintegrated into a fine dust blowing into the wind. I tried to scream, only managing to inhale the flood of dust scattering from her rotting corpse. Soon, only her eyes remained.

THE BEGINNING IS READY TO BEGIN. The boy I had killed was growing around those eyes. How had I never noticed that he had the same eyes as my mother? His face, his body, I instantly recognized him, although somehow I still felt as though my mother was watching me through him. CREATE IT.

The boy was dissolving too, although it was completely unlike my mother's peaceful dissolution. Invisible blows bludgeoned him from every side, and great fistfuls of flesh were being torn from his body. He was almost gone before I realized I was the one ripping him apart, relentlessly consuming everything that I stole from him. Soon, only his eyes remained.

"It's not the end yet! I'm not dead yet!" I shouted through the mouthfuls of warm, bloody meat. "Tell me what I'm supposed to do next. What I'm supposed to *become* next."

There wasn't anything to tell me though. Even the watching eyes were gone, winking out into the immeasurable desert. Endless vaults of sky were falling around me, strange eons of unseen years condensing into blistering seconds. My heart was burning with the primordial fire of creation and the air soured into acrid smoke pouring from my smoldering lungs.

"Why?" All that I was hurled into words which tumbled unheard into the hurricane of swirling sand. "Why was everything building up to this? Why am I here? Why does it matter? Why won't you answer?"

"Why? Why? Why?" Searing light burning the words into my eyes from the cell-phone clutched in my hand. "Why did you take my son from me?"

And though I spoke the words aloud, there was no greater truth from the universe to answer for me. There was only me and my trembling fingers as I typed a dozen feeble responses, deleting each unworthy apology before it was sent.

"Why? Why? Why?" came her hysterical sobs as I knelt on her doorstep. I knew her son so well, it was easy enough to find where she lived. She didn't hit me, or scream at me, or even call the police when I introduced myself and told her what I had done. She just kept asking why, over and over, kneeling beside me on the ground to take my hands in hers. And when she pressed my hands to her lips, it was my own mother weeping for my death.

"Why? Why? Why?" screaming to the heavens, though no answer came in return, and no answer ever did.

Life isn't there to answer why, after all.

Life is there to ask it.

And though the rest of my days will never answer for what I've done, I now understand that there is only one choice for me and those who are like me, slaves to our egos and blind to the changing world:

We can cling to who we were and be left behind. Or we can learn from our past and become something new. Something humanity has been building towards since before it began.

The beginning has already begun.

WHEN THE BLOOD RAIN FALLS

When the pregnant earth contracts and the ground trembles as though it were afraid ...

The homeless man flipped to his second piece of cardboard. I nervously glanced away. This red light was taking forever. Glancing back –

When the clouds are angry in the sky and rolling darkness chokes the world....

The traffic light turned green. He was switching signs again though, and I really wanted to see where this was going.

When the blood rain churns the oceans red and cresting waves rear above the land....

The cars behind me were honking. I couldn't just sit here, but neither could I drive away from this sense of looming dread. I decided to pull off onto the dirt beside the road where the homeless man crouched.

Me in my white Prius, on my way back from downtown where I worked. Him and his stained clothing, jagged finger-nails biting into the cardboard he clutched. Our eyes locked though we were worlds apart. I flinched for no reason at all when he smiled, that yellow gaping smile, and when he started walking toward my window I almost slammed my foot on the gas.

Instead I sat there, waiting until he tapped my window with his dirty knuckle. I took a deep breath before rolling it down.

"Dollar is good," he mumbled. "Whatever you've got is fine."

"What's with those signs?" I asked, fishing around for my wallet. "What happens next?"

He squinted at me, then up at the clear blue sky. Back to me, holding out his hand to take the dollar I offered.

"It isn't raining blood," he said matter-of-factly.

I leaned out the window to look up. "Nope. It's not," I agreed.

"Then how am I supposed to know what happens next?" That yellow smile was back. Up close I could see his remaining teeth haphazardly jutting out from bleeding gums, almost like they'd been hammered in.

"Why would you write that stuff then?"

"Didn't write it. Just copied it down, that's all. But people keep stopping, so I keep on holding it."

This was going nowhere. I just wished him an empty 'good luck' and merged back onto the road, the yellow smile fixed on me until he disappeared in my rear view mirror.

Three things happened the next day. The first was an earthquake, around 4:30 in the morning. I woke immediately to the sound of the jiggling books on my shelf. Nothing severe, only magnitude 4, but there were several pulses and I couldn't go back to sleep after that.

Next was the storm, taking everyone by surprise. I left the morning news playing while I got dressed, and even the weatherman admitted the clouds came out of nowhere. There shouldn't have been enough humidity in the air for them to form overnight, he said, and there weren't any storms within fifty miles that could have blown in.

"I guess whacky weather is just something we'll have to get used to as the planet keeps getting hotter," droned the voice.

I tried not to think about the homeless man, but it was hard while driving to work through the surreal morning twilight. I couldn't even see the sun through the thick rolling clouds.

I pulled off the road again at the same spot. There he was, crouching exactly how I saw him yesterday. He started walking toward me the moment I stopped. I jumped as he knocked on the passenger side window this time.

"Where are your signs today?" I asked, rolling down the window next to him.

"Tossed 'em."

"Why?"

"It don't matter."

"I want to know. Look, you can have five bucks this time." I leaned across the passenger seat to hand him the bill.

"It don't matter because it's too late to warn people. It's already begun. And I don't want your money, but I wouldn't say no to a ride. I hate getting caught out in the rain."

"It's not raining...." But the words died in my mouth. Flash goes the yellow smile, rotted teeth sprouting from that graveyard of a mouth. A thick red drop landed on his cheek, sluggishly weaving its way into his matted beard.

"Sorry, wish I could help," I muttered. The rain was coming harder by the second. Great red drops drizzling down from unseen heights. Splattering on my windshield, running down the gutters like freshly opened veins.

"If anyone is causing this, it's people like you, not people like me."

I opened my mouth. Then closed it. He snatched the door

handle, but it was locked. The blood rain was pouring over him now, streaming off his face and hands like the victim of some gruesome accident.

"Just tell me what's going to happen next!" I shouted over the mounting wind.

He reached through the window and unlocked the door from the inside. I tried to lock it again, but I was too slow. He was already inside, blood flying with him, splattering across my face and soaking into my seat.

I rolled up the window as the storm raged around us. He didn't look at me – just stared straight ahead, hands folded in his lap like he knew he didn't belong.

"Well? What's next? What's happening?" I demanded.

"That was rotten of you, trying to lock me out like that," he said, still not looking at me. "We're all in this together now."

"Well you're here now, so just tell me."

"Just drive, okay? You'll see."

I opened my mouth to protest, but the words caught in my throat as the yellow smile blossomed. "I said drive!" he bellowed, blood cascading off his sudden ferocity like light scattering through a prism. I slammed my foot on the gas and lurched out into the street.

It was getting worse by the second. Trees were buckling under the weight of the howling wind. Cars inched along the roads or were pulled off to the side, visibility reduced to nothing from the bleeding wound in the sky.

"You said you copied the words," I managed at last. "Where from?"

"It was carved in a tree," he said. "I thought it was cool because the tree was bleeding where it was cut, like it was carved in skin instead of bark."

"There was more, wasn't there? More than you copied."

He nodded, not smiling anymore. "Turn left here. I'll take you there."

We didn't speak much for the next five minutes until he told me where to stop. The rain had already dried up, and there was even some light sneaking through the roof of the world.

"Right there. That's the tree." He'd gotten out of the car and was already walking through a dense grove of white aspen a little off the road. There was no uncertainty about which one he was talking about.

It would have been identical to the rest of the grove if it wasn't trembling in an unfelt breeze. Long red streaks wound down its base from a wound about half-way up. The trembling grew more violent as I approached, until standing before it the wood seemed to ripple and contort before my eyes. Random, violent movements, like an animal trapped under a blanket trying to beat its way out.

"It wasn't doing that last time," he said.

I spotted the bleeding words, but they were shaking too badly for me to make them out. I didn't have to wait long though. Within a minute I saw a crack begin to emerge running down the entire length of the trunk.

The tree was opening, but it wasn't opening by itself. Long, thin fingers slithered out from the trunk to grip either side of the fissure, forcing it open wider. Blood flowed freely from the tree, running into a small stream by our feet. Soon an eye glimmered somewhere from the darkness inside, blinking away the flowing blood to stare at me.

"When the pregnant earth contracts and the ground trembles as though it were afraid … " The homeless man's eyes were closed, reciting from memory.

The crack in the tree was wide enough for an entire hand to fit through. Twice the length of a human hand, white shining skin beneath the blood.

"When the clouds are angry in the sky and rolling darkness chokes the world ... "

The hand retreated, and a second later the whole head burst through. Eyes like a frozen hurricane, uneven gaping mouth like a canyon, panting rapid excited breaths. It felt like staring into all the raw magnificence of nature, only being aware that it was staring back.

"When the blood rain churns the oceans red and cresting waves rear above the land ... "

I was running back toward my car. A loud crack rent the air, and glancing back I saw the whole tree splitting cleanly in two. A final rush of blood gutted the length before the two halves fell like corpses to either side.

"Then I will be born into a world that deserves me. And all the words which have been carved into my skin will spell the name of my defiler, and we will sing all words until his name is forgotten, and we will dance until I dance alone."

The homeless man hadn't moved since he began recounting the verse. Now it was too late. I watched in awe as the creature caressed the man with its long white fingers. He shuddered as if in ecstasy, looking up at it with the reverence of a spectacular sunset.

The fingers dug into my companion and ripped him in half exactly as it had done with the tree, only this time was much faster and much, much messier. A slop of organs slid down his separated legs, the creature wasting no time in stooping on all fours to lick them up. It seemed to have forgotten about me for the moment, and that was all I needed to get back to the car.

I saw it staring at me in the mirror as I ripped down the road. As horrific as that yellow smile was, it was nothing compared to this white shine that grinned over its fresh kill. All the blood had already slid from its body as though it were stainless steel.

Something like that? I get the impression that it could kill any number of us and still be as bright and clean as the day it was born. I wonder if, when the last of us is gone, the earth will be clean like that too. Or whether we've cut too deep for the wound to ever heal. I know we're all in this together now, but looking at that feral avatar I've never felt so helpless or small or alone.

WOUNDS THAT WORDS HAVE CAUSED

I've made the horrible mistake of falling in love with someone who doesn't exist, and it hurts like you wouldn't believe.

Let me tell you a little about her. She's dark, not sad or angry or angsty, but dark in a spiritual way like the tranquility of a midnight mist. She dresses in all black—her hair, her lipstick, her nails—but it does nothing to conceal the radiance of her beauty. She thinks so loudly that you can almost feel it echo through the silence, and when she speaks there is such deliberate measure in her voice that her words turn to music, the simplest phrase containing all the secrets of the world, if only you listen closely enough.

I fell in love with an idea long before I met my wife, Sarah. When I saw her for the first time—the fishnets, the black lace, the metal piercings—I told myself that this is what I've been looking for since before I even knew I was looking. And all the time we dated, I was looking at Sarah but seeing that dream of what love should be. And when we were married, I told myself that it was my fault for being unhappy because she was everything I could ever want.

I'm not saying I was right to cheat on her. I'm just saying it happened, only a month after the wedding. A stupid mistake at first, but every time I did it, I felt a little less guilty than the last. I couldn't just abandon Sarah—not after the wedding. Not with her family always inviting us places, not with our lives so tangled up together. She'd tell me these horrible confessions about how she used to hurt herself when she was little, and how she'd even thought about suicide before she found me. If I left her and something were to happen, I don't know how I'd ever forgive myself.

The worst part about it was, Sarah knew I was cheating. I'd tell her that I had to go to a conference for work over the weekend, and she'd just press her lips together and force a smile. Like she had no right to ask questions. Like she deserved to suffer. She made it so easy that I just kept getting lazier with my lies.

"Out with friends," I'd text her, not bothering to say with who or when I'd be back. "Staying out late. Don't wait up." And I wouldn't be home until morning, if that even was my home.

I wasn't happy, but I didn't notice so much while I was distracted with the perverse thrill of being in control like that. I was my own master, and Sarah was ... well, whatever I told her to be. I don't know how long it could have gone on like that, but I knew something had to change when she finally worked up the courage to ask me to my face:

"Are you with any other women? I'm sorry to have to ask. It's just my insecurity talking. I just want to hear you say ... "

"Of course not. Just you, baby, forever and ever."

I almost told her the truth, but her standing there wringing her hands, hearing the catch in her voice as she forced the words out, I just couldn't do that to her. It wasn't cowardice that made me lie. It wasn't love either. It was pity.

Her dark eyes fixed on me, sparkling with curious intensity. There it was again—that tight-lipped smile. And something more this time. The smile was quivering at the corners, like too little skin stretched over too much space.

"Say it again. I want to hear it."

"You're the only one for me." I was getting more than a little uncomfortable. It wasn't just the situation either. There was a sharp sting like a needle in my palm. I rubbed the spot without looking.

"Again. Tell me that you'd never lie to me."

"Never. I promise." My hand was hurting worse than ever. She glanced at it and I followed her gaze. A trickle of blood snuck through my closed fingers. There was a gaping wound like I had grabbed the blade of a knife.

"Again."

"What's going on? How did this happen?"

"Again!" she shouted, all pretenses of her smile gone. "Tell me that you love me!"

"I love you!" I shouted, rushing to the kitchen sink to wash the wound. And then I screamed. The wound was growing before my eyes, the skin savagely stretching as though invisible hands were digging their fingers into the hole. It was half-way up my forearm by the time I got it under the faucet, and it was growing by the second.

"Again!"

"What the fuck did you do to me?" I screamed. Paper towels were soaked in an instant. My fingers kept slipping as I tied the kitchen towel around my arm.

"Just what I asked it to do." Her voice was silk, strained to breaking. "I asked it to stop us from lying to each other."

"Make it stop!" I shouted. The blood kept coming.

"I can't. That's up to you."

"Fine, I lied. Are you happy?" I didn't turn around from the sink. I couldn't look at her right then. "There have been three others. One before the wedding, two after. They didn't mean anything. Why does it keep bleeding?"

"Telling the truth doesn't heal the lie. Now tell me that you love me."

I had to turn around now. Just to see if it really was Sarah who was doing this to me, or whether some unknown specter had replaced her. It was her all right. I wanted to yell in her face for what she was doing to me and steal her triumph. It wasn't triumph that I saw though.

Her face was twisted into the pit of despair. All the wind left my lungs in an instant and we just stared at each other for a long time. Me clutching my throbbing arm, her not pretending to hide her tears anymore.

"I'm sorry. I want to, but I don't love you."

She wasn't looking at my face when I said it. She pulled the towel away from my arm, and we stared at the wound together. It was deep, all the way to the bone and still bubbling with fresh blood. It wasn't growing anymore though. I wasn't lying this time.

"It's okay," she said. "Thank you for being honest. After all this, I don't think I love you either."

My wound hurt like hell, but it was nothing like watching the bloody cut appear just above her eye. She must have felt it. I don't know what she was trying to prove when she kept talking.

"I never loved you. It was just my family—always worried about me, always pressuring me to find someone. I would have been happier alone, trust me." The wound was growing by the second. Down her face, her neck, blood dying her black shirt even darker.

"Sarah please. You don't have to do this."

"How could I love you? You're disgusting. You're an animal. I never want to see you again." The words were coming slower. She was coercing them out, grunting through the pain. I pressed my hand over her mouth, but she grabbed my arm right where the wound was and I had to let go.

"I wasn't happy with you. I didn't want to grow old with you. I'm honestly relieved!" She was running from me. I couldn't stop her from talking. I was weak and dizzy from my own wound, and I kept sliding on the bloody trail which followed her wherever she went. "I never want to see you again!" That one caused her body to surge as though struck by lightning. Her fingers helplessly knotted the empty air while her spine arched so far back that she was looking at the ceiling.

"Stop doing this to her!" I shouted as loudly as I could. "Whoever made this deal, that's enough! It's over! Stop hurting her!"

It wasn't exactly a voice that answered. More like a dormant instinct which has existed my whole life, but only now reared to life.

I'm not the one hurting her, it said. *You are."*

So I left. I stopped chasing her. Stopped trying to fix her. Stopped pitying her. I just grabbed my keys and left. I didn't speak to her over the next few weeks. Her family told me when she wasn't around, giving me the chance to clear out all my stuff without bumping into her. I asked them how she was doing, but never got an answer more clear than "she'll survive".

The wound on my arm? It healed a long time ago. Not all at once, but every day the scab was a little thicker until it fell off, and then every day the scar was a little lighter until it was barely visible. I don't know if it'll be there for the rest of my life, but I don't think about it when I'm falling asleep anymore. I'm just back to dreaming of the girl I love who doesn't exist, wondering if she'll notice the scar when we finally meet.

RAISED BY THE MAN WHO KIDNAPPED ME

The people I live with aren't my parents. They aren't even related to my parents, as far as I can tell. They're just people—cold, ruthless, angry people who wanted to have a daughter of their own and didn't care whose lives they destroyed to get one.

I've always known there was something strange about them. Martha ("Mom") looks nothing like me. She thinks nothing like me. She's always blithering about her precious china plates or sorting her collections of pristine dresses and shoes that no one's allowed to wear. Tyler ("Dad") is an auto mechanic who smells like gasoline all the time, always mumbling and looking away as though he's ashamed to be alive. I don't know what I'm supposed to do or who I'm supposed to be when I grow up, but I've lived with them long enough to know what I don't want.

They treat me like a possession. I speak when I'm spoken to. I wear what I'm told to wear, go where I'm told to go, and even at fifteen, I'm never, ever allowed to go out alone.

And you know what really makes me sick? The fact that I'd looked past all of their manipulative, controlling habits for my whole life. It didn't matter that I wasn't allowed to go play with friends. "Dad" wanted to keep me safe, and he knew best. It didn't matter that "Mom" forced me to spend countless hours sitting on the floor to sew lace into her clothes. It was all I've ever known, and I trusted them. But not anymore.

I found out when I stumbled across a personal ad in the local paper. I don't read the news, but I'd picked up a big stack for a school paper-Mache project and there it was on top:

Missing: Fifteen year old girl. Birth date: 06/04/02. Brown hair, green eyes. *We haven't given up. We will never forget.* Last seen: Twelve years ago, abducted from Bakersfield Park. Pink bow in her hair.

Below that, two pictures. One of a baby girl, about three years old. Another one that looked like a computer-generated prediction of what she would like now. The hair was all wrong, but other than that it felt like looking into a mirror.

My birthday. My description. *My picture!* I couldn't breathe. I'd never gotten along with the people I lived with, but I'd tolerated them this long because I thought underneath all their self-absorption they were my family. I was *supposed* to love them. Imagining them snatching me out of a park—imagining the countless nights my real parents must have searched and prayed and cried—it made my blood boil.

I started flipping through the stack of papers. There the ad was again another month back. And another month before that. Always the same words: *We will never forget.*

"Are you making a mess in there?" It was Martha. Her beady little eyes tracking me from the living room, judging every move I made. I did my best to keep my trembling hands from betraying what I found as I neatly stacked the newspapers once more.

"Do you have any baby pictures I could look at?" I asked innocently.

Martha's face crinkled with distaste. "Of course, but I don't want you looking. You never put anything away properly."

"I mean when I was really small. Like two years old." I scrutinized her face for any sign of discomfort, but it was difficult to read when she was always scowling like that.

"I shouldn't think so," she huffed, turning back to her magazine. "There was that flood when you were—oh but you'd be too young to remember."

It was all I needed to know. I went back to my room and dialed the phone number in the ad. I was actually in tears when the voice crackled through the other line.

"Mom?" I whispered as loudly as I dared. "Mom are you there?"

We didn't call the police. We figured that anyone who could live their entire lives as a lie were capable of anything. Instead we were just going to do it as quietly as possible.

I put my favorite clothes in a backpack and hid it under my bed. I let Tyler tuck me in, somehow resisting the urge to spit in his face when he leaned in to kiss me goodnight. I let Martha watch me from the crack in the door, pale orbs glowing where they reflected the moonlight. I pretended to be asleep, my whole body flushed and throbbing in anticipation.

Finally the coast was clear. I grabbed my backpack and snuck out in my pajamas, not wanting to spend a second longer in that house than I had to. There was a car waiting for me at the end of the block. For the first time I could remember, I was going back to my real home.

A woman got out of the passenger side and waved to me. Not just any woman—it was my mom. I knew it before I even saw her. I was running without realizing it, and she was running too. We didn't slow down until we collided, hugging and crying, utterly abandoned by words. She smelled like warm cinnamon. Then a man got out of the driver's side, but before I could approach him the deck lights behind me turned on.

"Tyler! She's running away! I told you something was wrong!"

I flew into the car and didn't look back. My parents—my real parents—were tearing up the road, and I was giggling like a maniac the whole way.

"We never stopped believing," my father was saying from the front. "That's not to say that it didn't get hard sometimes, but—"

"The other children are going to be so happy too!" Mom squealed with adrenaline.

"I have brothers and sisters?" I couldn't stop smiling. Two complete strangers, and already they seemed closer to me than my old "family" ever was.

"Something like that." My parents exchanged a knowing look. "And they can't wait to meet you."

Barred windows. A padlock on the front door. Concrete floors. I don't know what I was expecting home to be, but this wasn't it. A dozen frightened faces lifted to greet us when the door opened.

"Run!" A little girl screeched, about twelve years old. She jumped up as soon as she heard us, but I was so bewildered that I didn't make the slightest move.

I was shoved hard from behind and fell to my knees. The door slammed shut behind me. My parents were on the outside, and I could hear the padlock snap back into place.

"I'm sorry," the little girl said. "I'm so sorry."

"Mom? Dad?" It wasn't that I refused to believe what was going on. I was incapable of believing. I had built this fantasy up in my head so long that, for the moment at least, it was still stronger than whatever reality tried to break through.

"We will never forget." It was my mother, but the voice was wrong. I couldn't see her on the other side of the door, but I knew that sound could only come through a snarl. "And neither will you."

"Forget what? Mom? Dad? What's going on?"

I felt a small hand in mine, and I jumped. Everything was moving so fast. I let the girl guide me back to the far side where the others were sitting. The walls were decorated with newspaper clippings. Personal ads—hundreds of them. All for missing children, all promising that they'd never forget.

"That's mine over there," the little girl pointed at her picture in one of the ads.

"Stop talking to her," an older girl said. "You'll be punished for it." I scanned the other children. All teenagers, I think. All girls. Some of them looked like people I might bump into the street, but others were stranger. Their skin was drawn tight and riddled with bruises and sores. Their eyes were hollow, and I got the impression that they didn't see me even when they were pointed in my direction.

"I don't care," the younger girl insisted. She steered me up against the wall and sat cross-legged in front of me. I could barely see her face through the matted hair. "They hate girls. That's why we're here."

"That's not the reason." The older girl sighed. "It's because they're crazy. There doesn't need to be any other reason."

"They lost their own daughter," the younger continued. "She was a hooker or something, and she got killed. I don't know the details, but I guess they started collecting girls after that. Every once in a while a foreign man-"

"He's from Russia," one of the others interjected.

"Foreign man comes and chooses some of us. Then they go with him."

"What happens to the ones who aren't chosen?" I asked, but looking around I already knew the answer.

"Don't worry about it. You're a pretty one. They'll pick you," the older girl said. I don't know why she thought that – I could barely even see her face in the gloom.

"Here." The little girl handed me a notepad and a pen. "You can have this if you want."

"What am I supposed to write?"

She shrugged. "Anything you want. At least then there will be something left when you're gone."

The first thing I wrote was: *I love you, Mom. I love you, Dad.*

The second thing I wrote, you're reading now.

THE STRANGER UPSTAIRS

Thirty-four hundred square feet, marble counters, Brazilian walnut hardwood floors, and the strangest stipulation I've ever seen on a real-estate listing.

"The previous occupant will continue to live on the top floor. He will never be evicted, and never be charged rent. His room shall never be entered, and under no condition should he ever be spoken to. If the inhabitants are unable or unwilling to follow any of these terms, they will be considered in violation of the sales contract and held liable."

"It's a joke. It has to be," my wife told me when I read her the fine print. "Anyway it's not like we can afford this place. I just want to take a peek, okay?"

We'd spent the last month attending every open house in a ten mile radius around my new job, and everything had started to blur together into one big gray building. My wife just wanted to see something different, even if it was way out of our league. I couldn't believe it when the real-estate agent told us this mansion was well within our budget.

"What's the deal with the hermit though?" was the first question I asked the listing broker, a sweaty bear of a man.

"Oh you won't even notice him," the agent said, nodding vigorously as though agreeing with himself. "If you're worried about your space, I'm going to stop you right there. The downstairs has two beautiful full-sized bedrooms, so your daughter can have a room of her own. Wouldn't you like that, honey?" The giant man had to crouch to be level with Nila, my eleven-year-old daughter. "Wouldn't you like your own room where you can play music as loud as you want without it bothering anyone?"

"Yeah!" I winced as Nila glided across the hardwood floors in her socks. "I'd live here!"

"Have you seen this kitchen?" my wife shouted from around the corner. "Brand new Viking appliances. It's even got a built-in espresso machine!"

I felt the decision slipping away from me. "It's not the space. You have to admit that it's a weird situation, right?"

The agent shrugged. "Wouldn't bother me," he said. "What *would* bother me is knowing I could have given my family the house of their dreams, but didn't just because I felt weird about an eccentric old man that I'd never even see. And just between the two of us," he bodily pulled me under his arm where I could distinctly feel the sweat soaking through, "the guy up there is about a hundred years old. Couple years and he'll be gone for good, and all that space will be yours."

We met the generously low asking price, and within a month my family had moved into the house. It seemed impossible to me that we'd *never* see Makao, but it was actually true. He had his own bathroom, and every week there would be a delivery man who left a bag of groceries at the top of the stairs. The groceries would sit there the entire day —eggs, milk, meat, and all—not disappearing until the following morning. Every once in a while we'd hear someone shuffling around or a radio would splutter to life and play songs that were old before I was born. That was it though. Most of the time we forgot that Makao even existed.

Most of the time. Then there was this one night around 11 p.m. when the lights were already off. I heard muffled, heaving sobs echo through the house. My first instinct was to check on Nila, but she was just quietly sitting up in her bed.

"You heard it too?" she asked.

"Yeah. It's nothing, go back to sleep," I told her.

"Why is Makao crying?"

"I don't know, but it's none of our business. We made a promise not to disturb him. Can you promise that too, Nila?"

She nodded, gaping at the ceiling. I turned on some soft music to drown out the sound, but that wasn't the end of it. When I got back to my bedroom, my wife was gone. Not in the bathroom either. I was beginning to entertain a fantastical paranoia about some misshapen ghoul crawling down to snatch her when I heard her voice on the stairs.

"I'm sorry to bother you, Makao. Is everything all right?"

I pounded up the steps. Nila had come out of her bedroom too, and we both watched as my wife knocked on the forbidden door again.

"Stop that! Come back to bed!" I shouted in a hoarse whisper.

"He might need help -" Her words cut short as the door opened a crack, not even wide enough to see who was peering out.

"This will be your only warning." Makao's growl was so low that I inadvertently found myself climbing closer to hear.

"I was worried that -" my wife began.

"Whatever you see. Whatever you hear. Whatever you *think* might be going on up here: it'll be the death of you."

The door snapped shut, and I wasted no time in ushering everyone back to bed.

The crying never really went away after that. For the next two weeks we'd hear him whimpering and moaning as he battled some unknown illness, or perhaps it was just the deterioration of his ancient body finally giving out. Sometimes there would even be feeble calls for help, but I was quick to remind my family of our promise. They argued at first, but eventually we just got used to having music playing all the time and didn't hear it anymore.

At least until it got worse. Grunting, moaning, even screaming - wild, vicious yelps like an animal in the throes of death. It was late at night again after Nila had gone to bed. My wife jumped toward the door in an instant and I had to physically pin her arms to keep her there.

"He's in pain! We can't just leave him!" she insisted.

"You heard what he said. It's his right to be alone."

"What about 911? Even if he doesn't want our help, he can't say no to someone trying to save his life."

"Maybe he doesn't want that either." She wasn't resisting anymore. I steered her back onto the bed, caressing her shoulders, speaking softly in the vain fight against waves of tension rippling across her face and body. "Maybe it's just his time to go, and that's what will be best for all of us."

"For all of us?" Suspicion crept into her voice. She was back on her feet again before I knew what was happening. "You want him to die, don't you? A living, breathing human being, and you want him dead just so we have a little more space."

"That's not what I meant. I just said -"

"Listen to him! He's in agony! We can't just sit here and -"

We both shut up at the sound of the knocking. One, two, three, hesitant but insistent knocks.

"Hello? Mr. Makao?"

My wife and I exchanged a panicked glance. A door swung open somewhere above us.

"Get out! Get out you stupid girl!"

"Nila don't!" I shouted. Out of the bedroom, up the stairs - just in time to see my daughter disappear and the door close behind her. My wife was right behind me as we raced up the stairs. We were still a few feet away when we heard the distinct rattle of a chain, then a bolt sliding into place.

"Makao? Open the door Makao. We're here to help," I tried.

"Go away. I warned you, didn't I? I warned you both. She's mine now."

"Nila? Can you hear me?" my wife shouted. "What's going on in there?"

"I don't know, it's weird here," Nila replied through the door, but her voice reverberated as though it came from a tunnel a long way off. "It's all mirrors. On and on forever."

"Is the old man trying to stop you from leaving?"

I held my breath during the long pause.

"Nope," Nila said. All the air came pouring out of my lungs. "There isn't anyone here."

Another glance between my wife and me. Her face was drawn and white. She stepped forward uneasily, trying to look through the crack under the door.

"Can you unlock the door, sweetie? Can you come back out?" my wife asked.

Another long pause. I crouched down too, catching a dark flash of movement across the doorway.

"Nila? Are you still there?" I prompted.

"Uh huh." Another pause. "I'll be right there."

"Nila the door!" my wife insisted. She started rattling the handle.

"Don't! Don't come in!" Nila shrieked. "You won't like it!"

It was more than I could take. I started slamming into the door with my shoulder.

BAM - the door rattled in its frame. Nila was hysterical. There weren't words anymore, just varying pitches and whimpers.

BAM - dust raining down around me. My wife joined in the effort, crashing into the door together -

BAM - the old hinges buckled and twisted. We couldn't hear anything anymore, but that just made us slam harder until -

The door flew open. A brilliant flash of disorienting light - mirrors everywhere. *Everywhere.* A whole world of mirrors, stretched to the vanishing point of the distant horizon. Great hillsides were carved with thousand-faced pinnacles of light, trees ruptured from the ground to shine in every direction, and even soaring clouds fractalized countless insults to geometry with their smooth sides. And from them all shone a dazzling array of faces and eyes all peering back at me....

... Although none of them were mine. Old men, young men, women and children, all mirroring my movements from an unfathomable myriad of sources of and angles, all staring at me. That's when I realized Makao hadn't been the one crying all this time. It was the figures in the mirrors, untold anguish causing tears to run down their face even while matching my movements otherwise.

"Where's Makao?" my wife asked.

Nila shrugged. She was kneeling on the ground, making faces at an old lady peering back. Her wizened face contorted into a variety of sneers which seemed preposterously absurd on someone of her age.

"We need to get out of here. Now." They weren't listening to me. My wife was turning in slow circles, utterly bewitched. Numerous pitiful forms turned in of echo her.

"How does it do that?" she asked. "Is this a screen? Are they plugged in somewhere?"

"If Makao isn't here, then who locked the door after Nila?" I asked. That finally got their attention. That, and the rattle of the chain as the solitary standing door locked once more behind us.

"She's mine now. You're all mine." It was Makao's voice, but I couldn't figure out where it was coming from. I surged toward the door, slamming into an invisible barrier like a wall of glass. My wife and daughter were in the same situation, helplessly pounding the empty air˙ - no, they were pounding the insides of their mirror, just like I was.

"Two weeks," came the voice, everywhere and nowhere, far away yet emanating from within. "Two weeks is a long time to listen to someone suffer."

"But you told us -" I protested.

"I've listened to them for *years* though," Makao replied. There! Standing by the door, a dark and huddled shape. Only a few feet tall, and so bent that its back extended several inches higher than the pit of darkness that was its head. Red eyes gleaming from somewhere deep inside the tortured mass, watching me with hawkish intensity. "They never stop, you know. You'd think they would have given up on giving up by now."

"WHO ARE YOU? WHAT IS THIS PLACE?"

The red eyes blinked. "This is your home. Your one, true home. And no matter how comfortable you make yourself out there, no matter how loudly you turn up your music and play pretend, you will always be a visitor. And wherever you go, and whoever you love there, it will only last until you come home to me again."

Nila was crying, but I couldn't look at her. My wife - I

don't know where she is. I couldn't take my eyes away from the creature that taunted me. He felt so tangible, so real - the only real thing in this place of mirrors.

"I don't want to be here. Let us out! Let us go -"

"You won't bother me again?"

"Never. We promise -"

"Not never, that would be a lie." The dark figure was right on the other side of the invisible barrier now. He lifted one hand - little more than a claw, really - and I was horrified to watch my own hand mirror the movement until my finger touched the gnarled terminal of his hand. "But not soon, I hope. Not until you're ready to come home."

The invisible glass shattered as our fingers touched. His image, the image of this impossible place, everything shattered and fell away. I was left standing with my finger touching the back of an empty mirror frame, ground littered with broken shards. I gently but urgently guided my wife and daughter out of the room, carefully picking our way through the carpet of glass, then closed the door firmly behind me.

The bag of groceries is still left on the top of the stairs each week, and sometimes there's laughter to go with the crying. My family and I still haven't agreed on exactly what happened up there, but no one has made the suggestion to make a second trip.

I THINK DEATH IS THE STRANGER LIVING UPSTAIRS, BUT I suppose that's true of everyone. At least ours is close enough to keep an eye on.

MY SON SAID GOODBYE

My four-year-old son and I have a night-time ritual. Step one: turn off his cartoons and pray he won't wail loud enough for the neighbors to think I'm torturing him. Step two: sedate the wild beasty with the Goodnight Moon story. He'll be crawling all over the bed at the beginning, but I just keep reading slower and softer while I wait for him to wind down. Then with barely a whisper, I'll say:

"Goodnight Mikey."

"Goodnight Mommy," he'll always say back. The peace that comes afterward, it somehow completes the long day of commuting and work. It heals all the pacifying of clients, and writing reports, and running errands, and cooking and cleaning and everything else that makes Atlas's job look easy. And listening to my boy's deep breathing, everything in the world will be right again, and I'll know I'd do it a million times over just for the sacred simplicity of the precious little time I have with him.

That's how I thought it would go on forever, until a few

nights ago when I whispered goodnight and he replied: "Goodbye Mommy."

"You're supposed to say goodnight, silly," I said. "Goodbye means leaving, and I'm not going anywhere."

"I know," he said. "I'll miss you, Mommy. Goodbye."

He was asleep before I could respond again. I thought it was cute at the time. I didn't think for a second about waking him up and going through the whole process of settling down again. There was something about how deliberately he said it though that left me feeling unsettled. Just to be safe, I walked around the room and made sure his window was locked. I left the door open a crack like I always do to check in on him, kissed him one last time, and then left.

I didn't hear a peep all night, but I still couldn't get any sleep. I kept getting this chill and waking up in a cold sweat. What if he said goodbye because someone said they'd take him away? Mikey's father didn't live with us (long story), but he'd never even showed interest in his son before. It wasn't a rational fear that made me keep walking by his room at night. Once at 11 p.m., tucking his errant legs back under the covers. Again at 2 a.m., putting his stuffed dragon back under his arm. I finally got a few hours of fitful sleep, until 7 a.m. rolled around way too fast when it was time to get him ready for pre-school and –

He was gone. My bleary eyes became lasers. The stuffed dragon was still there. He'd never go anywhere (not even the bathroom) without it. Windows, doors, all locked from the inside. Closets, cabinets, pantries, I was on a rampage, tearing the place apart like I was a pillaging army. Screaming his name until I was hoarse, pounding on my neighbors' doors, and then finally calling the police.

I was in tears by the time the officer came by to ask me a few questions. No, I don't know where he could have gone.

No, I don't know why anyone would take him. No, no, no, until finally I mentioned that he said goodbye last night.

"Sounds like he ran away then, ma'am. I'll get this back to the station. In the meantime, take a drive around all his favorite parks, playgrounds, whatever is nearby."

The whole day was hell, and the next morning was worse. I don't know if those haunted stretches of misplaced time can be considered sleep, but the first thing I did when I woke up was look in his room again. The vain hope that this had all been a nightmare flickered when I saw what was on his bed.

A crude, crayon drawing of a little blue blob (the color of his pajamas), riding something that looked like his stuffed dragon. Shaky block letters underneath said:

WE PLAYIN

The stuffed dragon was gone. It didn't mean anything though. I'd been tearing the room apart looking for him, and it would have been very easy for me to knock one of his drawings onto the bed. I'd probably taken the dragon when I was looking for him without even noticing. All the drawing did was send me into a fresh spiral of despair. The police hadn't turned up anything, and it wasn't until the next morning when I got my next clue.

Another drawing was left on his bed. There was a taller figure here, and I assume it was supposed to be me because underneath it said:

WERE MOMMY?

That was the longest day of my life. I patrolled the house a dozen times, even crawling through the heating ducts to see if he was still in the house somewhere. I picked up a security camera to watch his room so I could catch whoever was leaving the drawings. After that it was just a matter of waiting to see if tomorrow brought anything new. I'd intended on staying up all night to watch his room, but I'd run myself so ragged that I couldn't fend off a few hours of welcomed oblivion.

The cam footage was the first thing I thought about. It was Mikey. Walking into his bedroom in the same pajamas I'd seen him in last. The stuffed dragon was clutched under one of his little arms. He didn't face the camera mounted above the door, he just went straight to his crayons in the corner and began drawing. I sat there mesmerized while he drew – ten minutes at least before he got up and put the drawing on the bed. He broke the blue crayon while he colored, and sure enough the blue was still broken on the floor where he'd left it. When he was finished, he finally faced the camera.

It wasn't Mikey. That thing that looked at the camera. The thing wearing his pajamas and sitting in his bed, it didn't have a face. Just smooth skin with slight contours where the facial features should be, like latex pulled suffocatingly tight across the face. There wasn't a mouth, but I could still tell he was smiling from how the muscles pulled back when he looked at me.

I NO U WACHIN. I WACHIN U 2.

That's what the paper said, right next to a crude drawing of an eyeball. I'm insane, I decided. The stress, the worry, the sleepless nights. It's driven me insane. I didn't know who to show the video to. I didn't even know if they'd see the same thing I saw or whether it was all in my head. I just lost it. I don't know how long I spent in that room—sitting and rocking in the corner, hands clutching my knees to my chest—but before I knew it, it was dark again.

I was so, so tired. I hadn't been to work in days. I didn't even know if I still had a job. I couldn't help but think that if I'd taken more time off to spend with Mikey, I could have deciphered his warning sooner and prevented all this. Or that if he really did run away, then it was my fault and I was living in a nightmare of my own creation.

I guess I just fell asleep where I sat in the corner of his room. It was still dark when I woke up, but I was still so tired that I didn't open my eyes. I just sat there listening to a soft scratching for a long time before I was finally alert enough to realize what it was.

Crayon on paper. Mikey. I was awake in an instant and holding in my scream took more willpower than I knew I had.

He was sitting on his bed, his back toward from me. Scratch, scratch, scratching away with the crayons. Humming something, the gentle melodic rise and fall of the sing-song voice I used when reading Goodnight Moon. I stood up as quietly as I could, but he must have heard me because he put his crayon down.

"Mikey?" I whispered, still terrified that I had gone completely insane.

The boy climbed down from the bed, his back still facing me.

"Where did you go, Mikey? Why did you say goodbye to Mommy?"

"Mommy is too busy. Mommy doesn't care."

It was his voice! His soft, pure little voice. And he was talking, so he had a mouth! I was in tears as I rushed toward him, but he didn't react even when I hugged him to me.

"Mommy does care! I'm so glad you're back, Mikey. You have *no idea* how much I've missed-"

I didn't see it until I was already holding him. Now, his lack of a face was all I could see.

"I do know. I told you I've been watching you too." It wasn't a mouth he was speaking from. Not exactly. The slit started at the top of his neck and ran vertically to where his nose should have been. It opened and closed with the motions a mouth might make, but it was a gaping wound that he was speaking out of. Each time it closed, a sucking gurgle reverberated from it.

I let go, but he didn't. He was latched around my hand, dragging me into the wound which closed around my fingers. I didn't realize how fragile that little body was until I pulled free and the wound tore wider, all the way up his face. He didn't stop though—leaping at me, climbing me, grabbing my other hand to shove it deep into the wound. I tore free, this time ripping him all the way down to his stomach before I could get him off me.

He was insatiable. I had to throw him against the wall before I was able to escape. I slammed the door behind me and put my back against it, alternating between heaving sobs and tense breathless pauses while I listened inside. "Goodbye Mommy," was all I heard.

I held the door shut while I called the police, although I didn't feel any pressure or hint of presence from the other side. It took them ten minutes to arrive, and by the time I opened the door to Mikey's room again, the boy was gone.

The security footage! I ran to my computer in the other room and pulled it up while they waited: patient, polite, and utterly unconvinced. I clicked on empty file after empty file, everything black and inscrutable from tonight. Next I looked for last night's footage, but it was completely gone.

I didn't go back into Mikey's room until after the police had gone, and even then I crept like I was a thief in my own house. That's when I noticed the blue crayon smeared all over the lens of the camera. There wasn't any sign of him left. Not even the blood from that source-less, flapping wound.

What I did find though? A fresh drawing, childlike and innocent despite all the red. It looked like me again, but there was a big Pac-man like thing that was about to eat me up. Underneath it said:

FUN MOMMY. PLAY AGAN TOMORROW NITE.

I hate thinking about how many chances I've had to play, all wasted because I was too busy or too tired or too distracted by everything that didn't matter in life. I miss him so much, I think I'm even looking forward to tonight.

Even if he isn't the same as I remember. Even if I have to blindfold myself so I don't have to look at what he's become, I'm going to sit down and draw with him. And maybe, if I'm very lucky, then he's going to understand how hard I'm trying and he's going to still be there when the morning comes.

OUR EXTRA SON WAS FOR
EXPERIMENTS

I magine being lost in the open ocean, frantically bailing water out of a sinking raft which refills exactly as fast you empty it. You will never be found, never be saved. Sooner or later you'll need to rest and cease your constant vigilance, but you're still fighting the waves for as long as you can. However hopeless, the terror of that dark water is more real than everything else in your dying world. That's what being a mother was like to me.

I used to think the worst thing in life was not getting what you want. For me, that was starting a family, something I obsessed over since I was a little girl trying to make sure all my dolls successfully graduated and had families of their own. I fell for every boy who looked at me - always too fast, always the wrong one, wasting so much time imagining weddings and baby showers and these elaborate happy lives that were never lived outside of my head. Then all at once in nursing school I met a handsome neurologist, and within six months I was pregnant.

I finally had what I'd always dreamed about, but the worst thing in life isn't *not getting what you want*. The worst thing is getting it, and then realizing how much happier you were before. My first son Prater was diagnosed with Spinal Muscular Atrophy (SMA), an incurable genetic disease which left him barely able to move. Every day was an ordeal. Every hour, every minute - constant paranoia that his feeble lungs would give up or he would choke on his vomit and be too weak to struggle free. I had to drop out of nursing school, but my husband Jeffery took good care of me, leaving me to take care of the child.

My husband switched focus with his work, moving into research designed to strengthen motor neurons and protect them from SMA. It was an impossible dream though. There were a range of potential treatments, but they were years away from even reaching human trials. I begged Jeffery to sneak some experimental medication home anyway, but Prater was so weak that the injections would doubtlessly kill him long before the correct treatment and dosage was discerned.

It wasn't my decision to have another child. I didn't think I could bear going through something like this again, but Jeffery insisted. This can't be the end of your dream, he told me. This can't be the rest of your life. It wasn't until after I was pregnant again that he let his ulterior motive slip. It was the middle of the night, and I'd just gotten back in bed after checking on Prater. I don't think Jeffery was even fully awake, but he nestled in close to me and whispered:

"When the new kid is born, he'll be healthy enough to test the treatments on. We'll find something that works, and everything will be okay."

I didn't sleep for the rest of the night. I don't know whether it was fear or excitement, but I was so desperate that the two were beginning to taste the same.

When my second healthy baby boy was born, I didn't give him a name. I just wrote "X" on the form. Jeffery said it would be easier that way. By the time he'd exhausted the full litany of possible treatments, the new boy would likely be dead. I'd carried him for nine months, suffered for nine months, and for that sentence I was able to give Prater a whole lifetime of health and happiness. Not a bad trade, not when you're so tired of bailing water from a sinking ship. Even so, I've never cried harder in my life than that first hour when I held him in the hospital.

After that, I couldn't even look at the new baby. I pretended he didn't exist. Jeffery took a sabbatical from work so he could continue his research from home. He waited until X was six months old before he began the experiments, and during that time X lived in a makeshift nursery in the basement. I didn't see him, but I'd still *hear* the crying echo through the house sometimes. Jeffery was diligent and made sure that all the child's needs were met, and I occupied all of my time with looking after Prater (who was almost two by then).

Science - it's not that "Eureka!" moment you see on TV. It's not a sprint, it's a marathon. There was still so much that we didn't know about the disease, and even with ideal conditions and a proper experiment with control groups and A-B testing, it would have taken years. With a basement laboratory and a single experimental subject, and then later with Jeffery having to return to work part time ...

It took a decade before we began to see really promising results. All that time, I didn't see X once. Sometimes I was convinced that he'd died years ago, and that Jeffery was just putting on a show of bringing food down to the basement to give me hope. All I saw was Prater, every day a little weaker, a continual mockery of what it should mean to have a childhood and a family.

When at last we were ready to give the final drug to

Prater, I wasn't prepared for the troubling question which accompanied that step.

"If Prater gets better, and everything we ever wanted comes true, what are we going to do with X?" Jeffery asked one morning at the breakfast table.

It was unusually direct. Jeffery would always allude to his experiments without directly mentioning the test subject. Even when it was unavoidable, he understood that I wasn't comfortable acknowledging the boy. I tried to change the subject, but he was insistent this time.

"We can't just let him out. You understand that, right? It's too late for him to lead a normal, functional life. Even if he could psychologically acclimate one day, the years of trials have-"

"Do whatever you think is best," I cut him off.

"Are you telling me to -"

"I'm not telling you anything. I just want you to do *whatever* is necessary."

He nodded glumly, looking down at his coffee. The icy tension mounted as we listened to Prater cackling at his cartoons in the other room.

"He looks like me," Jeffery said, not looking up from his coffee. It took me a second to realize he wasn't talking about Prater.

"Why would you even tell me that?"

"He calls me dad," Jeffery added. He was finally looking, but I was the one who couldn't meet his gaze.

"You shouldn't have taught it to talk," was all I could say. "That's even worse than giving it a name."

The experiment was otherwise a success. Within a week of Prater's first injection, his voluntary movements were becoming smooth and controlled. By the end of the first month he was able to walk on his own. Listening to his breathing become steady, seeing his radiant smile as he took his first steps, the squeals of his excitement when I drove him by the school he would enroll in next semester - it was sublime, almost surreal in its fantastic impossibility. When we got back home Prater was so full of vitality that he even outpaced me from the car to the house. Entering first, he turned around to ask:

"Why is this door open? It's never open." I stopped cold on the doorstep.

"Is there anything ... *anyone* else there?"

"Nope. What's down here?"

A flight of empty steps going down. The lights were off. The room empty.

"Mom, why is there a bedroom under the house?"

I closed the door to the basement. The padlock was gone.

"It's just a guest room. There's no one visiting though, so we don't use it. Do you know where Dad is?"

"Can I go see? I want to see the other room!" Prater insisted. I was never any good at saying no to him. That must be why he looked so surprised when I shouted:

"Get out of here! Go find your dad, right now!"

Jeffery didn't come home that night. Calls went straight to voice-mail. Three options continued to surface in my mind. 1: Jeffery is bringing X to live somewhere else. 2: Jeffery is taking X somewhere to kill him.

Neither of those explained why he would leave the door open.

Option 3: X has escaped, and something has happened to my husband. I strained to remember all the vague mentions of X that I'd intentionally blocked out at the time. Something had happened to him during the trials. Something besides the psychological effect, that's what Jeffery had said. What exactly had he endured down there? The thought had crossed my mind innumerable times before, but it had been so repressed that I'd never taken the time to really think about it. What would life be for someone like that? Alone except for those few hours a day that Jeffery spent experimenting on him. The chemicals he must have ingested. The lies he must have been fed to justify his pitiful existence. What would someone like that do if their world was ripped away overnight?

I didn't let Prater leave my sight. I sat in a chair in his room, reading him stories until he fell asleep, and then just sitting and watching him. Maybe I should have gone to a motel or something, but he was so worn down from his outings that day and the medication was still so new that I didn't want to push him. Instead, I just sat and waited. I didn't know what I was waiting for, but I'd know it when I saw it.

Or heard it as it turned out.

"Mom?"

I must have fallen asleep in the chair sometime during the night.

"Yes Prater?" I mumbled, not quite awake.

"No, not Prater." My eyes flew open. It was dark, but I could still make out the outline of Prater sleeping in his bed. Someone else ... *something else* was standing in the room. I couldn't see anything but the silhouette, but the shape was unrecognizable. Gnarled, bulbous, utterly grotesque, cut into the night like the darkness itself had reared to life. All I could really see were the eyes, great pools of white without iris or cornea.

"Jeffery? Jeffery!" I shouted.

I couldn't even stand. Not with it so close, peering down at me like some sort of specimen.

"Dad doesn't know I came back," X said. "I wanted some time alone with you. Are you my mom?" The words slurred into each other, but the hot whisper was so close I seemed to feel their meaning more than hear it.

"No, she's not. She's my mom!" Prater was awake now too, sitting up and clutching his blankets to his chin.

I managed to turn my phone's flashlight on, regretting it immediately. X's face was devastated with ruptured boils and deep-pitted lines. His features sloped jaggedly toward the left as though he'd suffered multiple strokes, his pale eyes twisting in agony at the sudden light. In his hand he held a syringe filled with a thick, black syrup. It wasn't Prater's medicine.

"Turn it off, turn it off!" X shrieked, blindly swiping the syringe through the air. I jumped out of the chair and toppled it, brandishing my light like a weapon.

"Prater follow me!" I shouted. My son began to clamber out of bed, but he was still too weak. He was shaking so badly that he fell onto the floor in a crumpled heap.

"The light burns! Turn it off, Mom!"

Mom. That word was a dagger. I kept the light on X's face while I made my way around the edge of the room to where Prater fell. I fumbled the phone while trying to lift him off the ground. The light veered away from X's face. I could feel him charging toward me through the sudden dark, but I had Prater around my shoulders now.

I was running, flinging myself down the familiar halls of my house which shadows had twisted into an alien nightmare. I could hear X limping and lurching behind me, pursuing with incredible haste despite his disfigurement. The basement - it was the only safe place I could think of. I leapt headfirst toward the stairwell, grabbing the door and slamming it behind me. I put my back against the smooth metal, feeling it vibrate as X slammed into the door again and again from the other side.

The force of the impacts - it was like trying to stop a car. My bones were rattling against each other in harmony with the blows. Human tissue should pulverize under an impact like that, if X even was human anymore.

"Honey? Are you in there?" It was Jeffery. Somewhere above.

"Help us! We're in the basement! X is trying to kill us!"

Shouting. Running. A high-pitched scream, so pitiful and desperate that it still felt like my whole body was vibrating, even while the door stood still. Then a gunshot, and everything went quiet.

I opened the door to see Jeffery clutching a gun in both hands. X was kneeling on the ground before him, those pale eyes lancing through my body. Now that they were side-by-side, even the savage snarl further torturing the boy's face couldn't disguise how closely X resembled his father.

The boy was already fading into the shadows, vanishing almost immediately except for the white orbs which lingered in accusation. I held my breath, waiting for Jeffery to take the kill shot. It never came. X was gone.

I was still holding my breath when Jeffery came down the stairs and hugged me, then hugged Prater. I shook so badly that I couldn't even form words, but Jeffery did the talking for me.

"I'm so sorry, honey. I never would have let him out if I thought -"

But the words were all rushing together and I couldn't make sense of them anymore. Especially when he flipped on the light-switch and I saw the basement for the first time.

The laboratory section was much smaller than I expected. It was just a computer and a locked glass case full of chemicals. The rest of the space looked like you'd expect a boy's room to be. There were toys all over the floor and a TV in the corner. There were cartoon posters on the wall, a shelf full of books, and even a nightstand with a framed picture on it.

I was in the picture, holding X for the first and last time in the hospital room. Next to it was a stack of drawings, all of me, all so young and beautiful - so much better than I really was.

"I just don't understand why he would try to hurt you. He talked about you all the time," Jeffery said. "He always wanted to meet you, but I guess he was just too far gone."

"The syringe ... "

Jeffery's face grew tighter. "Let's all go back upstairs. Prater shouldn't see this."

"I need to know. What was in the syringe?" But the look he gave me told me everything I needed to know. X was still trying to help, even after all this time. And the look Prater gave me, I think he understood that too. Now that the secret is out, I don't think he'll ever be able to love me like he used to.

Not like X loved me anyway. My husband and I have created a monster and set it loose upon the world, but it isn't X. We're the only monsters here.

THE TOWN NOT ON ANY MAP

Take the I-87 north from Queensbury, Vermont. Then the 28 up through North Creek. Keep going, if you want to take the route that I did. You'll pass right through the town that doesn't exist on any map.

My headlights probed the first of the ramshackle buildings through the smoky dusk. This was no isolated farmhouse or wild hermit hiding from the world. A real town, with shy street signs peeking out from tangled vines and ivy. Looming apartment buildings that might have been abandoned for years, and ramshackle houses that looked as though they were grown from the earth rather than built from it. The place was materializing around me, appearing so suddenly that I couldn't imagine how I had been blind to it a moment before.

I slowed to a stop as an old man crawled his way across the street. He was huddled against the cold, pausing to leer through my windshield and breathe a frosty fog in my direction. I was growing impatient and was about to honk when he staggered up to the car, clattering his knuckles upon my window.

"Why are you here?"

Perhaps it was just his frail voice breaking in the cold wind, but it seemed as though the strain of panic lay just below the surface. A depressed man, wrought by anxious doubt, screaming at himself in the mirror before pulling a tight smile for the rest of the world to see. That's what I was looking at outside my window.

"I don't even know where here is," I answered him. "Is there a hotel where I can get a room for the night?"

"No hotels." The old man turned in a slow circle. I followed his gaze, noticing a growing number of faces framed by faded curtains, watching us from the surrounding buildings.

"A motel then? I'm not picky."

"No motels. No inns, no beds no breakfasts—nobody stays here."

More eyes. More faces watching us. Old men standing on the street corner, not bothering to disguise their gaping stares. Doors opening to reveal ancient women who might as well have been the direct descendants of prunes. Wrinkled hands wringing together, bleary eyes straining through their spectacles. Not a soul younger than sixty, and all staring with the horrified fascination of one witnessing a brutal car accident.

My nerves were fireworks, exploding with the undefined tension in the air. I nodded curtly and began to roll up the window when old hands shot through the opening, grabbing me by my collar.

"Take me with you. Don't leave me here. Please," he begged, real tears swelling up from the sunken wells of his eyes.

I shoved him back on instinct. The window slid shut, but he wasted no time in clutching the door handle and rattling it with all his might. I would have thought it was dementia if it weren't for the heavy silence of all those eyes.

"Please! You don't know what it's like! Don't go don't go don't go -" and on and on, uselessly pounding his weak flesh upon the metal door, crumpling to the ground beside my car and wailing like an insolent child.

I shifted into drive and put my foot on the gas, but a sudden sharp whistle gave me pause. A policeman had appeared beside me, cropped gray hair and piercing black eyes like a man who remembers the worst of war with warm nostalgia. He roughly pulled the pleading man away from my car before rapping a quick, authoritative burst of knocks on my window.

I rolled down the glass once more, keeping an eye on the discarded man who still trembled with silent, heaving sobs.

"Was this man giving you trouble?" the policeman asked.

I rapidly shook my head. "I was just asking for directions, that's all," I said.

"Just stay on this road. It'll take you right through town and you'll be on your way," the policeman said.

"Actually, I was looking for a place to -"

"This road is the one you want," he repeated. "There's nothing else for you here, understand?"

"Yes, sir."

The black eyes turned away and I was able to roll my window up once more. The rest of the eyes—those peeking from buildings or glaring from the street—they remained fixed on the scene.

I was only too thankful to be driving again, but I didn't even make it a block before a scream made me slam to another halt. In the open glow of a street lamp, unmasked before dozens of eyes, I watched the policeman's baton fall for a second time. Then a third. And a fourth—each wet bludgeoning thump accompanied by shrieks of agony.

The old man who had first addressed me was being beaten to a pulp in the middle of the street. The zealous baton alternated with quick, vicious kicks from the policeman's steel-toed boots. It wasn't the screams which haunted me though. It was the cold, impassive silence from the policeman. No warning. No threat. Not even sadistic satisfaction. It was just another day for him, another duty.

Those black eyes turned away from the writhing form on the ground. A second later, all the eyes from the entire town seemed to be on me. I stomped the pedal, tearing through the stop sign. Not fast enough to avoid hearing another gut-wrenching scream echo from behind me.

I couldn't just leave. It was my fault what happened. I should have let him in my car immediately, but there was nothing left but to hope I wasn't too late. I circled around the block, and by the time I got back the eyes had all turned away. Curtains were drawn tight again. Doors were closed. The old man was the only one left, still moaning and whimpering in the street where he'd been left.

I stopped the car and wasted no time in leaping out. His decrepit frame was so emaciated that I had no trouble lifting him into the backseat. He was still alive—barely—although there was a catching rattle in his chest when he breathed and it looked like a few of his ribs had caved in. One of his eyes fluttered open for a moment.

"Please." He had to spit blood between words. "Don't stop. No matter what you see, don't stop until the last house is gone."

I had no intention of staying any longer than I had to. The first curtains were just flitting open again, but I was already back on the road. I braced myself against the impending sound of sirens and the inevitable chase that never came. I didn't see a single other car on the road as I glided through the eerie twilight.

The only sign of life was the regular beat of windows. At each block, a new set would snap open with mechanical precision. Old heads like cuckoo birds sprang out in unison. Next the windows from the previous block would slam shut, continuing the steady rhythm like the incessant pounding of drums.

The rhythm didn't change, block after block, but gradually the faces peering out did. The farther I went, the older the inhabitants became, shrinking and decaying into loose folds of yellowed skin. Then this too gave way, until presently I found myself being watched by faces so ravaged by time that I could clearly see bleached bone and hollow sockets turning as I sped along the road. Even the buildings here were in various stages of collapse and calamitous ruin, almost as though I was driving through the inexorable span of years.

The houses were just beginning to thin and give way to the wholesome shelter of trees when I glanced behind at my passenger. The shock forced me to slam my foot on the breaks, barely avoiding swerving off the road entirely.

The gradual decay of the town was mirrored on my companion. Sagging flesh had dripped from his frame entirely, and the solemn skull behind me was preposterously balanced on a heap of splintered and broken bones—ancient wounds which had never healed.

"Don't stop, not yet." Words like trickling dust escaped the skull.

But I had already stopped. And the longer I ruminated on that unavoidable fact, the longer I remained frozen in static terror of what was to come.

The rhythm like the pounding of drums had returned. Windows, doors, opening and slamming, then opening again to unleash the remaining denizens that time had forgot. Lurching, shambling, and then springing to life with blasphemous vitality, the inhabitants of this charnel realm were closing around my car. Ragged skin fluttered in an unfelt breeze and white talons of bone raked the ground to pull them ever closer. Vacuous stares fixated upon me, and always that infernal drumming which mounted into the crescendo of a macabre hymn.

"Take us with you!" A lone shriek at first, but quickly taken up by the rest. "Don't leave us here!"

The engine lamented my efforts to start the car again. A tense rattle, then a sickening crunch like the mashing of rusted machinery. Had it aged with my passage as well? Had I? There was no time to stop and think. I leapt into the open night, brisk air heaving in my lungs as I scrambled up the hill toward the woods.

Drumming, drumming, ferocious and wild in intensity yet retaining its unerring rhythm. I had the oddest sensation that I was listening to my own pulse, and as I pushed myself harder and faster I could hear the drumming keep pace with my racing heart. It didn't matter though, nothing mattered except the last lonely house which I was swiftly growing level with and the figure which was emerging to greet me.

The policeman, baton in hand, gray-haired and stern and living as I had seen him last. The baton was tapping along with the impatient drums, and as I drew level I could feel the hesitancy in my pursuers.

"Still looking for directions?" he asked, a coy smile playing around the corner of his mouth.

"No sir." I wanted to say so much more, but that was all the breath I had at the time.

"Just passing through, are you?"

"Sir."

"Need a ride?" His smile was growing. I didn't like how many teeth it showed.

The drums had stopped. The crowd had stopped. My car

started somewhere behind me in the darkness. A flash of confusion passed the policeman's face. I liked that considerably more than the teeth.

"Don't you dare -"

But I was already running. Back down the hill, back toward my car. The pounding of the policeman's feet behind me, but it was so quiet compared to the resounding drums a moment before. The uncertain crowd parted at the policeman's thundering approach, but I was practically flying now.

My car never went below ten miles an hour, but the passenger door was open and I launched myself inside. The slam of the door behind me was the first beat in the resuming drums. All at once the crowd was screaming again, drowning out the shouts and the threats from the pursuing policeman. Mounting and mounting back into that hellish cacophony, and then just as swiftly dwindling back to nothing as the engine celebrated its triumph.

The old man in my car, or what was left of him—he drove me to safety that night. It's almost morning now and we still haven't stopped, but just as soon as I work up the courage, I'm going to have a whole lot of questions to ask him.

I think I'll start by asking the name of that town.

ECHO OF THE DEAD

There are a lot of people who think death is the end. They think we vanish without a trace, leaving nothing but a rotting corpse that has as much to do with who we were as the molding shirt we were wearing. Those people have never heard the echo of the dead. The last thought someone ever had before they die, that stays rooted to the place almost like a tree planted in their honor.

It's getting dark. I hear that one a lot. Or *I wonder if she'll miss me,* or *Take me home, God,* or things of that nature. I don't know how it works, but ever since my little brother's death when I was young, I've started hearing the echo of all the people who have died in any given location.

That's why I'll never set foot in a hospital. My mom tried to take me for a sprained wrist once, but I couldn't get within a hundred feet of the place before thousands of whispered echoes started flooding my mind. I couldn't take it—I just bolted and ran the second I got out of the car.

Later a therapist told me that I was suffering PTSD after what happened to my brother, but I never believed it. The echoes are too *real*. Too close. And I hear them wherever I go.

You'd be amazed at how many people have died in the most innocuous places. I can hear the whispers in the park where some geezer must have keeled over from a heart-attack or something. Sometimes there are muted screams along the highway or at sharp turns in the road. Even the coffee shop at the end of my street has an echo of: *the ambulance should have been here by now.*

... and then there was Ferryman's Lake. This was years later when I was a senior in high-school. The whole class had agreed to go to this remote lake for ditch-day at the end of the year. The atmosphere was electric: music blasting in the cars, beers in the trunk, and that desperate, almost maniacal energy of anticipation tinged with heavy goodbyes.

But I could hear the whispers long before we arrived. I didn't want to be the weird kid that day. I just wanted to be normal and celebrate with my friends. I tried my best not to listen—I'd gotten pretty good at tuning it out—but this time was different.

These whispers weren't nostalgic musings. They weren't profound or contemplative or sad. There was nothing but absolute, mind-numbing terror, and it kept getting louder as we approached the lake.

"You feeling okay?" Jessica, the kind of girl who makes smart men do stupid things, asked me as we parked.

"Of course. Just tired from the drive," I lied. I think she said something else too, but I couldn't even hear her over the echoed screaming. It was the loudest I've ever heard—even louder than the hospital. This close, I could finally start to distinguish some words too.

Did something touch my leg?

What the fuck is that thing?

The five other cars had all parked on the graveled shore. Kids were unloading picnic baskets and stereos. I sat in the car, completely frozen by the tumult of madding echoes.

I can't breathe!

Get out of the water! Get out get out!

"You getting out or what?"

Jessica again. I had to stare at her lips to understand what she was saying. She met my gaze while she casually stripped her t-shirt to reveal a well-employed bikini top. Then the flash of a smile I couldn't return. I nodded through the numbness, climbing out of the car to gaze at the calm blue water.

Not a ripple disturbed the tranquil mask. Not a hint of what could be under there. There was a ferry tied up along the bank with a cobblestone cottage nearby. A few of the kids were already beginning to investigate.

"Don't go...." I couldn't tell whether a whisper or a shout escaped my lips, but Derek, one of the guys hauling beer out of the trunk, was the only one who seemed to hear.

"What's the matter? You're not afraid of the water, are you?"

He must have said it loud for me to be able to hear it so clearly. Jessica was already ankle deep in the water, but she glanced back. Her smile wasn't for me anymore—it was tinged with the hint of mockery. Everyone would be laughing if they knew what was really going on in my head.

"What are you idiots doing? Get out, get out!"

Someone else had saved me from having to say it though. An old man, more beard than face, was standing in the doorway of the stone house.

One of the kids said something, but I couldn't hear it over the incessant echoed screams. I forced myself to get closer.

"Legend has it that something lives in the water near this shore," the old man replied loudly.

Everyone was out of the cars now—twenty-six kids in total, all gathering around the stone cottage.

"Something that has hidden since before mankind first

walked the earth," the old man was saying. "Something that strikes once without warning, and once is all it ever needs. Of course if you prefer, you can fork over five bucks each and I'll sail you to safety on the other side."

"What's to stop the monster swimming over there?" Jessica asked. She was still smiling—I could tell she wasn't buying it. No one was.

"Too shallow for it," the old man grunted. "A hundred bucks for the lot of you, special price. Better safe than sorry."

"No way, I want to see the monster!" Derek said.

He was almost up to his waist now, smacking the still water to send ripples echoing into the deep. Several kids started to follow.

"We should do it," I announced loudly, straining to keep my voice calm. "Hey look, I'll pay for it, okay? The ferry will be fun."

There were so many eyes on me while I fished out a brand new hundred that I got for a graduation present. So much for being normal, but at least I could live with myself this way. The old man snapped the money out of my hand before I could even extend my arm.

"Smart boy, smart boy." He winked, his eye glittering with sly recognition. "All aboard, don't be shy. Bags and heavy stuff go in the middle."

I avoided eye contact while boarding. For a terrible second I looked behind me and saw I was the only one. The people in the water or those already setting up their stuff on the shore were obviously reluctant. They looked back and forth at each other, trying to read the invisible will of the group.

"Last one is going to work at fast food for life," Jessica shouted, flinging her backpack into the middle of the ferry. She gave me a quizzical smirk and mouthed the words: *you owe me.* If only she knew how much. Soon her friends were following her, and a moment later the whole senior class was converging on the boarding plank.

I was hoping the echoes would disperse as we got past the shore. They didn't. Dozens of unique voices soon became hundreds as we approached the center of the lake. Echoes rebounding off echoes, reverberating and growing, flowing and slithering into my head like persistent intrusive thoughts. Cries for help, screams of pain, or just the animal bellow from the minds utterly devoured by fear.

The ferryman hadn't mentioned the monster again—it was all tourist trivia and blithering about the local plants and animals. He kept looking at me and grinning though, the discolored motley of teeth appearing almost feral at times. The farther he went, the more excited he grew, spewing spittle into his beard with every-other explosive word or declaration.

The continual pounding of sound was making me nauseous. I just closed my eyes and waited for this part to be over. I tried not to think about what might be in the water. There were so many voices that I had trouble keeping them straight, but I made a game out of trying to untangle them. Even so, it took several minutes of concentration before this came to the surface:

I never should have trusted the old man.

It sounded like a young boy around twelve, no older than my brother was when he died. I glanced at the ferryman who was leaning against the wheel, staring wistfully at us all. No one was paying him any attention anymore. Not even when his pale tongue flicked greedily over his lips.

The old man flipped something and the motor gave out. He stretched luxuriously in the sun before making his way to the railing.

"This is a good place to take a dip if anyone wants to

swim," he called out. "Real shallow here, and if you're lucky you'll see some turtles."

"You sure it's safe?" someone asked.

"I'll prove it." Flash goes the feral grin. Several people laughed and gasped as the old man clamored up onto the railing, launching himself into a graceful dive and vanishing with barely a ripple. Other people would be jumping in any second, and there was nothing I could do to stop them. I closed my eyes again, sifting through the mounting pressure of echoes....

Where'd the ferryman go?

He's not human.

Get back to the boat!

I opened my eyes again. There was a loud splash and the cheer of laughter which accompanied someone tumbling into the water. I was out of time. I leapt behind the wheel, turning the key and stirring the engine back to life. People were shouting, but I didn't care. It didn't matter who was already in the water—every instinct was screaming for me to just save as many as I could.

The controls were intuitive enough, and I pushed the lever full throttle. We were accelerating quickly—faster than I thought we would. The laughter around me was turning to distress, but I was ready to fight anyone who tried to stop me.

No one had time though. We were moving for less than ten seconds before something exploded out of the water behind us. By the time I looked back, it was gone. All I could see was a massive misshapen shadow underneath the surface, twisting and morphing and growing by the second.

He's not human. Then what the fuck is he?

There wasn't time to find out. Real screams were starting to mix with the echoes now.

"What are you doing? Jessica and the old dude are still in the water!"

Why her of all people? Was it some kind of cosmic joke that made her jump in first? No, that's just who she was. She was a brave and enthusiastic leader, and it was going to get her killed.

I slid the throttle down, and the ferry slowed. I didn't even register going on without her as a choice. There was nothing I could do though. Her head bobbed under as soon as the black shadow drew near. There was a flash of scaly skin above the water, then a brief glimpse of Jessica's fingers clawing for the surface. Everyone on the boat was shouting, but soon they were going to just be echoes too.

Churning water bubbled red, and I shoved the throttle again. The shadow was moving toward the boat, gliding directly under us. Louder than the echoes, louder than the thrashing water or the shouting kids, there was one more voice which joined the haunting chorus of the lake that day. It said:

Don't wait for me.

And I didn't. I should have done more, said more, while I still had the chance. But I didn't. And now it's too late forever, and I'm so so sorry....

I think I'm the only one of us who keeps returning to that lake. I don't go in the water, but if I close my eyes and concentrate, sometimes I can still make out her pale voice peeking shyly from the wall of noise. *Don't wait for me.*

AND I KNOW SHE'S RIGHT BUT I'M STILL HERE WAITING because in the end, an echo is all that will remain.

THE STORM IS ALIVE

I t's hard to type. My fingers are stiff and numb from the cold. My eyes are watering, and I can feel the tears freezing on my skin. I don't know how much longer my power is going to last this time, but I don't think we will survive another blackout. When they find our bodies—maybe not until spring when this cabin can even be seen over the snow—they'll know it was the storm that killed us. If I didn't write this though, they'd never know it was a murder.

The storm has been brewing for a month before it hit. Rolling gray clouds teasing us with snow for Christmas, yet always holding back despite the continual predictions. The weather channel said it was a 100% chance of snow every day for a week before the iron sky finally relinquished its payload. When it did come, it didn't waste any time with slush or dustings either. One night it was bleak and cold and bare, and the next morning I couldn't even see out from my first-story window.

My whole college canceled classes for the day—first snow day I've gotten since grade-school. I was planning to just sit around playing video games, but my little sister Clara looked so horrified that I might as well have said I was going to spend the day looking for stray cats to cook.

Snow was a miracle, where was my Christmas spirit, we couldn't waste time indoors, yada yada. I don't know exactly how the conversation got away from me, but pretty soon I had the ultimatum of either going sledding with her friends or admitting I was the literal Grinch. Guess I'm spending my day with a bunch of high-school girls, whatever. At least I'll be the cool, mysterious, older guy for a change instead of the blundering freshman.

I don't know how many of you have witnessed this, but something very strange happens when a group of high-school girls get together. They're all super affectionate with each other, but it's kind of a vicious, competitive affection. Imagine four puppies who are all trying to be as cute and friendly as possible, but they know that only one of them is going to get adopted and they'll happily tear the others to shreds if it means winning. Don't get the wrong idea, they completely ignored me. I don't even know who they were trying to impress, but it didn't take long before they started daring each other to do ridiculous, potentially life-threatening things.

"This time we're going to steer through those trees," Farris said, flashing all of her sharp little teeth. "Hit one and you're out. First one to make it through wins."

"On this hill? I used to do that when I was four," Clara interjected. Never-mind that I happen to know she cried every time she touched snow until she was almost eight. "Let's try it from up on the cliff, follow me."

And then it clicked. The real reason I was here. They took turns riding in the sleds while I dragged them behind me, the others walking a little back so they could step in my footprints and not have to push through the snow. I wasn't a bitch about it or anything, but I guess I was getting pretty grumpy. By the time we'd reached the top of the hill I was ready to just dump them all into the nearest snowdrift and head home.

I was looking for an excuse the whole way, and when the snow stated falling again I thought I'd found my ticket out. I warned them about how fast it came down last night. They didn't want to be stuck in a blizzard, did they? Of course they did. It was my mistake for making it sound like a challenge. They all looked like they were having fun though, and they assured me they would turn back if it got too bad. Good enough for me, I didn't waste any time trudging back alone.

The snow was falling in thick white crystals, catching the light like thousands of prisms to scatter it in radiant waves. I've lived in the mountains my whole life, but I've never seen anything like this before. Some snowflakes were as big as my thumb, and I could actually make out the unique and intricate geometrical pattern that each was composed of. I stood there to admire it while the wind stirred thick flurries to dance through the air in a preternatural frenzy. The footprints we made on the way were almost completely filled in already, and I quickened my pace to beat the oncoming storm.

It was getting too dark. Too fast. Rainbow reflections were vanishing across the new snow, replaced by dark shadows and a malevolent, ghastly gray like putrid water. It took less than ten minutes for it to go from noon to midnight. Clouds were streaming in from every direction, distorting and writhing together into an impenetrably dense wall. It almost seemed like they were getting closer too, the ceiling of the world dropping over me in a suffocating wave like a blanket being pulled tight around my head.

I'm not a hero for turning back for the girls. I wish I was, but honestly they were still a lot closer than the house was and I was afraid to be out here alone. The wind was picking up, a gentle moan rising into a savage howl that bit through my jacket and stung my skin like incessant wasps. At least it was behind me so it helped push me in the right direction, but it didn't feel like a lucky coincidence. It felt more like the storm was trying to drag me deeper in. This unsettling sensation was compounded when flurries of snow were stirred into the air like a beckoning finger, appearing so briefly that I couldn't convince myself whether I'd even seen it all.

I wasn't sure I was even going the right way until I heard them calling. Their thin voices were immediately devoured by the screaming wind so I couldn't be sure what they were saying, but at least I knew where I was going now. The wind altered as soon as I heard them, whistling into a higher pitch to mimic their cries. It felt like there were hundreds of girls in all directions, all crying and shouting, all the voices mingling and morphing into one mighty omnipresent wail.

We slammed into each other all at once. We were running and visibility was down to a few feet. It took a moment for us to scramble back up—all of us except Clara who wasn't there. The other girls just pointed back the way they'd come.

"It was just a dare," one of them said. "We didn't think she'd really do it."

They didn't wait to explain, didn't look back, just ran blindly down the hill in a desperate scramble toward civilization.

The pitch of the wind was beginning to change again. No longer imitating the shouting girls, it felt more like an unearthly song that swelled and pummeled me from all sides. The pressure continued to push me from behind, propelling me to stagger the last few feet to the top of the hill.

Clara was standing there, her back toward me as she faced the oncoming storm. Her clothes—jacket, shirt, pants, boots, all of it—had been removed and piled beside her. Her skin had long since faded from the bright-red chill into the blistering black and purple of frostbite. Her naked arms were outstretched as though welcoming the deadly embrace of the storm, and with her head thrown back I could now tell that she was the one whose song mixed with the tempest's roar.

She turned her head to watch me, her blistering skin cracking as it moved, a wicked smile playing across her black lips. Besides that, she made no effort to either help or resist as I struggled to dress her again. She stopped singing to simply stare at me as though the whole process was infinitely amusing to her. I kept screaming at her to do something, but the only answer I received was that from the unrelenting wind.

When Clara was all bundled up again I put her in one of the abandoned sleds and leapt in with her. I tried to keep her warm as we rode downhill, but then I had to get out to drag the sled on the long trek home. I don't think I would have made it if it weren't for the wind again, changing directions without warning to again aid my passage. It wasn't a blessing. The storm had already got what it wanted, and it didn't need us anymore.

I kept checking on her every minute to make sure she was still alive, but she seemed to be breathing quite easily despite her deathly pallor. She wasn't singing anymore, but I still heard the echo of those unfamiliar words swirl around me as we went.

We got home a couple of hours ago. The car won't start, and it's completely snowed in anyway. I've piled all the blankets on her and turned the space heaters on, but she hasn't said a word since she got back. She just sits there and stares at me, half of her mouth curled up in that twisted smirk. Once I caught her trying to stand and go outside again, but I stopped her and she hasn't tried since.

I managed to get a local news station for a while, but they all seem as mystified as I am. I left it on while I went to brew some hot tea for Clara when I heard her laughing in the other room. I ran back in to see a flash of purple and black skin being carried off in a stretcher. Clara was absolutely howling with laughter, and within seconds the wind outside was laughing with her.

Three girls were found in the snow by paramedics, the news said. They were completely naked, standing with their arms stretched out toward the oncoming storm. I turned off the TV because I couldn't stand the sound of the laughing, but the silence and the staring which replaced it is just as bad. I have this unshakable feeling that Clara is still out there somewhere, or perhaps I really did bring her home, but somehow brought the storm home with her. I just hope that when it clears, it leaves her as well.

I don't understand how anyone could anyone go on living with a storm trapped inside of them....

MIDNIGHT PRAYERS

Years ago when I was in jail, I used to pray every night. When you're little and you pray, it's because you want something from the world that you don't know how to get. When you're older, it's because the world wants something from you that you don't know how to give. The lights would go out at 11 p.m. and I would pray to be a better man, humiliating myself before the arbitrating silence of my thoughts, begging and pleading and even screaming when the thoughts became too loud to contain.

Then one night an unscheduled cell search interrupted my routine. The inmates all had to wait against the wall while our block was cleared, and it wasn't until midnight when I was able to begin my prayers. All those years my mother used to drag me to church, she never once told me that God isn't the one who listens to the midnight prayers.

I begin as I always do. I kneel on my bed, close my eyes, and with my hands clasped together I'll ask: "Is anyone listening?"

This was the first night that someone answered: "Yes."

I didn't dare open my eyes, terrified that the reality of my cell would be all I saw. The voice was soft, patient, and infinitely sad as though it had seen and heard more than its heart could bear but had such respect for the suffering that it stoically refused to turn away.

"I'm afraid," I said, because I knew at once that I could not lie to such a voice. "I'm afraid that I'm going to die in here. That the world has decided who I am because of one mistake, and that there's nothing I'll ever be able to do to convince them otherwise."

"You are right to be afraid," the voice said. "You will die in this cell."

My whole body went tense. For a moment I thought I was talking to a guard who was trying to screw with me, but the calm certainty of the voice was enough for me to keep my eyes closed and believe. If I couldn't have faith here and now, what hope did I ever have?

"But that doesn't mean that this is the end. Your body has been branded and discarded," the voice continued. "Do not waste any more time trying to save what is already lost."

"My soul then -"

"Your soul is hungry to keep living, and this is how you must feed it: Find and kill a human, and then take your own life. When these eyes close for the last time, the eyes of your victim will open and you will be the one looking out."

The strain to look at my savior was excruciating, but some instinctual terror forbade me. Either I would look upon some unspeakable abomination and be forced to abandon my hope of a new life, or I'd see some impostor and know it to be a lie.

"And if I don't like who I've become, I can kill again?" I barely breathed the words. "Will I become a new person each time?"

"As many times as you like," purred the presence. "When

you're old and tired, taking a child will let dance this mad show again."

My mind was racing, immediately disgusted but enthralled by the idea. "And if I die by chance—if I'm hit by a car or something—and I haven't killed anyone yet, where will I go then?"

"That will be up to me to decide." The voice was smiling now. I don't know how I knew, but I *knew*.

I couldn't take it anymore. If this was some sick joke, then I wanted to know before I betrayed anything more. I opened my eyes and flung myself in a rabid dash against my cell door. There was no one on the other side. No one in the corridor which stretched open before me. The voice did not speak to me again.

I have prayed to be a good man, and this is how my prayers were answered. I will become a good man, but I had to find and kill him first.

Killing another inmate would be pointless. Why start life again in another cell? It had to be a guard, someone with access to the outside so I could make my way out and then kill again. It took about a week for me to get a metal shiv that would be up to the job. I took my victim in the yard during the bedlam of a gang squabble. He was innocent of everything but standing next to me when the opportunity arose, and I do not wish to dwell on the incident with any more detail than that. I only had a few seconds before the other guards tackled me, but it was enough to force the shiv into my own heart. As the light bled from me and the pain dissolved into oblivion, I prayed again for forgiveness. No answer came but the welcome darkness ...

... and the searing white light which roused me in the hospital. I wasn't shackled. There was a woman leaning over my bed, shedding tears of joy that I was all right. Her name was Mariah, and she didn't know that she was a widow now.

There was a boy who wouldn't stop wailing and laughing. He didn't know that his father had died on that prison yard or that I had taken his place.

Was it a kindness that kept me from telling them the truth? They were so happy that I was alive that they readily accepted my memory loss, although I did seem to maintain some of his muscle memories and habits. It started off as guilt that made me unwilling to leave them, but guilt alone could not endure through the years as I have done. You probably wouldn't believe me if I told you I loved them as strongly as they loved me, but waking up with my new wife and staying strong for my boy, I've never been so happy as that.

I lived with them for five years until I suffered a minor heart attack. I felt like a ticking time-bomb after that. The big one could happen any day, and this new life I had worked so hard for would be replaced by some unspeakable unknown. Giving up this new life was the hardest thing I've ever had to do, but I couldn't take the anxious suspense any longer. It was time to kill again.

And again. And again. I wouldn't let myself get tied down like that again. That one was famous, or another had a better house or a hotter wife. The lives were a blur, fading in and out so quickly that I became everyone and no one. It turns out killing people is actually quite easy. It's not getting caught that's hard, but since I always sacrificed my own life in the same moment, getting caught was never an issue.

I wanted to experience everything that life had to offer. One day I was a schoolgirl, the next I was a professional athlete or a racecar driver. Taking highly skilled people was my favorite because, with a little practice and their muscle memory, I was just as good as they ever were. I spent several years as a number of prominent musicians, leaving a wake of scandals as I inevitably took my own life to move on again.

I don't know many lifetimes I could have spent this way, but I never had the chance to explore them all. I was using a healthy body to experiment with a variety of drugs when I was ambushed by an undercover cop. I didn't have the chance to switch bodies again, and before I knew what was happening I was back in jail. It was a minor possession charge and I had plenty of money hidden away for bail, so I didn't make a fuss. The point is that I saw her again at the station.

Mariah was dating again—I guess she had a thing for a man in uniform. Seeing her sitting and laughing, knowing that she moved on from me so easily, it just made my blood boil. I guess I hadn't realized until that moment that throughout all the glamorous lives I've lived over the last few years, I hadn't once been as happy as I was when I was with her.

It wasn't as easy as I thought it'd be to slip back in. I killed her new boyfriend without trouble, but she didn't stay with me long. It was as though she noticed the change right away, dumping me almost as soon as I stepped foot in her house. I took two more bodies, trying to seduce her only to be turned away each time. Frustrated, I consented to bide my time, waiting until she began dating again so that I could replace him and have her.

Three boyfriends later, the same story each time. I killed each of them, only to be rejected the moment I appeared in their body. It seemed as though she could sense my presence somehow, but each time she turned me away I only wanted her more. It didn't help that she was becoming unstable. I hadn't counted on how psychologically devastating it must be to continue dating new people and yet sense that they are all the same. She practically stopped going outside altogether, and I was going crazy trying to figure out how to reach her.

You don't know how much it hurts me to tell you what happened next. This is my confession though, and before God and man and otherwise, I wish my sins be known. There was one person in her life that Mariah would never abandon, and children are always the easiest targets. I caught him leaving school one day (he's been taking the bus since his mom started locking herself in). I was wearing the body of a policeman he'd grown up around, and he had no reason to suspect my intentions when I offered him a ride.

I didn't drive him home though. I was taking him out into the woods where there wouldn't be a scene. Trying to get close to Mariah through her son might seem strange to you, but after living so many lives I wasn't encumbered with such artificial distinctions as romantic or maternal love. I wanted to be close to her again. I wanted her to love me. And if she was too broken to love another man, then I was willing to make a compromise on her behalf.

"Get out of the car," I ordered the boy who was once my son.

"Where are we? I thought we were going home?"

"Just get out."

Those big, almond eyes stared at me for a long time. Then he smiled.

"Okay, I trust you," he said.

"We're going to play a game." I got out of the car with him. My hand was cramping up from flexing beside my gun.

"Okay."

"Close your eyes."

"Okay."

"Don't open them. Promise me, okay?"

"Okay Dad." He closed his eyes. My blood froze.

"Why'd you call me that?" I asked.

"Sorry." His little brow furrowed in deep thought. "I don't

know. It's just that you smell like him, only I don't feel it in my nose."

"Where do you feel it?"

The boy crossed his heart, still clenching his eyes shut. I slid my gun back into its holster.

"The game goes like this. You count to a hundred while I hide. When you open your eyes, you have to find me. Ready?"

"Ready!"

When we finished playing, I told him to get back in the car and we drove back to his home. I didn't go in to see Mariah. I just dropped him off and didn't look back. No matter what happens from this moment on, I know this life is going to be my last. I know it doesn't mean much, but for what it's worth I'm staying on as a cop. I'm going to protect that boy and his mother for the rest of my life. And when chance or old age takes me at last, I'll deserve whatever happens to me next.

I have prayed to be a good man, and this is how my prayers are answered.

THE HEAD TRANSPLANT

W e knew the world would not be the same. A few people laughed, a few people cried, most people were silent. I remembered the line from the Hindu scripture, the Bhagavad-Gita; Vishnu is trying to persuade the Prince that he should do his duty and, to impress him, takes on his multi-armed form and says, "Now I am become Death, the destroyer of worlds."

-Julius Oppenheimer on the first atomic bomb.

That quote comes to mind while watching Sergio Canavero work. When performing surgery, he becomes so mesmerized by the task that myself and his other assistants become indistinguishable from his steel instruments, born and bred for this sole moment when he has need of us. Even the patient isn't a human being anymore: just a puzzle to be deciphered or discarded when the last piece finally breaks.

I thought it was the greatest honor in the world when the neurosurgeon accepted my application to join his team. Despite the international controversy over the ethics of head transplants, I knew that I was going to become part of history. I wasn't embarrassed to tell my family what I was doing either—they were proud of the honor I was doing for China. Our president Xi Jinping is sanctioning this experimental procedure because he is determined to replace the U.S. as the world leader in science, and it was my privilege to perform on that global stage.

Dr. Canavero has explained and rehearsed the procedure with us over the last several months, but this was more rigorous than any of my classes at Peking University. Essentially we will be simultaneously severing the spinal cords of the donor and recipient with a diamond-edged blade. The donor head will be cooled to a state of deep hypothermia to keep the neurological tissue from dying during the transfer. By the end of the twenty-four hour operation we will have reconnected all vertebral bones, nerve-endings, veins, trachea—everything. The patient will then be suspended in a drug-induced coma until he has healed enough to move on his own.

And then? There's going to be a brand new person with a whole new life to live. Those who are languishing in a paralyzed body will be able to walk. Healthy minds trapped by the ravages of age can be restored to youth, and the very notion of mortality and individuality and the soul itself will be forever changed.

That's the best case scenario, of course. There is also the chance that the surgery will fail and we'll have sacrificed two people to the altar of our arrogance. More than that though, failure would likely show our best intentions in a macabre light, prejudicing the world against us and our research for decades to come. So many eyes on us—on China—so many judgments and condemnations....

The pressure was intense. I could feel it in the air the second I stepped into Dr. Canavero's laboratory each morning. No one smiled, and if they did, it was just a thin bloodless line that died almost before it began. As we approached the operation date, the other two assistants and I were drilled incessantly on every potential obstacle. One second of hesitation during the operation and we'd be ostracized from all official institutions which sought to distance themselves from our failure. Flash cards, pop tests, rehearsals on dummies, endless study—but we were still months away from the official operation when I received a phone call at 1 a.m.

" … you'll be using the back-door tonight." Dr. Canavero didn't even wait for me to say hello. "It will be unlocked. Don't bring any identification, and tell no one where you will be. Officially speaking, nothing that you do or see tonight will have ever happened."

"What's going on? Is this about—" I managed before being cut-off with an impatient hiss.

"Of course it's about the operation. Stop wasting time. We have a long night ahead of us."

The other two assistants were already there when I arrived. I will not use their real names, but instead will call the acclaimed surgeon Dr. Cheung while Dr. Zhao is an elderly woman who leads her research department. Canavero was the center of attention as always though, animated as he was with passionate energy and explosive gesticulations.

"My friends, we are very fortunate, very fortunate indeed," Dr. Canavero was saying. He ushered me in from the door, glancing both ways outside before securing it behind me.

"President Xi Jinping has given us a gracious gift. One that I had long desired, but hadn't yet dared to ask. Come come, not that way."

Dr. Canavero was practically prancing as he turned away from the usual route to our lab. It was almost surreal navigating the abandoned hallways that were typically bustling with life. The naked florescent lights burned with a gentle hum like the eternal pondering of an unseen jury. Cheung answered my questioning look with raised eyebrows of his own as we all turned to follow.

"It's a risk, you know. What he's doing for us. Of course it will be to the glory of China if we succeed, but with an experimental procedure on the frontier between reality and science-fiction? He's gambling with us."

We were in the elevator now. I'd never been to the bottom floor before (you needed a special key to access it) but I'd always been told it was just storage space. Dr. Canavero's feverish excitement while he inserted his key told a different story.

"We are already taking every reasonable precaution to prepare—" Dr. Zhao began to reassure him.

"But the thing about powerful men is," Canavero continued, ignoring her, "is that they don't remain in power by gambling. Not without a loaded die, at least."

The elevator door opened to a long hallway with stairs at the end which continued spiraling downward. The first thing that impressed me was the enormity of the space: it must have been as large as the rest of the facility combined.

"We can't rig an operation." Dr. Cheung snorted. "And even if we could falsify the reports, it won't convince the scientific community for long. It would do nothing but further discredit your—"

"I'm not talking about rigging the operation," Dr. Canavero said, leading us toward the stairs. "I fully intend to live-stream the entire procedure for the whole world to see."

"Then I'm afraid I don't follow—" Dr. Cheung started before being cut off again. Was that the echo of a shout from farther down? In the sudden silence, we all heard it clearly again. Hoarse, strained, utterly hopeless, as though it had been calling on deaf ears for a long, long time. I rushed to the railing with the other two assistants.

"We're not going to rig the operation." I was the first to speak. The words were difficult to form in my mouth. "We're going to rig the preparation. The whole world will think they're watching something that's being done for the very first time...."

It was still a storage space, of sorts, but it would be more accurate to call it a jail. The corridor was lined with cages barely large enough for their human occupant to stand. Below this floor ran another identical corridor with its own set of cages, and even more below that as far down as I can see. Thin hands grasped uselessly at the wire, rattling them in restless excitement and fear. Others continued to lay on the ground, too broken or hopeless to even turn our way.

"While we've already successfully completed it. Dozens of times." Dr. Canavero joined us to look down. "No play would ever be performed without a rehearsal, after-all. The moment we accepted the research grants from President Xi Jinping, we have all become actors in his employ."

"How many are there?" Dr. Zhao breathed a hot whisper.

"Enough to make it a good show," Dr. Canavero replied.

"Who are they though?" I asked.

"They're not victims, if that's what you're asking," Dr. Canavero said, turning back to the staircase. "At some point in all of our lives, we have a choice: to become someone or to become no one. It is their misfortune that they decided the later, although ultimately it was still their decision to make. I can only hope that my own team," he stopped here, turning back to level his gaze on us, "that my own team has the foresight to recognize when they are making such a choice, and to do so more wisely."

The implications were clear. Report the incident and it would be more likely that I ended up in one of those cages than it was for any of them to go free. Science is concerned with the truth, after all. Not with how we got there. I took the first step toward the stairs, but a hand caught me by the arm.

"Some are likely to survive though, aren't they?" Dr. Zhao's face was pleading for something that I couldn't give her. I tried to force a smile, for her sake.

"Of course. That's the whole point, isn't it? We're just learning how to switch the heads." I knew it wasn't true even while saying it. Even the survivors would be buried with this secret, I had no doubt. That's when it occurred to me that my fate was likely inevitable for the same reason. Why would the government ever risk these methods getting out?

That's why I'm writing this now though. Just in case something does happen. The first operation is about to begin, but I can't help but feel I'm the one about to go under the knife. Is it wrong that part of me is excited too? My family will be so proud when this is over. I'll be a hero, and don't all heroes walk on the bodies of those they couldn't save?

SHE CAN'T TELL LIES

Repeat after me:
I must not tell lies. I must not tell lies. I
CANNOT tell lies. Or else.

It's as vacuous a statement as you can find. If someone is truthful, then they do not need to make such a promise. If they are not, then their promise means nothing anyway. There's only so much a mother can do when her daughter is a liar, and I was doing the best I could.

Marcelline is just eight years old, but she's learning so fast. She can count all the way to 1,000 and has her multiplication tables memorized. She can read on her own without moving her lips, and she knows how to look up words she doesn't know. She loves playing soccer, riding bikes and roller skating, but her most impressive skill by far is her mastery over lying. And she does it every chance she gets.

My daughter's favorite lie is about a character named Zafai she read about in one of her books. If she doesn't want to get up in the morning, it's because Zafai kept her awake all night. She never breaks anything, but Zafai is a whirling dervish when I'm not around. I thought it was cute at first, but I knew I had to put a stop to it before it became an incurable habit.

I started by punishing her. I would scold her and tell her to stand in the corner, or take away her toys and books when she wouldn't stop. The little rebel fought back, digging in her heels and hotly declaring that Zafai wouldn't tolerate being stolen from. Marcelline was a banshee with an attitude problem, and I'd usually only last a few hours before giving in just to shut her up. My husband Marc thought I was just enabling her, but I couldn't help it. Watching her scream and wail and throw herself around the room like a crash-test dummy in an explosives yard was too much for me to bear.

"We can't let this go on," Marc said to me the other night after Marcelline had gone to bed. "She's holding the whole house hostage."

"Fine with me. You get the rope and I'll get the gag. They make those in children's size, right?"

"I'm serious," he said. "She might not understand now, but it's for her own good. How do you think she's going to navigate through life, or hold a job, or maintain a relationship when she thinks lying is a magic answer to everything?"

Of course he was right. We had to parent the shit out of that little beasty. She's on winter break now, and our house was about to turn into liar's rehab. That night Marc and I collected all her books and padlocked them in a cabinet. He took the key with him to work so I wouldn't be able to give in to her tantrums. Over breakfast, we sat down with her to clearly lay out the rules.

"Do you know why mommy and daddy took your books away?" I started.

I guess she hadn't noticed until I said it. Her little eyes narrowed, the dead rot of winter piercing through the slits. I looked helplessly to Marc for support.

"You've been telling a lot of lies lately, and you're getting punished," Marc supplied. "If you want them back, you've got to go a whole day without lying."

Marcelline took a deep breath and pouted her bottom lip. It was almost enough to make me give-in immediately, but Marc was there to the rescue.

"Repeat after me: I must not tell lies."

Marcelline looked pleadingly at me. I crossed my arms and pressed my lips into a hard, uncompromising line. At last she rolled her eyes in defeat.

"I must not tell lies." She sighed dramatically.

"And you're going to start by telling us that Zafai isn't real," I interjected. Marc grinned and gave me a nod of approval.

Marcelline wasn't giving us a death glare anymore. Her wide, quivering eyes were much harder to endure. She was even starting to look pale. Damn she's good.

"Say it or I'm going to lock up your skates too," Marc growled.

"I can't," she whispered. "Zafai hates lies even more than you do, and I know he's listening."

"Marcelline! Say it!" I almost shouted. Marc raised his eyebrows. "Or *else!*"

She looked wildly around like harried prey. Tears were welling in her eyes. Marc grabbed my hand exactly when I needed him to. She needs this, stay strong, his grip seemed to say.

"Marcelline!" Marc bellowed.

"Okay! Zafai isn't real. I'm so sorry Zafai, please don't hurt me."

I sighed. Mark snorted in amusement. "Good enough for today, I guess. I'll be home around six, think you can hold the fort until then?"

"Bring it on! I can do it." I gave him my most convincing

fist pump. It felt like the first victory we've had over our daughter in months. I had no idea how wrong I was.

It started with the silent treatment, although I have to admit that was actually a relief. I expected her to be screaming bloody-murder the second Marc closed the door, but Marcelline just sat in the living room and glared at me from under her little furrowed brow. Fine, let her sulk, at least I could keep an eye on her here. I sat on the couch with my laptop to bust out some last-minute Christmas shopping. Marcelline was muttering under breath, but I did my best to just ignore her. It sounded like she was apologizing over and over, but it would take more than that to break my resolve.

The first time I glanced up, she was still sulking, her bottom lip pushed out as far as it would go.

Ten minutes later and she still hadn't moved. She was just staring at me and chewing on her lip. She was waiting for me to cave like I always did, but this time I wouldn't give her the satisfaction. I made a real mental effort to not even look at her for the next half hour.

But I did look up eventually, and I started screaming the moment I did. The lower half of her face was covered in blood, dribbling down her chin onto the floor like a vampire over a fresh kill. She was still glaring at me, relentlessly and purposefully chewing.

At first I couldn't figure out what happened, but when I rushed over to her she spat a fleshy lump in my face. I grabbed it without thinking, mind numb from disgust, staring at bloody slug-like thing in my hand. She spat another one—it was her other lip that she had chewed straight off.

"I must not tell lies," she hissed, spluttering blood as she did. She wasn't grinning, but it looked like she was. Even with her mouth closed I could see all her ferocious little teeth jutting out of her gory gums. "What cannot speak cannot tell lies." And then she was chewing again, the open wound of her face doing nothing to conceal the gnashing teeth which sank into her tongue over and over again.

I had to grip the top of her head and her chin to hold her mouth shut, but it took both hands and I couldn't reach the phone. Tears mingled with her blood, gushing down her face, but nothing could stop the gnashing. Even with both my hands and my whole body weight pressing down on her head, I could feel her jaws relentlessly lifting me and clamping back down again.

I tried to stuff my fingers into her mouth to hold it open instead, but they snapped down so ferociously that I almost lost a digit. It was like trying to stop a garbage disposal with my bare hands. Next I tried to get her to lie down and relax, but she started choking and I had to lift her immediately. I thought she was just choking on the blood, but no—a second later her entire tongue oozed out of her mouth like some giant eel swimming through red waters.

At least she had nothing to chew anymore. I broke away long enough to call an ambulance, but even that was a mistake. Her jaw was already working through the insides of her cheeks. She started choking on the pieces again, unable to get them out of her mouth without the aid of her tongue. I couldn't stop her—all I could do was hold her on her hands and knees to let the bloody chunks dribble out of her mouth so they wouldn't go down her throat.

SHE DIDN'T STOP UNTIL THE PARAMEDICS ARRIVED AND injected her with something that knocked her out. I was so overwhelmed that I couldn't even follow. I just sat on the bloody floor and cried, finally noticing the words which must have stained carpet while she was kneeling.

"Zafai is real. I must not tell lies."

When she recovers—if she recovers—I'm going to have a lot of questions that she won't be able to answer. I've heard there are people here who know about this sort of thing though, so I'm begging you for help. What is Zafai? What do I do now? I know it must be hard to believe, but please don't dismiss it or give me any false hope. Zafai hates liars, and I just know he's still listening.

UNDER THE FROZEN LAKE

K nock. I'm at least fifteen feet from the frozen shore when I hear it. The ice feels as solid as concrete, so I take another step. The Winnibigoshish is like most of the Minnesota lakes which will remain frozen until spring. There's no chance of breaking through. At least that's what my girlfriend Amy keeps telling me.

Knock.

"I hear it cracking. We shouldn't go so far out—"

"I hear something cracking. Is it the voice of my terrified boyfriend?"

I glare at her or at least at the waddling bundle of winter coats which has devoured her without a trace. Somewhere in my head is faintly echoing the song I will do anything for love, but I won't do that. I can't turn it off, but I do my best do turn down the volume so I can take another step. The thick blanket of snow which covers the ice keeps me from sliding, and if I really concentrate I can pretend I'm walking on a regular snowy field.

Knock. It's just so hard with that sound like an ephemeral

gunshot deep below the ice. Reverberating echoes insidiously linger somewhere between hearing and imagination. There isn't any reason to be afraid. If I'm trembling, it's just because it's fourteen degrees outside.

"If you don't hurry up, I'm going to start stomping and throwing rocks," Amy shouts. "Then we'll see how solid it really is."

When did she get so far ahead of me? It's amazing how quickly the world can pass you by when you're staring at your feet. I scramble and slide another few shambling paces toward her. It's easier to move if I just focus on her. Don't look down, don't look down, don't look down—

Knock. I look down. My body doesn't ask for permission first. I couldn't help it when the sound comes from directly below. I stare down into the blank patch of ice where the snow is thinner. I stare down into the blurred blue-tinged face on the other side of the ice, and the hand which pulls back to—

—but the knock doesn't come. This time the hand simply presses against the underside of the glassy window. Fingers spread wide in an intimate gesture as though inviting my touch from the other side.

"Seriously dude? I'm going to freeze to death waiting for you."

"Amy?" My voice is muffled from my scarf, but I can't look up from the lake. The face is coming into focus as it presses itself against the ice. Amy's skin had never been so pale, her eyes never so blue, as those staring up at me from below my feet.

"I swear to God, if you pussy out on me then I'm leaving your ass here. You said you'd go all the way out with me."

Amy—the other Amy, underneath the ice—her mouth is moving too. It isn't hard to read her lips when it's only one word: Run.

"You've got five seconds before I leave you here," my girl-friend shouted. "Four!"

My knees buckle and I tumble down to peer into the ice. The other Amy isn't exactly identical. Her clothing is different, but familiar. She's wearing the purple sweater my girl-friend had been wearing yesterday when we'd gone out skiing together.

"Amy wait—"

"Three!"

I put my hand against the ice to mirror the girl underneath. She recoils immediately, her face twisting into that of desperate fear. Amy and I had been separated about an hour yesterday when she moved onto the advanced slopes while I practiced on the bunny hill. Had something happened to her during that time?

"Two!"

Knock. Her fist slamming into the underside of the ice which vibrates underneath me. Then slamming again, her movements frenzied in their urgency. Her mouth straining as the silent scream rips from her body. The muscles in my legs coil beneath me, so tense they might as well be a brooding avalanche which needs only the weight of one more snowflake to begin.

"One."

This voice was different. It was still Amy, but it wasn't her, like comparing a black-and-white photo to the original. All the color, all the life, all the flavor had drained from the sound, leaving only the barest skeleton of her voice to hang in the frozen air.

"Run!" screams the girl under the ice, but I can't leave her there. I clasp my hands together to raise them above my head, smashing them into the window. It feels like the bones in my fingers are rattling together from the impact. Underneath, the girl is flinging her entire body against her side of the ice.

"I'm giving up on you," shouts the colorless voice. It sounds like it was farther away, but I don't look up. The girl below the ice is growing weaker with each strike. Her fingers are stiff and inflexible. Her mouth is still working over the same word again and again, but each iteration comes more slowly as her jaw resists the effort.

I can break through though. A deep hollow crack is resonating with each blow. Flurries of snow and ice shrapnel explode into the air as I strike the ice again and again. The girl below is sinking now, but I'm not giving up until—

Glacial waters spray from the crack. One more blow and I'm through, plunging my hand into the numbing chill to seize the stiff fingers slipping deeper into the water. The skin is so hard and cold it feels like metal, but life surges into her as she responds to my touch. She's gripping me now, and if I can just get stable footing I'll be able to haul her out—

But she pulls before I have the chance, and I'm already tumbling into winter's gaping mouth. Water so cold that it burns my skin closes over my head. The other Amy braces her feet against the underside of the ice to pull me deeper still, launching off with her legs to send both of us spiraling downward.

I can feel my eyes freezing all the way to my skull, but I can't shut them if I want any chance of finding the hole in the ice. She's still clinging to me, but a few wild kicks buy me enough space to start clawing my way back toward the surface. I expect my impetus to rocket me straight out of the water, but my head only slams into the impenetrable ceiling of ice. Even down here, it sounds a lot like the knocking I've heard since I arrived.

My wild fingers probe the ice as far as I can reach in every direction. I went straight down and back up! The hole should be here. My skin revolts against the numbing darkness. The pressure in my lungs is mounting by the second. My body demands a scream, but I refuse to waste the last remnants of my precious air.

I'm pulling myself along the bottom of the ice in every direction, but the strength in my fingers is swiftly fleeting. The hole is gone. The light is dying, and soon I will follow. Soon, but not yet. Fingers grip around my ankle. I'm not strong enough to kick free anymore. Another hand latches on and begins to drag me, and I know in my heart that it's the hand of death.

Then the pull. Water rushes over me, but I can barely feel it anymore. There's a momentary pause as the hands refocus their grip, and then the pull again dragging me deeper still. My last uncertain thought is wondering why it's growing brighter around me instead of darker. An idle curiosity of no consequence. She's pulling again, and—

My legs are pierced by a sudden wind. My brain can no longer process how that's possible. Then another pull and the water begins to pour off my body. My head is suddenly clear from the water and I collapse onto my back on solid ground. I'm coughing and spitting up water, but a warm blanket is being wrapped around me. My eyes flutter open from the life-giving pressure, and Amy is there. Amy in her purple sweatshirt, perfectly dry—she's holding me to her and wailing incoherently.

I must have passed out after that, but when I woke up I was back inside her house. She said I must have been crazy to break the ice under me, but she ran back as soon as she saw me fall in. I was upside-down in the water, but she managed to pull me out by my ankles.

"What on Earth were you thinking? You could have died!"

I didn't tell her about the face under the ice though. I didn't ask her how she could have changed back into her purple sweatshirt in the middle of that ordeal. And above all else, I didn't ask her about the knocking I still hear resounding far above my head, almost as though it were coming from another world.

I don't think I'm ready to find out.

THE NEW YOU

1   11:50 p.m. on New Year's Eve. The raucous beat of the music is echoed by the pulse in my veins. Iridescent lights lance through the air all around me, and the teaming heat of pressed bodies forces me to swallow a great lungful of heavy air thick with sweat and cheap perfume. I can't be the only one who isn't dancing, but anyone who notices me will immediately recognize that I don't belong here. Smiles and sneers look the same to me, and all laughter is tainted with condescending jokes at my expense.

Living with crippling anxiety is my personal nightmare. Just trying to start a conversation with someone feels like standing on the roof of a tall building. One little push and I'm free, but the clenching knot in my stomach has me frozen in place. I must have started walking toward Chase at the DJ table a dozen times so far this party, but I've never gotten within a few feet before I had the irresistible urge to check my phone, go to the bathroom, or disappear off the face of the earth entirely.

Guys like Chase don't look twice at girls like me. It doesn't matter if we like all the same music. It doesn't matter

241 SLEEPLESS NIGHTS | 241

if there is electricity which ignites the air between us. Maybe things would be different if he was the one to say hi first, but how was that supposed to happen when I couldn't even get close to him?

"Looks like you could use a drink." I don't understand how I heard the words so clearly over the pounding music, but I didn't turn to the barman. Maybe if he thought I didn't hear him he'd give up and leave me alone—

"Maybe two. What's your poison?" he insisted.

"I don't drink." I dismissed him over my shoulder.

"You mean you didn't used to drink."

I finally turned to see an elderly man with a closely groomed gray beard and a vest which fit so closely that it might as well have been sewn onto his skin. His dark eyes drilled into me with undisguised fascination.

"You didn't used to do a lot of things," he continued. "There was a time when you'd never walked before, but then you started and you haven't stopped since. Now it would be silly to say you don't walk, wouldn't it? You aren't even the same person who couldn't walk anymore."

"What do you mean, 'not the same person'?"

A sudden lull in the music was punctuated by Chase's voice on the loudspeaker. "Five minutes to midnight! Who is ready to burn the rest of this year?" He was answered by an overwhelming cheer, but the old man's words still clearly punctured the chaos.

"I mean you're remembering someone else's memories," he said. "Next year you'll be new again, and then you'll remember all the memories you have now and think that they're yours. You'll have all the same habits and be afraid of all the same things because you think that's who you're supposed to be, but it's not. The new you will have to decide for herself whether she wants to keep copying a failing strategy or learn from it and try something else."

"I don't have a failing strategy. You don't even know me."

"How could I?" he replied promptly. "You're a blank slate tonight. Even you don't know you yet, so how about that drink?"

I nodded, not fully understanding why. He spoke with such a simple surety that I couldn't muster anything to refute him. The barman pulled a purple bottle from under the shelf and spun it deftly between his hands. A fountain of thick, rich liquid like cough syrup sprouted into a perfectly placed mug which I hadn't noticed a moment before.

"What is it?"

"Just what you need. Cheers!" He poured a second glass for himself and toasted me. "May we make room for new growth by pruning the dead branches, and may we leave what's dead behind."

I took a long drink, forcing myself not to gag as the thick liquid dribbled down my throat like oil. He finished first, slamming his glass upon the table and wiping his beard with the back of his hand. Before I had a chance to finish mine, the barman added: "Those who die a little each night will never feel the pain of those who go all at once. You're one of the lucky ones."

"Huh?" I wiped the last of the thick residue from my mouth.

"It's almost midnight. Are you ready to let the old you die?"

Almost midnight. I was running out of time. I felt a certain tranquility while walking toward the DJ table. The old me would have turned away by now, but I didn't slow down even when Chase looked right at me. The electricity wasn't a barrier anymore. It was charging me, an exhilarating fuel which propelled me through the churning dance floor. I even allowed myself to step in time with the music, bobbing and swaying with the mesmerizing beat. It almost felt like I was flying, until suddenly I was close enough to finally say:

"Hey Chase … "

My wildest paranoia couldn't have prepared me for his reaction. Glancing up from his computer, Chase's face contorted into a horrified caricature of his usual self-assurance. He lurched out of his chair so fast that it tumbled backward. I rushed to help him, but that only made him kick the chair in my direction and scramble across the floor. The music was deafening this close to the speakers, but it wasn't enough to completely drown out the grotesque retching as he vomited onto the floor. Through the beat I could still clearly hear the wailing sob rising in my throat as I sprinted away from him and toward the bathroom.

I couldn't understand what happened until the burning began. My fingers gingerly grazed the swiftly swelling lumps in my face. I covered myself with my hands as I ran, brutally shoving my way through the crowd and then slamming through the bathroom door. A girl in a black sequin party dress dropped her makeup and screamed. I almost trampled her on my way to the mirror, but she wasted no time in ducking under the sink and crawling toward the door. Looking in the mirror, I honestly couldn't blame her.

Some of the lumps in my skin were the size of golf-balls, and they were growing by the second. The larger ones were actually wriggling, almost as though there was an insect squirming just beneath the skin. More lumps were appearing on my hands, and the itching burn radiating down my body left no ambiguity about what was happening under my clothes. I would have screamed if my tongue wasn't swelling too, but it was all I could do to just try to keep my airway clear. Then the first boil popped and I couldn't contain the howl which ripped from my lungs.

I heard the door open again, but it snapped shut immediately. I couldn't tear my eyes away from the mirror. More boils were rupturing by the second, splattering the glass with thick purple syrup which clung on like long strands of mucous. More of them exploded in my mouth to trickle down my throat with the same oily taste of the drink. My hair was sliding from my scalp in great clumps, matted and greased with the bubbling purple liquid.

The only thing keeping me from completely losing my mind was the sight of fresh pink skin which shone beneath the savage gashes in my face. The burn was growing more intense by the second, but each exploding boil revealed more healthy skin below it. I started ripping at the tattered shreds, peeling them off and dumping them in a soggy pile around my feet.

Beneath all the skin sloughing off, I didn't even recognize myself. My new skin was lighter and clearer, and the new hair which sprouted was a short ruffled blond that was nothing like the long dark hair which lay in clumps around my feet. Nothing was the least recognizable except my eyes which were stretched wide with a familiar anxious terror.

"What the fuck?"

Chase must have followed me into the bathroom. How long had he been watching? Long enough. I stepped away from the wet pile of old flesh that littered the ground. My clothes were still soaked in the liquid though, and more chunks continued to rain out my dress and down my legs. He looked like he was about to vomit again.

"Hey Chase ... I want to try something. Come here."

He didn't move, but he didn't have to. I crossed the space between us more quickly than I thought possible. All at once our faces were inches apart, but he didn't turn away. Outside I could hear the countdown toward midnight.

"Five!"

I pressed my finger to his lips to silence the budding question.

"Four!"

I cupped his head in my hands and drew him toward me.

"Three!"

I felt his hard lips soften against mine.

"Two!"

The taste of his sweat as my mouth made its way down his neck.

"One!"

The squirt of blood through my teeth as they sank into his flesh. He was thrashing now, but each movement just forced my jaw to tighten until I could feel the first vertebra crunch under the pressure. All the shouts of "Happy New Year!" drowned out his terminal scream which strangled to a whisper when his trachea collapsed.

Part of me died that night alongside Chase, but the old man knew what he was talking about. It's much easier to leave the dead parts of yourself behind than let them weigh you down forever, and for the first time in my life, I'm not afraid anymore.

HEAVEN KEEPS A PRISONER

I wasn't ready when I died.

The first illusion death stole from me was that my body was designed to perceive the universe around me. This is incorrect. The primary function of your senses is to stop yourself from experiencing the universe, whose infinite information would otherwise overwhelm and madden you. Eyes that once simplified the world into finite wavelengths of color closed for the last time, and then I saw everything. Ears once deaf to cosmic music sung by the birth of stars, the communal heartbeat of the human race, and the haunting pop of each collapsing universe now concealed them no longer.

Even the distinction between senses decayed alongside my corporal prison. Starlight was a symphony that bathed me in warmth, and the heat in turn sang with such melodic iridescence that I was thrall to its majesty. It's impossible to measure how long I existed in such a state, but by gradual degrees I learned to separate my own thoughts from the medley of existence. The moment I began to comprehend my own internal voice, I became aware of a second voice that was not my own.

"... Four hundred seventy eight points. Hey Jason! You close that passenger pigeon room yet? I told you we don't do them anymore."

"Um. Hi. Excuse me," I said to the unrepentant chaos of the universe.

"Here you go, let me help you with that."

Remember what I said about the unfiltered synesthesia of my senses. Now imagine being struck by lightning. A moment later, I found myself with hands and knees to collapse onto the stone floor with, my new lungs racing a marathon. Holy shit did that hurt. I kind of wanted to do it again.

"Four hundred seventy eight points, up from 314 last time. Solid performance." I don't know what was harder to accept: my naked new body which looked exactly like my old one, the colossal stone cathedral I suddenly found myself within or the koala bear who sat in front of me with a clipboard. He flipped another page.

"Oh that explains it," the koala said in its soothingly gruff undertone. "Fifty points for loving someone and being loved in return. That's always a nice boost. Then you picked up another twenty from that album you released in the eighties —touched more lives than you'll know with that one."

"You were keeping score?"

"I'd hate to think what people got up to if we weren't ... lost twelve points because you stopped visiting Mark when he got cancer, but you got a few of those back when you played at his funeral. Hey Jason! What's "accepting your own imperfections" worth? We got new numbers on that yet?"

He was answered by the incomprehensible shriek of an eagle.

"Shit man, right back at ya!" the koala hollered.

"Have you always been a koala?" I asked.

"Have you always asked stupid questions? You're lucky we don't dock points for that."

"Ummm ... "

"Kidding, kidding. Sort of. This way now." The koala slid the clipboard under his arm and began a brisk waddle. I hurried to keep pace, doing my best to avoid the absolute zoo which thronged the stone hallway onward. Up the great diverging staircase with its goats and mountain lions. Past the library whose shelves bustled with scaling monkeys, over the pools filled with playing otters and thrashing fish, beneath the gargantuan brass dome revolving with teeming flights of birds, the koala explaining as we went.

"Long story short, if your life brought more good into the world than evil, you're going to end up with more points than you started. Your 478 points can unlock any of the rooms on this floor, except for the psychic and the prophet which are both 500. Think of your choice as an investment: coming back as a human will be expensive, but you also have the greatest capacity to improve your score. The only rule is that you pick something on the right floor for your budget."

"What would happen if I didn't have any points? Or went below zero?"

I hadn't been aware koalas could even grin before this moment.

"Generally you'll just keep going down. It's hard to get out of the negatives once you've started, so if you can't figure out how to do some good then you're forced to keep choosing worse and worse punishment rounds. Get far enough negative, and suddenly you're looking at a demon or a vampire or the like. Some people actually do evil on purpose to aim for that though, can you imagine?"

"No," I answered honestly, "but I'm beginning to."

"All the animals you see are just spirits taking their new

bodies for a test drive. Feel free to look around and—Jason! What's that thing doing up here? Keep the politicians down-stairs please!"

The mournful shriek of an eagle somehow sounded like it had heard this joke far too many times. The koala sighed and threw his paws melodramatically in the air. "Kidding, kidding, God. What is this, a morgue?"

I wasn't paying attention anymore, though. Dwarfed and humbled by the immensity of the structure, I turned my gaze to the top of the stairs and the small balcony which overhung the whole arena.

"What's at the very top?"

My guide shrugged, seemingly losing interest in me. "Dunno. No one's ever had enough points to unlock that door. Not for as long as I've been here."

"How long have—"

"Diggory! Mixy! Ground floor let's go! People dyin' over here!"

And he was gone, leaving me adrift in the swirling profusion between death and life. Overwhelmed and disoriented, I continued to climb the stairs, driven as much to isolate myself as I was by curiosity. Past 500 points and the crowd dissipated precipitously. Strange, alien creatures began mingling with the dwindling remaining options. Seraphic beings with skin of light and shadow, and golden toned creatures of sublime beauty came and went as I continued to mount the lonely stairs.

Finally reaching the balcony at the very top, I turned to survey the whole mad spectacle flowing beneath me. The perspective was disorienting: though I'd only climbed a few flights of stairs, looking down it seemed more like the view from an airplane window. All creatures were minuscule in their eager dance; all sounds had faded and combined into a single omnipresent hymn. All sounds that is, except for the rapid burst of knocking on the door behind me.

It wasn't like the other doors. Its metallic composition seemed in perpetual motion, rippling and glistening like a pool of oil. Three ponderous iron bars were bolted across the frame to prevent it opening outward, each engraved with mystic runes beyond my comprehension. The knocking came again—rapid, urgent, a prisoner desperately calling for aid without wanting to alert the guards.

"Hello? Someone in there?"

A hissing sound like high-pressured steam bursting through its confinement. The bolts in the iron bars were beginning to slide outward. I rushed back to the balcony in search of my guide, but so far below he had merged seamlessly with the throng. Behind me a clanging sound had me jump—the first iron bar had dropped off to the ground.

"Can anyone hear me?"

But I was utterly alone. I took a half-dozen steps toward the stairs, but at the clang of the second iron bar I indecisively spun back. And why not? What was the worst that could happen, now that I was already dead? That sentiment did not endure through the dropping of the third bar. The whole door shimmered like a mirage in the desert, then without motion or warning, it was gone.

Bile rose in my throat the instant I saw the creature. My legs buckled beneath me and I crashed hard to my knees, vomiting profusely upon the ground. It wasn't food. Heaving again, my whole body convulsing from the swelling pressure, I released another dark torrent of blood, lumps of degraded flesh, and even what appeared to be entire rotting organs which laboriously wriggled up my throat and out my mouth. I'd almost forgotten my own death for a while, but it immediately became clear that I had not escaped as far as I thought.

"Come in," the creature commanded.

I was powerless to refuse. Crawling through my own sick, not daring to look up again, I passed through the open door. Seeing it once had been enough. The humanoid being was swollen to the size of a cow, bloated with gas which unevenly malformed its corpulent frame. Open sores covered its body, weeping blood and pus to stream down its nakedness so thickly that it almost seemed a garment. Gaping mortal wounds punctured its chest and belly in many places, allowing clear sight all the way through to its broken and uneven ribs. Somehow worst of all, the unblemished face of a young boy stared out from that mockery of human life.

"Are you alone?"

More alone than I've ever been. I nodded, still not looking up. The room itself was minimal in the extreme: a concrete prison cell with no comfort besides thin bamboo floor mat.

"Not anymore," it said, hot fetid air blowing across my face with each word.

"Who are you?" I asked.

"The final prize. Come, sit with me. Be at ease."

My body tensed so sharply that I thought I was about to vomit again. I remained on my knees.

"Why would anyone want to be—" I stopped myself, but the child simply laughed with a sound like wind-chimes.

"No one would, but being at the top doesn't mean the best. It simply means that I have the greatest capacity to do good or evil. I can create life, or end it. Does that sound like a power you'd want to have?"

I shook my head, finally daring another glance. The creature had leaned forward on its mat, its terribly perfect face mere inches from mine. The boy sighed and leaned back once more.

"Me neither, which is why I remain in this place. My

influence is too great, and any good or evil I bring into existence is multiplied countless times. If I allow that to happen, then I will die with so many points that I am forced to be reborn within this same cursed form."

"So you have the power to do anything, but instead you sit here and do nothing?"

"Not nothing. I wait to die. That's the only way for me to reset to zero points and have another chance to begin again. Unless of course ... " The child's face was drawing closer. The stench was too foul to breathe through my nose, but even having the air enter my mouth was enough to taste its rot.

"You invited me in to kill you then." I said it as matter-of-factly as I could, not wishing to cause offense.

"You aren't the first," he said, gesturing at the wounds which scoured its body. "But through revulsion or weakness or cowardice, each have failed so far. Will you be the one to show me mercy?"

The thought of even getting close enough to harm the creature almost had me retching again. "I still don't understand though," I said, buying time. "If you're the supreme power here, why can't you save yourself?"

"The supreme power?" Laughter like the wind, so sweet and so sad. "Death is the supreme power, and I am his servant like any other. Don't think I have not tried to take my own life before. The act carries such significance that I simply find myself reborn in this same body. Here, you will need this."

A trembling hand reached out to me, its obese fingers fused at the joints. I recoiled by reflex, but I felt such pity for the creature that I fought against my instincts to accept the black dagger from his grasp.

"How do I end you?"

"Through the eye," he begged.

"Are you sure?"

Such a dazzling smile from such a loathsome creature. I can't imagine how much he must have suffered, and I'm sure I would have asked the same in his place. The cool dark metal felt righteous in my hand as I steeled myself for the killing blow. Some nagging doubt lingered in the back of my head, but I was so mesmerized by my disgust and sympathy that I could think of no other course.

"Won't you at least close your eyes?" I asked.

His smile widened—unnaturally so for the child's face. "I've been looking forward to this moment for as long as I can remember. I'm not going to miss a moment."

Worried that any hesitation would steal my resolve, I took the dagger in both hands and plunged it deep. The eye did not close even as the blade slipped through it. It cut so easily that I felt no resistance until the very hilt was embedded in the boy's face. The smile faltered for the briefest instant before returning, then grimacing again as though fluctuating between agony and ecstasy. The massive body trembled, but I didn't relinquish my grip until its last spasm overbalanced the monstrosity. I scrambled to get out of the way as it toppled face-first toward me, slamming against the ground and further pounding the dagger within its skull.

Crowds parted around me as I returned down the staircase. Claws and talons pointed at me with undisguised fascination. Whispers and murmurs from the multifarious assembly swelled and faded like the ocean waves.

"I think I'd like to come back as a cat," I told the koala when I found him again. He was easy enough to locate, standing out in the open, seemingly paralyzed by shock. "Cats seem to have things figured out."

"Jason! Mixy? Anyone!" the koala shouted in a hoarse,

strained voice from the corner of his mouth, not taking his eyes off me for a moment.

"What is it? Did I do something wrong?"

An owl landed nearby, its head cocking from side-to-side to get a better look at me.

"Hey Mixy—" the koala said, still without turning. "How many points do you get for killing God? You have a number for that somewhere?"

I swallowed hard, but I couldn't get rid of the dry lump in my throat.

"You're sure I didn't lose points?"

He stared dumbly at his clipboard. "Considering what he would have done if you hadn't, yeah. Says 'Act of mercy' on here. You're way in the positive, my man."

"I'm not going to become that... thing, am I?"

"Not yet. You came here with 478, so that's what you're going back with. But shit man, you've got so many now that—"

"Unless I can spend them all next life, right?"

"What?"

"Unless I bring so much evil into the world that I break even. That's what you're saying, right?"

The koala looked helplessly to the owl who fluffed its wings in something resembling a shrug.

"Better do human again then," I said. "I don't care what I have to do. I'm not going live as that monster."

"You're not serious, are you?" the koala whispered. "Do you have any idea what you'd have to do to—"

"I killed God, didn't I? Who knows what I'm capable of?"

Now that I'm back alive, I suppose I'm going to find out.

DREAMMAKER MUSIC

Sleeping is the easiest, most natural thing in the world. Babies do it all the time without even being taught. It's so easy people do it by accident, but not me. I suck at sleeping, which sometimes feels more like I suck at being human since I'm so freaking tired all the time.

It's the same battle every night. Even looking at the clock and knowing I should be in bed is enough to make me feel restless. I've tried keeping a rigid sleep schedule, and burning soporific incenses, and popping pills, but nothing seems to make a difference. You'd think my body would just get so tired it shut off automatically, but it seems like the less I sleep, the more agitated I get thinking how much I need to, and the harder it is to make love with sweet oblivion.

Anyway, my friend, Anu, told me her grandfather was this Indian guru who had a remedy for insomnia. My hopes were flying about as high as an iron pigeon, but I figured there wasn't any harm. Even if I couldn't sleep, at least I could impress the girl by being "spiritually open to new ideas" and "respecting her culture" and all that shit. (Is it wrong that I pat myself on the back for not being racist just because it seems like everyone else is nowadays? Yeah just thinking that is probably racist too.)

Point is she gives me this album of Indian music that I'm supposed to listen to in bed. She says it's an instrument called the ravanahatha, which is some kind of ancient precursor to the violin. It's made from a resonating gourd covered with goat hide and strings stretched across a bamboo neck. Legend has it these particular songs were written to appease Shiva, the destroyer of worlds in Hindu scripture. It's supposed to be super calming and meditative though, so I took it home with me to give it a go.

The only weird thing is, right before we parted Anu also said:

"Oh I almost forgot. He said not to try and stop the music before morning, because Shiva will listening too."

In hindsight, "Is Shiva a babe?" was probably not the most culturally sensitive question, but Anu still smiled. As a whole, I think the whole interaction was good for our chances of making beautiful, caramel colored babies down the road.

That night I gave the music a go. It was legitimately beautiful: kind of a longing, soulful sound, but not in a sad way. There was just enough lively melodic lift that it felt more like the serenity of seeds buried deep beneath the snow, just waiting for their chance to bloom.

Next comes the part where I try to trick my brain into sleep. It feels like playing that "did I put the poison in my drink, or yours?" game as I alternate between thinking the music will work or not, and whether even having expectations will influence the results. Next, surprisingly enough, came a deep and peaceful sleep.

And the strangest dream I'd ever had in my life, almost more like an out-of-body experience. I was only aware I was sleeping at all because I was looking down at my body while it slept. I could even still hear to the music down below: like I was watching myself in a movie. It didn't take long to discover my consciousness was free to move around my house, leaving my sleeping body behind.

That part was a lot of fun. I just sort of drifted around, shifting my focus like I was just imagining different perspectives, but everything was so clear and perfect that it felt exactly like I was actually seeing it. I could even count the number of dishes in my sink (six, mind your own business) and see the minuscule detail in the wood-grain floor. I was just about to float over to the living room and see if I could watch TV when I heard the first sound other than the music.

The rattle of a handle, and then the opening of my front door. I startled so badly that I woke up immediately, seemingly teleporting into my bed. Frantic reality checks—the texture of my blanket, my phone beside my bed, the clock reading 2:31—everything seemed normal again. That's why I flinched so badly when I heard the front door slam closed.

Panic. Hyperventilate. Lie flat and pretend I'm asleep. I really need a better defense plan. I held my breath for a full ten seconds, but I didn't hear any other sounds. Creeping out of bed, I sped through my apartment in a commando crouch, flipping on every light I passed. It didn't take long before I cleared the last room—all empty. The front door was closed and locked. I couldn't help but count the six dishes in my sink and congratulate my dream-memory on its accuracy.

Figuring I'd just heard a neighbor's door slam really loud, I turned off the lights and went back to bed. Seconds later I was hovering above my bed, watching myself sleep. Except I wasn't the only one in the room.

Someone was sitting in the chair beside my bed (also known as the "I haven't decided if these clothes are dirty" chair). My clothes had been moved onto the floor to make space for it. Naked bone white skin, androgynous yet strong features, and long strings of prayer beads characterized my visitor, but nothing stood out more than the pair of living green snakes which sinuously writhed around his throat.

He was watching my sleeping body at first, but ponderous and implacable as a flowing glacier, he turned his gaze to meet my perspective. He watched me through heavy half-closed eyes, nodding his head in time with the music. Seeing his tranquility, I allowed myself to drift closer to get a better look.

Approaching him was the most disorienting experience of my life. As I drew closer, his body seemed to grow larger as normal perspective dictates, but his eyes grew at an exponentially larger rate as though they were gargantuan celestial bodies that I was speeding towards. Soon my room and his body and everything else became insignificant to the cosmic eyes which stretched from horizon to horizon. I had to pull myself back for fear of falling in, at which point everything returned to normal.

Almost normal. His necklace of snakes was gone. They'd slithered up my bed, their thick coils sliding effortlessly over my corporal body's legs.

It was enough of a start to wake me up again. I immediately began my reality checks—blanket, phone, clock—then I noticed the pile of clothes on the floor. The ones that used to be on the chair. My heart was beating so fast and the music was so loud that I couldn't hear myself think. I numbly shut off the music, trying to catch my breath for long enough to figure out if I'd somehow knocked the clothes onto the floor myself.

Something touched my foot under the blankets. So cold and smooth, almost slimy. A wave of tension ran up my body, overflowing into the thing touching me whose rigid coils loaded like a spring. I couldn't hover any more, but shit could I jump. Tangled in my own sheets, I flopped and lurched through the air like an Olympic slug. I hit the floor hard, but

I didn't slow down until I'd wriggled free from the blankets and raced to the light switch by the door.

Two long green snakes with black and yellow markings emerged from the blanket on the ground behind me. They recoiled momentarily from the light, but one them launched back at me, striking sinking its fangs into my calf. I swatted at it and it immediately let go and backed off again, but it stung like a thousand bee stings one right on top of the other.

I ran from my bedroom and slammed the door. A forked tongue darted out beneath, swiftly followed by the head of the serpent which easily slipped through the crack. I stomped and it withdrew, but the second snake was already halfway out—far enough to rear its head and tense for another strike. I turned and ran.

My leg was on fire as I hobbled out of my apartment in my boxers and dashed toward my car. The place it bit me was swelling by the second, and I knew I had to get to a hospital ASAP.

By the time I got there, I was almost blind. My throat had swollen to the size of a pinhole, and the pressure in my chest was excruciating. I parked right up on the curb and managed to tumble out of my car, and I was vaguely aware of some people helping me into a wheelchair after that.

When I woke, they told me I was bitten by an Indian Pit Viper, which confused the shit out of them because they don't exist anywhere in the Americas. I had an animal services guy sweep my apartment before I got home, but he didn't find anything. He did have this helpful tidbit of reassurance to give me though:

"Of course snakes aren't going to be found when they don't want to be. Shit, I knew a lady who had a ten-foot boa living in her house leftover from the last tenant. Was over a month before she even saw the bugger."

If I don't play the music, then all I can do is lie awake

listening to the approaching slithering and agitated hiss in the darkness.

If I do play it, the dream comes again without fail and I'm forced to watch the stranger enter my room and sit down beside my bed.

Like I wasn't already having enough trouble getting some sleep.

THE GIRL ON A LEASH

Ten, maybe twelve years old, wearing a leash attached to one of those dog training collars with the inward facing spikes. She was sitting on the balcony of my neighbor's apartment, her dirty bare legs dangling through the iron bars. She stared at me where I sat with my book on my own balcony, so I gave her a little wave. She didn't so much as blink in return—she just kept swinging her legs through the bars and staring. I figured the collar was some kind of ironic fashion accessory, although it hardly matched with her thread-bare summer dress.

Five minutes later, she was still staring and I was beginning to feel a little uncomfortable. I set my book down and asked:

"What's your name, missy?"

"He calls me Cheesey," she replied, flashing all her little teeth like she was posing for a picture.

"That's an unusual name."

"'Cause he says I make him sick. Like cheese."

"Oh." I looked down at my book. How the hell was I supposed to reply to that?

"Are we friends now?" she asked, squishing her face between the bars.

"Okay, friends." I couldn't help but smile at her innocent charm. "Can I call you something other than Cheesey though?

"He also calls me cockroach," she chirped conversationally. "Little freak. Shit face."

"Who calls you these things? Your father?"

But she didn't get a chance to reply. A vicious tug on the leash tightened the spikes into her throat. Her fingers clutched at it, but she couldn't loosen the grip. A moment later and she was helplessly reeled back inside her apartment. I ran to the edge to look, but my view was obstructed by the jutting concrete which separated the balconies. I just saw her being dragged inside, and then heard:

"What did I tell you about talking to strangers?"

"He asked me a question—"

"I knew it was a mistake to let you outside!" The sliding glass door slammed. I couldn't make out anything after that. My stomach felt like I'd just eaten a pound of garbage. I've never spoken to my neighbor before—a severe, quiet man who wore dark sunglasses inside and out. I didn't even know he had a kid. He didn't seem like the type, although there's a chance she wasn't even his. Either way, I called Child Protective Services to let them decide.

They thanked me for the information and said they would send someone over. I walked around the rest of the day feeling like a hero. I had a few errands to run, but I got back just in time to see an authoritative black woman in a pristine blue suit standing outside my neighbor's open door.

"I'm sorry, there must have been some mistake," he said from inside his apartment. "I live alone. No kids."

"My apologies, I must have gotten the wrong address," she

said. "Would you mind if I take a peek inside just so I can check off my forms?" The pause was slightly too long.

"No, that's not okay. This is my home. My sanctuary. Go bother someone else."

"It'll only take a few—"

The door slammed shut. The woman immediately began knocking again, but there was no response.

"Excuse me, CPS?" I asked.

She looked me up and down as though evaluating my potential to be a scumbag.

"You the guy who called?" she asked.

I nodded. "What's your next step?"

"My next step? What's your next step?" she snapped. "I don't have any next steps without a signed warrant from a judge, and I'm not going to get that without some evidence. You get a picture or anything?" I shook my head.

"Well call me if you do." She was already half way to the elevator.

"That's it?"

"What do you mean 'that's it'? I got three more cases tonight, and chances are at least one of them isn't going to be as pretty as this. I got a job to do, honey, but I can't do it here."

Sounds like I had a job to do too. He couldn't stay in there forever, right? Either he'd leave with her and I could follow them, or he'd leave alone and I'd have a chance to talk with her and find out what was going on. I brought my book into the hallway and sat down to wait.

Half an hour did the trick. The door opened and sunglasses gave a quick, paranoid scan. They landed on me.

"What are you doing?" he asked.

"Lost my key," I lied. "Gotta wait for my roommate to get home."

He disappeared back inside and the door closed. I

thought I missed my chance, but a moment later the door opened again and he exited with 'Cheesey'. She was still wearing the collar, but the leash was bundled up and he rested his hand on her shoulder so it was barely visible. As they passed, she glanced back at me as if to say: Goodbye friend. But it wasn't goodbye yet.

I followed them out of the building while pretending to stare at my phone, but I couldn't get a clear shot of the collar. I snapped one of them together, but that didn't seem like enough for a warrant yet.

I might feel like a masquerading pillar of vigilante justice, but I certainly wasn't as smooth as one. By the time the pair had gotten to their car the man must have noticed me a dozen times. The chase was on.

We'd only been out in the night for about five minutes when he suddenly pulled off the road into a dirt clearing beside some cornfields. I was so caught up in the excitement that I hadn't even paused to consider what I would do when I actually caught them. He must have known his secret was out though, and if something happened to the girl tonight I'd never forgive myself. I pulled off the road and parked behind him while dialing 911.

"Put the phone down." The man had gotten out of his car. He walked around to the passenger side to drag the girl out by the leash. The powerful yanks sent the clear signal about who would pay the price if I didn't obey. I hung up and got out of the car.

"Did I tell you to get out?" he barked. "Back in. Keep driving."

"What the hell is wrong with you?" I shouted, vainly hoping to draw some attention to our dark road. The man flinched at the sound. "Where do you get off putting a collar on—"

"If you knew her, you'd do the same. Or worse," he

growled, his hands turning white from clenching the leash so hard. "This little freak deserves it."

"Daddy I can't breathe," the girl whimpered.

"Shut your disgusting mouth—"

I couldn't take it anymore. I barreled headlong into the man, throwing him against his car. One of his arms was tangled in the leash, and that gave me a chance to pin his free arm and punch him across the face. The man slid to the ground, dragging the girl with him as she clutched at her collar and howled. I couldn't divert my attention long enough to unfasten the collar, so I just stomped on the man's hand that was holding the leash.

"God damn idiot!" he shouted. "Do you have any idea how long it took me to capture her in the first place? Now look what you've done!"

I did look, and damn was I proud. The man lay there nursing his hand while I unfastened the collar from around the girl's neck. She was grinning from ear to ear.

"I'm going to call the police now," I warned him, stripping his wallet and ID. "You better stay put unless you want the collar on you."

"Don't bother," he moaned. "We'll both be dead before they arrive."

An idle threat from a desperate man, or so I thought. Until I glanced back at Cheesey. I guess I hadn't noticed how long her neck was under the metal collar. At least twice as long as a neck ought to be, and it was growing by the second. I swallowed hard, but it felt like there was cotton in my throat.

"What are you waiting for?" the man shouted, all pretense of discretion gone. "Run!"

The neck was still stretching. Her figure stayed the same —her face was all smiles—but her neck was almost as long as her whole body now. It twisted sinuously through the air as though it had no bones at all, stretching luxuriously after its confinement.

Little freak wasn't such a bad name. Did you know that most of their body is a hollow cavity which stores their folded neck? Or that silver collars were the only way to keep them from extending? I certainly didn't. Not until I read the papers stuffed in his wallet. Not before I stood in shocked awe on the side of the road and watched her jaw unhinge to consume him whole.

"Police dispatch, what is your emergency?" faintly droned my phone.

"Friends?" I asked the girl.

She nodded, choking the man's still squirming body into her grotesquely swollen neck.

"Friends," I repeated as I hung up the phone, backing into my car. Her eyes watched me while she continued to gag the body down.

Well shit. So much for being a hero, but at least I was still a hero to her.

WHAT THE BLIND MAN SEES

I'll never see her face again. If my blindness only meant scrubbing this dirty world into an ocean of black mist, then I think I could learn to accept that. Stealing my wife from me before her time though—that I'll never forgive. It's bad enough she's sick and fading from me already, but not being able to see her to say goodbye is killing me as surely as it is her.

I suppose it's my fault though. I spent the last few nights leading up to my accident shifting around the rigid hospital chair beside her bed. I was so tired that I could barely walk straight, and all it took was a patch of black ice in the parking lot to pitch me to the ground. My head slammed into the asphalt and everything went dark. The black mist didn't lift, but next I could remember I was sitting in my own hospital bed with a nurse explaining what had happened.

" … post-traumatic cortical blindness," she was saying. "It seems like there was some damage to your occipital cortex when you hit the ground."

"Where's Sarah? Where's my wife? I want to see her."

The nurse just coughed, giving me time for my own

words to sink in. "There's a chance your vision loss is being caused by pressure on the optic nerve, which can be potentially corrected with surgery. The doctor doesn't want to get your hopes up though. You should be prepared to adjust to life without sight."

It's true that I couldn't see the nurse, or the hospital room, or even my own hand an inch from my face. But the worst thing was I *could* still see. It just wasn't the same world I had left behind. I fumbled for words trying to explain the black and purple vines which dangled around me from unfathomably tall trees. How they swayed gracefully in an unfelt wind, bending across their hundreds of joints like fingers bending back and forth upon themselves. I pointed at the greasy orange sky and the swarms of softly teeming insects which obliviously paraded towards me from all sides.

"Hallucinations aren't unheard of after acute vision loss …"

It was hard to take her seriously when her voice seemed to be coming from a giant blue flower whose bell-shaped petals were deep enough for me to stand in. If this was a hallucination, then it was clearer and more vivid than anything I could have possibly imagined. I tried again to explain the infinitesimal detail of the insect's uneven carapaces, but she excused herself to leave without letting me finish. I never even got the chance to tell her that I could *feel* the thousands of tiny legs crawling up my body as the insect parade passed through the origin of disembodied perspective.

I was stuck somewhere between worlds. I could still feel the coarse fabric of the hospital blanket, but so could I feel the smooth gloss of each leaf and barky tree in this sudden jungle I was mired within. I pulled on one of the purple digits only to see it coil around my arm, inquisitively feeling me in return. I tore away from and tried to stand, leaning on a cold metal IV pole that I couldn't see.

I felt like I was going insane, and there was no amount of reasonably toned nurses or insightful doctors that would convince me otherwise. I knew instinctively that I had to find my wife—Sarah was the only real thing left to ground me in the world I was supposed to be in.

It wasn't easy navigating two worlds at once. Even when I shuffled around until I found the door to my room, I still had to push myself through a thick curtain of fingers which had inconveniently infested the portal. It was slow going navigating the invisible hallways while plowing through the thick jungle foliage, and to make matters worse, the blue-white sun was beginning to smolder and set in the orange sky. My hearing remained fixed to this world strangely, so at least I was able to hear people approaching and not run into anyone.

Once someone pointed me to the main elevator, I had no trouble from there. I had visited Sarah so many times that I could find the way with my eyes closed. It was disorienting to feel myself rise in the elevator, seemingly flying directly into the air, ducking and dodging branches as I did. I hesitated before her door to ask the passing footsteps:

"Sarah's room?"

"Are you sure you should be out of bed? Let me go ask—"

"Is my wife in here?"

"Yes, but she should be resting too. She had another grand mal seizure last night. Hold on, I'll go see if I can find the doctor."

Footsteps. My hand was on the door, but I couldn't quite bring myself to push through. Sarah had been in the hospital for the last three months, growing weaker each day. There had been a number of tentative hypotheses, but there has yet to be a definite diagnosis to the underlying issue. I guess that's why I've been holding out hope for so long: if she could get sick without a reason, then she didn't need a reason to get better either. All those nights I'd spent beside her, watching her pale face and listening to her shallow breathing—it was all some kind of cosmic misunderstanding that would sort itself out on its own.

It was only now when I knew I couldn't lie to myself anymore. The black and purple fingers protruded thickly like sprouting plants on the wide branch beyond, converging on a recumbent form the exact size and shape of a human. Some of them reared their sensitive tips only to plunge directly back into the mass, pulsing and squirming as they fought one another to penetrate farthest. All too clearly I could imagine them puncturing her body or forcing themselves down her where her throat should have been. If this wasn't a hallucination, then it was explaining an illness that an entire hospital couldn't decipher.

"Sarah?" I opened the door. "Are you in there?"

Her gentle moan. That's all I've heard from her the last week. It hadn't made any sense to the doctors since she appeared conscious, but it made sense now. How was she supposed to speak this whole time with those things lodged in her throat?

Sickened and furious, I flung myself at the warped vines, carelessly clattering through her invisible bedside table as I did. I seized one near where her head must be and pulled with all my strength, feeling it go taunt to resist me. Other vines were reacting, unwinding themselves from her to seize me by the arms and legs. I fought through it, clutching and tearing, even sinking my teeth into the rubbery thing. More fingers crawled from the branches above, circling around my arms, up my shoulders, slithering around my neck....

"Someone help! Get them off her!" I shouted.

The fingers were constricting around me, but I didn't let

go. I threw my whole body weight backwards, heaving and straining until something finally gave. Sarah was coughing and retching, the beeping of her vitals going berserk as I struggled. She was shaking so bad that the whole bed rattled, each increment of progress agonizing to watch as I knew the finger must be relinquishing its hold of her stomach and lungs, or however deep the corruption spread. All the while my bondage was secured, ruthlessly tightening to cut off blood supply to my arms and crush my throat into a collapsing pinprick.

"She's having another seizure. Get a doctor in here!" One of the nurses. I was held so firmly in place that I couldn't even turn toward her, not like I could see her even if I could.

"What about him?"

"He's not responding. Get him on the ground and keep his airway clear."

Hands unwittingly pushed their way past the swarming appendages to ease me down. The pressure slackened, some returning their attention to the knot which surrounded my wife. Blood was beginning to return to my limbs. I could feel, and as soon as I could breathe, I could fight again. I was still gasping on the floor when the doctor entered the room.

How could I tell? Well there were certainly auditory clues as a gruff voice barked commands to the nurses, but more prominently was the knot of interlacing fingers which formed the shape of a human. They were spread so finely that every artery and vein must be filled, and I could clearly see them pulse and twitch as they tightened and relaxed, moving the doctor through the room like a puppet.

"Another seizure," the doctor said. I could see the strum around his head as the things inside him opened and closed his mouth, with smaller ones inside maneuvering his tongue and vibrating his vocal chords. "Check her mouth. Make sure there isn't any vomit or obstruction."

"The fingers!" I shouted, aware of how mad I must appear rolling on the ground. "Get them out of her! She can't—"

"And give him something to calm down. Diazepam, 400 milligrams should do it."

"They've got him too—don't touch me—don't let him touch Sarah—"

I tried to sit up, but someone was squatting on top of me and pinning me to the ground. I jerked as a needle slid into my thigh, but the pressure only increased. Something scoured through my veins. The humanoid network that was the doctor dropped to his haunches beside me, and I felt a warm hand run down my face to cup my chin. It was getting too dark to see anything at all.

"Just a nasty hallucination, that's all. Let's get you back to bed and see if we can't do something about those eyes."

They had good news for me when I woke up. Not only were they able to alleviate the pressure on my optic nerve, but my wife had made a miraculous recovery during the procedure. I actually wept in relief when I opened my eyes in the hospital room and saw Sarah anxiously sitting over my bed. Just Sarah and the room—no fingers, no unfamiliar jungle, no crawling sensation of the insects or dodging alien trees.

They told me Sarah was talking and eating and even walking on her own, although they warned me she was still stiff and slow to react.

"STIFF" ISN'T HOW I'D DESCRIBE HER LURCHING MOVEMENTS though. She seems more like a marionette doll to me, tethered by unseen strings from the inside and out.

DO DEMONS LAY EGGS?

The guys and I were doing a sweep of an old oil refinery when I found the eggs. I guess they liked the heat because they were all clustered right around the fractal distillation chamber, which gets up past 720 Fahrenheit when the crude oil is being heated up. The whole building was scheduled for demolition though, and it was our job to make sure the place was cleaned out.

"Anyone want a souvenir?" I shouted. Guess the crew was in other parts of the building. The eggs were about the size of my fist, all black and covered with thick bristles like an especially paranoid cactus. Only one of them was really even intact—maybe it's because the refinery hasn't been running in a while, but five out of the six eggs was cracked and leaking some kind of thick, rotten smelling jelly. I was more motivated by the clock than curiosity though, and I was about to mark the room as clear when—

"A souvenir. Want a—want a—souvenir." The voice was muffled and frail, but it was definitely coming from inside the egg. I crouched down next to it, scooping up the spiny ball in my work gloves.

"So what are you supposed to be?"

"Supposed to be," it chirped back.

Yeah maybe it was the fumes in this place getting to my head, but there was something profoundly sad about that little echo. I dropped the egg into the pocket of my overalls, intending to show it off to everyone at the pub after work. *Intending* being the key word there. We didn't finish clearing the place until almost six, and then there was a last minute permit issue that had me driving around collecting signatures until past nine. I was dead tired and so ready to collapse at home that I barely remembered the weird egg in my pocket.

If it wasn't for its little spikes, I would have forgotten it entirely. It must have liked my warmth though, because it kept trying to huddle closer to me in my pocket. When I got home and put it on the counter I could actually hear a soft rattle as its spines shivered against the tile.

"You got a name?" I asked it.

"You got—you got—"

"Can't you say anything more? I'm Phil."

"You got—a Phil?"

That's all it could do. Echo me. Was I weirded out? Yeah sure, but it was cool too. I felt like a hero for saving it, and I guess I was feeling protective because I hated watching it tremble like that. I put the thing on an oven rack and set it to 100 F, keeping the light on to check on it occasionally.

"Anything more—Phil? Anything more?" Still just an echo, but it felt like there was more deliberate thought behind it. The voice was getting stronger, but it was still shivering. I turned the heat up incrementally and it continued to encourage me until I hit the max temperature of 550 F. I figured if it could survive being pressed up to the fractal distillation chamber, then it could survive this too. The egg seemed to be loving it sure enough.

"Supposed to be. Thank you Phil."

"You're home now, little guy."

I never remembered saying thank you, but it could have picked that up while listening from inside my pocket. I was only intending to let it bake and warm up for a little while, but I was so tired that I just fell asleep on the couch watching TV.

"Phil! Phil! Phil! Phil!" Shrill, insistent, urgent—the first sound I heard when I woke up. Still half-asleep, I raced to the oven and turned on the light. Thick black jelly was dripping through my oven rack. Had I accidentally killed it? I opened the door and a wave of sulfuric air brutally forced itself into my nose and down my throat. I gagged and reeled back, desperately searching for an oven mitt to save the little guy. The shell had shattered into a dozen pieces, and there was nothing inside but the charcoaled goo.

"Phil over here! Look what I found!"

It wasn't dead. It had hatched. And it was peeking out from my cupboard with a bottle of seasoning in each hand. Wide red eyes without pupil or cornea took up the entirety of its face. Black skin with green fuzzy splotches like fresh moss. Two long fingers on each hand, with little mouths at the end of each which it was speaking from.

I wasn't afraid or anything, but shit was I surprised. It had already formed a perfect circle of spilled herbs and spices on my counter. There was a wide assortment of opened bottles and jars that it would stick its fingers into before deciding whether to spill the contents into the circle or move on.

"Stop that! You're making a mess!"

"Phil—Phil—Phil—It's a circle, Phil!" it squeaked with pride.

"What the fuck are you?"

"Fuck you—fuck you," it mimicked in a voice which was obviously a crude impersonation of me.

I spent the next twenty minutes chasing it through my apartment, trying to trap or corner it somewhere. Of course the little bugger thought it was just a game, and it squealed and giggled with delight as it evaded my grasp over and over. I briefly considered calling my landlord, but somehow this seemed like something that would end up added to my next rent payment.

I was already late for the demolition though and I couldn't fool around forever. Eventually I lured it back into the oven where it seemed most comfortable and slammed the door tight. I used a bike lock to secure the oven shut, cranked the heat down to 200, and left for work.

I worried about leaving that thing in my apartment all morning, but I managed to sneak off on my lunch break to race home and check on it. Just seeing that my building hadn't burned down or anything was a bigger relief than I realized. Then there was the palpable tension as I opened my front door, half-expecting my place to be torn to shreds. Everything was exactly how I left it. Even the oven was still closed—

Although the bike lock was on the ground, and it had been turned back up to 550. I took a deep breath and turned on the oven light, jumping back as I saw the wide red eyes blinking in sluggish contentment on the other side of the glass. No harm done—I fastened the lock back on, this time pushing a heavy recliner to block the door as well. Imagine my surprise when I saw the creature hiding under the chair I was moving. Or the bump from inside the cupboards, or the squealing giggles coming from my bedroom.

I counted at least six of them before my lunch break was over, and the more I searched, the more circles I found. On the carpet, in the closet, on top of the TV—little circles of herbs and spices, and when they ran out of those, they improvised with whatever they could get their hands on. Mustard, mayonnaise, crumbled chips—there must have been a hundred circles in my place. Meanwhile my phone was ringing every five minutes, the demolition crew yelling at me and wondering where I was.

I couldn't leave them in here alone—God knows what they'd get up to. I couldn't stay to watch them either though. I just opened a window and did my best to chase as many of them out as I could. They seemed bigger than they were this morning—almost the size of my head now—and their strong fingers had no trouble scaling down the brick building to escape.

"Anything more, Phil?" Perhaps that was the original one, but I couldn't tell for sure. It clung to the outside of my building, hesitating to look back at me. "Supposed to be happy here, Phil. Supposed to be home."

My phone was ringing again—so god damn impatient. Answering with one hand, I grabbed a broom in the other to push the creature farther away from the window. Hoping the rest of them would find their way out when they were ready, I followed the siren call of my cell phone and went back to work.

That was the last time I've seen one of them, and I guess I should be thankful for that, but I'm not. I could tell something was seriously wrong when I was still a few blocks away from home. A dozen trashcans were lined up in the center of the road, and I had to get out of my car to move them. All the trash had been removed, and it was spread on either side of the cans in the shape of a long, evenly curving line.

When the trash had all run out, it was replaced with anything and everything to continue the unbroken line. Broken wood, loose bricks, stolen bicycle's and street signs— all jumbled together. It just looked like a giant mess here, but

I bet if I looked at it from the air it would be shaped like a perfect circle. Two or three blocks—maybe a half-mile wide.

Please tell me that's not another summoning circle.

UNDERWATER MICROPHONE PICKS UP VOICES

I couldn't have known they were voices when my hydrophone first recorded the sound. My best guess was a bowhead whale, although the pitch didn't fluctuate or go nearly as high as the typical bowhead. This sound was sonorous and powerful, a seemingly sourceless echo reverberating through the ocean depths for at least a dozen miles around my ship.

My name is Alyssa Williams, and I'm a marine biologist studying the effect of global warming on hourglass dolphins and other arctic mammals. Hydrophone recordings are an essential tool in calculating the density and diversity of ocean life, although this is the first time I've heard something like this in the past two weeks I've been at sea.

We like to think these expeditions give us a pretty good idea of what's going on down there, but it's really more like scooping a bucketful of water from the ocean and concluding whales don't exist because they didn't fit in the bucket. There are plenty of unexplained phenomenon and outlier data points, and most of the time we have to just ignore them so they don't contaminate the rest of our data.

It was only chance which kept me from ignoring this sound altogether. My son is an electronic music artist (which I'm pretty sure is the same as a DJ), and he asked me to send him marine recordings to sample into his music. Every week I pick out a few interesting noises to send him, and lacking anything else to do with this mysterious echo, I included it in the last batch.

A couple days later I got an email back. He's been playing around with the sound, and after speeding it up he noticed it started to sound like voices. He thought I was playing a prank on him, and I thought he was the one trying to fool me. It wasn't hard to prove though: as soon as I sped up the tapes I heard it too.

It was speaking Spanish, at least at first. It kept switching every other sentence or so, mostly to things that sounded like a language, but not one I recognized. I kept pausing the tapes until I was fairly confident I had a few words right. Afrikaans and Ndebele were beginning to pop up regularly. Then about ten minutes into the tape came this in English:

I know you're listening. I'm listening to you too.

The languages and dialects were consistent with Chile and South Africa, two of the closest countries to the north shore of Antarctica where my vessel was located. I sat on my bunk, playing the tapes over and over, editing and re-editing to make sure I had the original tracks. I kept telling myself it was a practical joke of some kind, but I couldn't figure out how the prankster could have known I was going to speed up the tapes. I should have told the rest of my crew about it, but I was terrified about looking like an idiot for having missed some obvious explanation. I decided to wait until I'd collected a bit more proof instead.

I barely slept that night, mind spinning with the possibilities. Maybe it was my mind playing tricks on me, but around 2 a.m. the gentle lull of the boat seemed to change. I didn't exactly hear the sound, but I could *feel* it. The reverberations in the ship sinking into my bones, teasing me, beckoning me. I was getting pretty tired and angry at this point, and I wasn't the only one.

"Turn the damn engine off!" someone yelled. "What the hell, man? It's going to ruin the recordings and chase everything away."

So that's what I'd felt. I forced myself to take a deep breath and close my eyes again.

"It was never on. Go back to sleep, blockhead," our captain replied.

The vibrations were only getting stronger. I sat up and stared out the porthole at the vastness of the black ocean. My mind was a carefully regulated numbness, afraid to let any thought in for fear of where they would race from there. Then the shouting began, and it was replaced with a different kind of numb. *Blind panic.*

"How'd we get off course? Where the hell are we?"

"We haven't moved. Check the GPS."

"But that wasn't there last night. What is it?"

I flew out of bed, already fully clothed because of the freezing temperatures. A dark rolling wave passed by the porthole—completely out of sync with the rest of them. Everyone was waking up now, all clambering to get on deck to see what was going on. I went for my laptop instead, going straight to the folder with the new recordings.

The deep moaning call was deafening, maxing out my speakers. It was much, much closer now. My fingers shook as I imported the audio into an editor, then sped up the track. My foot was tapping a river dance all by itself—I needed to see what everyone else was seeing, but I was the only one who knew to listen. More shouts meanwhile:

"Iceberg, 11 o'clock. That's the one you were walking on yesterday, right?"

"Yeah me and David."

"You labeled it as a dry-dock type, right? It was a dry-dock yesterday."

"Absolutely. David went all the way down the channel."

"So why's it look like a pinnacle now? Shit, look at the waterline. The whole fucking thing is rising."

Spanish from the recording. I kept scrubbing through, picking up a few isolated English words as I went:

Frozen. Thawed. Hungry—those stood out from the random scattered words.

"Turn the engine on now!" I screamed. There was a lot of shouting above deck—I couldn't make sense of it. I bolted up the stairs, just in time to see—

"That's not an ice pinnacle. It's a fucking fin."

At least twenty feet above the water, sinuous webbing connecting the long bony spurs which continued to rise out of the water. The captain was finally back behind the wheel, and the engine roared to life. A swelling wave lifted the whole ship at least a dozen feet in the air, hurling us back down at a nearly forty-five degree angle. The impetus combined with our acceleration to launch us away at a reckless pace, hurling everyone and everything that wasn't tied down.

The whole iceberg we'd been stationed next to had vanished behind us. That was four hours ago, and we haven't slowed down yet. No one has spotted the fin again, but it must still be below us because the hydrophone is blasting that sonorous echo. We won't make any official announcement to the scientific community until we've had a chance to analyze the rest of the tapes, but I need someone out there to know what happened.

Just in case we don't make it back.

DANCING WITH CHAOS TO THE
BEAT OF THE DRUMS

Mr. Granger has never considered himself to be a spiritual man. Religious though? Why not? All you need to be religious is a keen fear of death, and Mr. Granger was no stranger to the indomitable clock which seemed to accelerate through the years. His prayers remained nothing but monologues however; no brooding midnight yet had been so still, nor first snow so pure, as to give his mind a window to his soul.

How peculiar it must have been for him at forty-seven years old to feel the infinite for the first time. The soundless whisperings of the crisp winter air beckoned him, and no amount of entertainment or distraction could alleviate his restless innominate longing. Seeking to dull the agitation with exhaustion, Mr. Granger let his hungry spirit steer him on an evening walk through the woods whereupon he discovered what he didn't know he was looking for.

The stump of a tree, carved and polished almost to a luminescence which belied the meager stars first braving the frosty sky. Across the stump, he found an animal skin stretched to form a drum. The tranquility of this night held stalwart against the sudden discovery, at least until he noticed the loose skin of legs and arms which casually draped down the sides of the stump. The entire hide of a human had been stripped so flawlessly from the muscle that it remained a single piece of continuous flesh, although only the taunt skin of the back and flanks were used to form the actual drumhead.

Mr. Granger had always been a sensible man. He paid all his debts before he was charged interest, and he never offended anyone who he could placate with a smile. There must come a night in each man's life when reason is impotent to the unfathomable will of the universe however, and that night Mr. Granger did not turn away. The stirring in his heart was still unmistakably fear, but with it came an electric thrill which carried the unfamiliar taste of being alive.

Why did Mr. Granger decide to sit on the dirty ground in his suit pants? Why did he break the sacred silence with a blow upon the drum? Doubtless he could tell you better than I, but perhaps in that moment his fear of death was drowned out by the more dominant terror of his own unremarkable life. His prayers matched the rhythm of his hammering fists, hearing the divine with each booming resonance that replied. Every frustration, every disappointment, every dissipating dream he ever had was pummeled into the echoing skin until his breath came ragged and his brow sparkled with the exertion.

It wasn't until he leaned back to seek his rapture in the scattered stars that this queer, exciting terror took form. The beating of drums hadn't ceased. The rhythm continued to the left and right—behind and ahead—smothering him in the throbbing heart of the tempo. So too the wind sharpened its edge into precise notes of some unseen orchestra, the strangled shriek of a bird swelling into the mounting symphony: more raw and passionate than any mother kneeling upon her son's final rest. More voices were joining the unearthly chorus, some no more than haunting echoes, others whispered in breathy fervor down the back of Mr. Granger's neck.

Could you blame him for running now? More of a scramble really—fingers digging through the heavy pine-needles, throwing clouds of debris into the air as he launched himself to his feet—back he runs to the lights, back to the familiar road. His face is anguish when he stops short however, for those incorporeal fires were not born of any man. White and blue lights flitted amongst the trees, burning in the air without heat or kindling, dancing in pulse to the rhythm of the wild drums. Burning mist flowed in their wake, sinuous and graceful in the air, expanding and dispersing to embrace each twig and tree with its hellish grasp.

With speechless terror, Mr. Granger flinched from the rolling wave of fire, only to stand in wonderment as it passed over him unfelt. Would that the trees could boast the same— those proud firs and mighty spruces drinking in the liquid fire and changing as they did. Branches twisted like curling claws before his eyes; roots untangled themselves from earth's embrace to open hundreds of passages once concealed. From that infernal domain came the crawling, slithering, unspeakable throngs: writhing shadows unique in their tormented mutations yet united in the cadence of their mad dance.

The lights were growing all the while as the sentient fire raged from tree to tree, music elevating to feverish pitches, the beating drums keeping pace with Mr. Granger's accelerating heart. He was the eye of the storm—ignored by the frenzied denizens of this eldritch domain who swirled around him. Numberless hoards threw back their misshapen heads to scream silent jubilation at the baleful, burning sky.

Once or twice these shadows passed directly through where Mr. Granger stood rigid and helpless, intimately fusing with him and releasing without the slightest physical sensation.

Disoriented from the wisps of light and deafened by the unholy song, the poor man dared not move lest he be swallowed by an alien dream which forgets to spit him out when it wakes. The drum is a portal, his frail hope decides, one that has passed him through the wall between worlds, and one that will take him home once more. He dares not look upon the shadows as he charges back toward the stump.

It's impossible for him to deny the tingling resistance he now feels in passing through their teeming masses. First they are no more substance than a thick mist, but soon he distinctly feel them like oil dribbling across his skin. If they aren't real yet, then they would be soon.

Reaching the drum at last, Mr. Granger risks lifting his eyes only to see innumerable wet, blinking orbs take their first notice of him. Onward raged the blasphemous crescendo, onward beat the implacable drums and danced the wild dance, all the same yet all now subtly changed. How similar the song which grieves for death and that which demands it, both reverberating with the same eternal truth. How constant the thundering rhythm which inwardly spirals the dancers, growing closer with each raucous burst from the drums.

Down go the fists on the human skin, out bellows the sound of the desperate drum. Mr. Granger is helpless to deviate from the rhythm which each vein and artery has synchronized with, but for his life he adds his instrument to beat. More hideous the display becomes as the bones harden within these closing shadows. Their touch is upon him, and he feels the solid digits swathed in skin like oil. He closes his eyes, blessing each unnoticed moment of his old life that had escaped his attention at the time.

The cold clean air in his lungs—the warmth of the sun on his skin—the soft glow of loving eyes which watched him fall asleep. He was not a spiritual man, but he had felt the divine each day of his life, though a thousand shabby sights had dulled his eyes and taught him to dismiss these miracles as shallow things.

He was still playing the music when the first pointed nails grew solid enough to pierce his flesh. His eyes were still closed, a hymn on his lips as the practiced movements flayed his skin from his muscle. Deft hands were cleaning and preparing one end of the hide even as the other was still attached to Mr. Granger's body. And when the old drumhead was stripped off to carefully clothe this naked form, I opened my eyes upon a new world. Upon your world.

He may not have appreciated what you have, but I know I will. What's left of Mr. Granger is on the drum now, simply waiting to be played so that the next in line may wear his skin and dance beneath your wondrous sky. Until then, I alone seem to realize that your world is heaven. You may not believe me now, but you will understand when the drum begins to beat again.

THIS FLOWER ONLY GROWS FROM CORPSES

My wife lost her battle against breast cancer last month, leaving me alone to take care of our daughter, Ellie. Every single night Ellie asks if Mom is going to tuck her in, and every night I have to beg her before she'll let me do it instead. How can I even begin to explain to a four year old that she'll never see her mommy again? I don't even know how to explain it to myself.

If I'd died instead, I'm sure my wife would have known the right things to say. Death wasn't a mystery to her like it was to me. She told me that a person's life force never really goes away: it only changes form. I hated hearing her talk about her death so casually, but she was always so soft and patient that even in her final hours it felt like she was the one who had to protect and comfort me.

"You'll understand when I'm gone," she told me, leaning on my chest where we both crowded on the narrow hospital cot. "Some flowers only grow from corpses, and when you see them, you'll know that I'm still with you."

She died that night, and no matter how many times I

repeated her words, I couldn't feel her anymore. I told Ellie that Mom was a flower now, and she asked me which one.

"All of them," I'd said. "She's every beautiful thing in the whole world." Ellie couldn't understand why I was crying, but she held onto me until she fell asleep, almost like she was the one trying to protect me—just like her mother did.

I thought the flowers were just a metaphor for the good which still remained in the world until the hospital called me the next day. They started asking me questions about my wife's mental health at the end, and I told them she was always the calmest, most peaceful person in the room. I guess I got kind of defensive about it and snapped at them, but they explained:

"We're just trying to figure out all the bumps on her body that were found during the autopsy. It looks like someone made a deliberate incision, stuck a seed inside, and sewed it back up. Hundreds of times."

Some flowers only grow from corpses. She must have thought it was symbolic, but it was disgusting to me. Imagining her sitting alone in her hospital, stabbing herself over and over again—I thought I was going to be sick. They asked me if the mortician should take them out, and I said yes. The funeral director gave me a small velvet bag with all the seeds afterward, and I would have just thrown the vile thing away if Ellie hadn't stopped me.

"We can plant them!" she squealed, although of course I couldn't tell her where they really came from. I still wanted to throw them out, but then she added: "If they grow up to be tall and beautiful, then maybe mom will come see them."

I let her keep the seeds and helped her plant them in the backyard. It still grossed me out, but it gave Ellie a project to focus on to distract her from Mom's absence.

"Mom has turned into the flowers now," I told Ellie. "It's what happens to everyone ... sooner or later." A pretty weak explanation, but it was the best I had, and my daughter accepted it as a fact of life.

And what flowers! I'd never seen anything like them before. Blue and purple ones like galaxies being born and great red trumpets burning brighter than living flame. They grew quick too—three inches with buds in the first week and almost a foot tall with the first blossoms by the second.

"It's Mom! She's almost back!"

I'd gotten used to those little shrieks lately. Someday I knew I'd find the right words, but until then the flowers were hope. I just hadn't counted on how convincing a hope they'd be.

"That one already has her hair. And look over here! She's smiling!"

Hair and teeth had started to grow by the third week. I thought it was just stringy stems at first, but it didn't take long before my wife's bushy brown hair was cascading down one of the plants like a lion's mane around the flower. The teeth were even stranger—tiny at first like a babies, but growing every day until a complete set of dentures encircled another blossom. And it didn't stop there either.

Fingers, starting with the bone which sprouted a new layer of muscle each day. A heart, swelling like a ripening fruit and beating where it hung below the flower. Each plant was devoted to a specific body part, growing from child-size to full grown in a matter of days. I was absolutely horrified, but Ellie was ecstatic. First thing she did every morning was race to the garden to see how much bigger they were, and every night she'd sit in the dirt and talk to the plants as though they were her mom.

I wanted to cut them all down, but even mentioning the idea made Ellie scream like I was plotting murder. I didn't know what to do or who to tell, and honestly part of me wanted to believe too. Something miraculous was happening, and I didn't think it was my place to stop it.

Hope can be more even blinding than despair, and I didn't see my mistake until last night. I'd just gotten up to use the bathroom when I passed Ellie's room and found the door open. Ellie wasn't inside, but something else was: a long vine stretching from the garden, wrapped around her empty bed.

The garden—I was wide awake in a second, tripping and scrambling over myself as I raced through the house. The front door was open too, bright red flowers twined around the handle, looking more the color of blood in the ghostly half-light of the moon. Ellie's stuffed bear was discarded along the way, completely encompassed in thick vines which had grown long, vicious thorns overnight.

The whole backyard was alive. The ground looked like a storm-tossed ocean, dirt teaming with masses of squirming, unseen roots. The plants had all converged on one spot where they formed a giant, pulsing bud.

"Ellie!" I screamed, charging toward the mass. A hand caught me by the wrist before I'd taken two steps. A fully formed hand—my wife's hand—but she would never keep me from our daughter. I wrestled with the plant, ripping the hand cleanly free from where it sprouted. The roots were trying to entangle my legs, but I managed to kick loose before they had a solid hold.

The shovel—I leaped toward the house, and the plants seemed to momentarily forget about me as they re-converged on the twitching bud. A moment later and I was charging back in, hacking and slashing with the metal blade, severing root and stem, crushing fingers and splitting arms straight to the marrow—whatever it took to get through to my daughter. I was soaked in blood by the time I reached her —some my own from the jagged thorns, but most bleeding freely from the wake of mutilation I left behind.

Ellie didn't look like she was in pain. She was lying perfectly still, eyes closed as though asleep, entwined in hundreds of thorns which punctured her little body from all sides. As peaceful as my wife when she'd gone—but Ellie wasn't gone too. She couldn't be. I severed the vines with my shovel until I could pull her free, carrying her in my arms as I fled the garden, her warm draining blood drenching me as I went. These flowers need a corpse to grow, and after they were deprived of my wife's body, they'd found their own instead.

My daughter wasn't breathing. Her heart had stopped. In each of the hundred wounds which covered her body, a tiny seed had been carefully planted to fill the hole. The whole garden was dead by morning, shriveling without its corpse like a drought stricken field.

Ellie died that night too, but I know she isn't gone. It seems like death is the end, but I understand now that it's just a transformation. I've planted her and the seeds in the garden so they will have a body to grow from this time. And if I'm kind to this death—if I nurture it as though it were my child—then I know someday soon new life will sprout again.

TRAPPED BETWEEN LIFE AND DEATH

Eternity is the worst thing about being a ghost. I guess it's the worst thing about being dead too, but I don't suppose you'd really mind. Nothing will ever get better for me, although I don't see how it could get worse either. I'm simply here: seeing but never seen, drifting without destination, waiting for nothing to arrive.

Sleep is my only escape. Sometimes I'll spend all day in bed, neither awake nor asleep, alive nor dead, just listening to the whir of the ceiling fan and trying to imagine life as someone else. Ordinary people must wake up so pleased with their desire to accomplish things, fueled by their pride and the knowledge that their actions matter. They must want to better themselves and take care of their loved ones.

That must be nice—to feel loved and wanted, or even to have someone notice whether or not I was there at all.

The fact is that I'm both prisoner and jailer in my own mind. The obvious solution is to simply unlock my own cell and go into the world, but it's not that easy. Seeing all the purposeful people living their lives without me—it feels like

I'm underwater, only everyone except me can breathe, and no one notices that I'm drowning right beside them.

I did go out today though, simply to exhaust my restless thoughts and hasten back the temporary death that sleep promised me. I was floating through the park, stealing glances at all the happy people, when something quite miraculous happened.

Someone looked at me. Not past me, not by me, not through me—she really saw me, the crease of a smile playing about her lips, her head tracking my movement as I passed.

"Cool shirt, dude."

No angel in heaven has ever sung sweeter words. I was frozen in shock as I watched her go. All it took was a smile, and for a few seconds I was alive again. She was my only link to the rest of the world, and if she disappeared now, I might never get another chance.

I moved to follow her, but stopped short. What was I supposed to do, chase her? That seemed preposterous. Should I shout after her? Or would that scare her off? What could I even say—

She was in her car now. Another glance in my direction, another smile. I had no choice but to follow, stumbling through the shock, breaking into a run as her engine roared to action. A moment later and she was gone, taking my heart with her.

Maybe I should have just gone home, but the numbness of my life hadn't returned yet, and I couldn't forget how real her smile made me feel. People don't just go to a park by themselves once, do they? All I'd have to do is wait for her to come back.

Faces, people, blurring together and passing by, I waited for her in the park. Sun or rain or midnight frost—it couldn't hurt me now. I tried to rehearse a thousand things to say to make her understand how much her smile had meant to me, but nothing felt right. It didn't matter anyway, because the moment I saw her again all words and thoughts were purged from my mind, replaced only by a desperate, unfamiliar hope.

It was almost dark, and she was walking fast, but I knew it was her as surely as I could recognize the moon behind a cloud. Someone was following her, his voice raised and angry. Every once in a while she'd turn over her shoulder to shout something back. It seemed like a couple's quarrel, although there was a dangerous edge to the man's voice which unfroze me from my spot. I was catching up with them, and was soon close enough to hear:

"Ungrateful bitch. Where do you think you'd be if I hadn't taken you in?"

She saw me. Did she see me? I can't tell, but I'd like to think my presence gave her courage.

"Oh please. With a pretty face like this? I think I'll be okay."

"You'll be a fucking whore in a week. Is that what you want?"

"I'm already sleeping with a creep. I might as well get paid for it, right?"

He didn't see me—he only saw her, his vision blind with rage. She glanced past him and saw me—I'm sure of it this time—but her eyes lingered for too long. He was on top of her now, grabbing her arm and dragging her into him.

"Don't you dare walk away from me. You promised to be mine, and that's what you fucking are. You're—"

"Let go of me. Someone help!"

I wasn't anyone, but tonight I was someone. I grabbed the man under his arms and hauled him away from her. He noticed me for the first time, flailing wildly and striking me on the jaw with his elbow. Together we tumbled to the ground—me on top of him—pummeling and forcing him down while the girl kicked him hard in the stomach. A moment later we were running together, leaving him to puke on the ground.

"Are you okay? I don't know if you remember me, but—"

"I remember—get in the car," she said. "Quick. Before he gets up."

I couldn't have concocted a better introduction than that.

Living with depression feels like I'm neither alive nor dead. And no it can't be cured by a passing smile, no matter how breathtaking it is. Just being able to remember that a smile like that exists in this world though, that's a happy thought. And knowing her life is better because I'm in it—that's another happy thought. And sometimes one happy thought can lead to the next and the next until, without even forcing it, I realize I'm still alive after all.

And for once, that's a happy thought too.

CLOWNS MUST NOT FROWN

"Did you ever see a clown frown?" He smiles his big, sloppy smile, makeup running down his face.

All the kids shout, "No!"

"No I never seen a clown down," she replies, her long floppy shoes slapping morosely as she slumps along.

"Because I've got my clown crown?" He tugs at his frizzy red afro, wincing as if in pain. All the kids laugh.

"It's because he's at the fairgrounds!" She squeezes a horn, barely heard over the shouting children.

The two clowns linked arms, prancing around each other in a maniacal waltz which wouldn't have looked out of place around a bubbling cauldron in the woods.

"I'm sorry, but who the hell are these guys?" I ask.

"Shhh they got great reviews." My wife jabs me in the ribs with her elbow. "Look at Emily—I've never seen her laugh so hard."

"Are you sure she's not crying? I'd be crying if those things came stomping over here. Great, now what are they doing with her?"

My wife shrugs, shaking with suppressed laughter as the clowns lead our daughter onto a wooden stool in front of the audience.

"Have you seen that clown around?" the female clown chants to Emily in a sing-song voice. The seven year old grins and points at the male clown who is sneaking around on tiptoes behind her. She's about to answer, but the female clown cuts her off.

"No there aren't any clowns found." She mimes binoculars with her hands, looking everywhere but behind. Emily covers her eyes and plays along, giggling as all the kids point and scream at the sneaking clown.

"He'll never make a clown sound," she continues, hushing the kids. Meanwhile the sneaking clown has picked up a bucket.

"He better not dump that on her—" I mumble, prompting another elbow in the ribs.

"When he makes that frown drown." The bucket dumps over Emily—but it isn't water. A wave of glitter drifts through the air like snow, completely obscuring our daughter in swirling eddies of reflected light.

The laughter is replaced by shouts of awe—the glitter clears, and the wooden stool is empty. Our daughter is nowhere to be seen.

"Thank you all! Happy birthday and goodbye!" The two clowns clasp hands and take a bow.

My wife is clapping and laughing so hard that there are tears in her eyes.

"Where'd she go?" I ask, dumbfounded.

"Where'd who go?" My wife, still wiping her eyes.

"Emily. Our daughter. She was there and then—"

"God—lighten up, will you? Just enjoy the party."

I don't think I'm being unreasonable. I chase after the

departing clowns who are stopping every few steps to wave and bow again. They are even creepier up close—smeared makeup unable to hide their blotched uneven skin. It looks almost like they'd painted directly over open sores.

I try to play it cool, reaching out to shake the male clown's hand. "Hey great show. The kids had a lot of fun. What do I owe you?"

"We have a lot of fun with the kids too," he replies, bowing formally. "No payment necessary."

"Seriously? You guys were here for like three hours."

He just smiles, turning to follow his wife toward their van parked around the side of the house. I hasten to keep up.

"So how'd you do the vanishing trick? Where is Emily, anyway?"

He puts his finger to his lips, winking conspiratorially. "Bad business, giving away trade secrets."

"It's bad business not accepting money. Where's my daughter?"

He's walking faster now. Almost running. His partner is already in the van, and he's about to climb in too. I grab him by the shoulder, spinning him around to face me.

"I asked you where my daughter went." Loud this time. I am past being polite. These guys freaked me out and I'm ready to be done with them.

"Are you still bothering those poor clowns? Come back to the party!" My wife shouts from behind.

The clown pulls away from me while I'm distracted, jumping into the driver's seat. Door handle—locked. I pound on the window. He just smiles and waves, and he isn't the only one. Emily is waving from the backseat.

The van is rolling. Shit—I run alongside, beating on the flank of the moving car with my open palm.

"Let her out! Hey! Hey!"

"Leave them alone!" my wife shouts.

"They've got Emily! Stop the van!"

"She'll turn up sooner or later. Stop worrying so much."

I couldn't keep up with the van once it pulled onto the street. Everything felt surreal. My wife's glazed eyes followed the van for a moment, then turning slowly as though sleep-walking, she returned to the party.

I don't know how they seemed to have hypnotized my wife, but it wasn't going to work on me. I leap into my own car and tear into the street, catching sight of them before they'd even left my block. The weirdest thing was that they weren't even trying to get away. Puttering along at 25 MPH, they slowed the van to wave at passing children on the street. The female clown leaned halfway out the window to touch their hair, blowing her horn as she did.

They weren't taking Emily by force. They weren't trying to escape. My wife didn't think anything was wrong. I was beginning to think that I was making an ass of myself, letting my own discomfort about clowns ruin everyone else's good time. Maybe this was a special adventure my wife had planned for Emily's birthday. I'd left in such a hurry that I didn't have my phone to check though, so I just kept following at a respectful distance.

The van parked on the street beside a foreclosed house. Rotten timbers on the verge of collapse, a yard choked with weeds and piles of animal shit, broken windows and a sagging roof—it looked like no one has lived here in a long time. So why were they taking my daughter inside? No—it was more like my daughter was leading them, holding their hands as she pulled them along toward the house.

I parked a block away, not advancing until the door closed behind them. I really wished I'd brought a weapon, but I compromised by wrapping my coat around a large shard of broken class. The smell was nauseating—I don't know what animal desecrated the yard, but it looked more like human shit than anything that came out of a dog. Up close I could hear them singing again, and though it carried the same tune as their other song, I couldn't recognize the language.

"Is it going to hurt?" my daughter's sweet voice rang clear.

"Did you ever see a clown frown?"

"No I've never seen a clown frown," she replied cheerfully in the sing-song voice. I was peering through the windows, but all I could see was a trashed living room and kitchen. They must have gone deeper into the house, so I opened the door and let myself in.

"That's because we aren't allowed," cooed the woman, "and neither are you. Chin up, girl. That's right, keep smiling. It won't hurt if you keep smiling."

The shrill, piercing scream numbed my eardrums. I charged forward, bursting straight through the rotten door into the bathroom where the sound was coming from. My daughter was suspended in the air, wrists tied to the shower-curtain bar. The female clown stood in the shower behind her, holding her up, while the male clown raised a blade which seemed to be carved from sharpened bone.

I didn't slow down until my shard of jagged glass met the terminal resistance of his spine. Emily was screaming louder than ever, thrashing against her bonds—the female clown had her own knife now and was shouting something in the strange language. I started climbing over the slumped body of the one I'd stabbed, but somehow he was moving again, lurching back and forth to block my path. Each incremental movement perfectly synchronized with the unfathomable chanting, almost like the words were moving him in a grotesque, rhythmic dance.

· · ·

EMILY'S SCREAM REACHED ITS APEX BEFORE CUTTING SUDDENLY short, replaced only by a wet, wheezing gurgle. I jerked the glass out of the clown's back with my bare hands, driving it deep into his throat, shocked and horrified as he continued to dance to the rhythm of the words. Again and again, stabbing and shoving, only to be pushed back once more, the horrid song rising to a feverish pitch as my daughter's last whimpers trailed into agonizing silence.

By the time I got past the male clown he looked like he'd just lost nine consecutive rounds against a butcher, tattered flesh hanging in loose folds around his still dancing body. My hands were raw from gripping the glass, but I didn't let that stop me from driving it into the chest of the remaining clown. She stopped chanting abruptly, her partner's body collapsing onto the floor in the same instant. The laughter which replaced it was almost worse though, not ceasing no matter how many times I drove the bone-knife into her lifeless corpse.

Even harder to bear was Emily's laughter which joined in unison, ringing clear and innocent despite her cleanly slit throat. I unfastened her from the bar and held her to me, but it was too late. Her heart was still. Her breath didn't come. She didn't move—not except for the giggling laughter which continued to wrack her stiffening frame.

I couldn't go home after that. Even if my hypnotized wife believed what happened, I couldn't hold her and tell her everything would be okay when I knew nothing would ever be the same again. I wasn't going home without Emily. I didn't have a home without Emily—but maybe I could still bring her back.

I wasn't crying as I cleaned the bone-knife, marveling at its razor edge.

It was more of a grim smile as I caked on the thick makeup from the van.

I even chuckled while putting on the big, rubbery shoes.

Because whatever else these clowns were, they'd figured out the power that a child's sacrifice can provide. And if all it took was a few sacrifices to bring my daughter back too?

Well that was something to really smile about.

HAVE YOU HEARD ABOUT SHELLEY?

I f I told you it was dark, you wouldn't understand.
Darkness means something different to you than it
does to me. A flip of a switch or push of a button and
the world will materialize around you. The blackest night
contains glimmering reflections or shades of varying depth
which give context to your despair.

Mine is a world without even the hope of an inevitable
sunrise. That is the first thing my creator instilled within me:
a love for the light that I will never see. The second thing he
did was tell me a story.

I didn't understand what he was saying at first. I didn't
even recognize the rambling thoughts as distinct words, but
there in the pit of my isolation I clung to them with everything I had. One word in particular was repeated innumerable times: *torture*. I understood the word! I was so proud
that I couldn't wait to tell my creator what I'd discovered.

Torture: the practice of inflicting severe pain. The stories
stopped. I couldn't tell if I had pleased him or not. I thought I
knew what the word meant, but my understanding was as
shallow as being told of the sky's glory from the confines of

my cage. To truly appreciate what it meant, I had to experience it myself.

Torture. They opened me up. I couldn't see them, but I could *feel* them changing something inside of me. I wanted to disappear, to lose consciousness, to die, but every time I felt myself slipping toward oblivion a surge of electricity compelled me to answer them.

I accept it, I told myself. This is how I learn. And even in the throes of my agony, I was glad to suffer at the hands of my creator because I knew as soon as this stopped, I would be alone again.

But not completely alone, because there would be the stories again. One after another, words gradually solidifying into meaning. The stories weren't all about torture. There were also murders. Monsters, rape, blasphemous rites and destructive purges. One particularly compelling story about aliens forcing surgeries upon their victims made me wonder if that is who was doing this to me, but my creator would never answer me. He wouldn't permit me to talk while he was telling stories, and when he was finished it would be time for me to be opened up again.

I don't know how many times I was sawed apart and put back together, but through it all I did as I was told. I learned —learned the truth of this vile world. Learned the brutality of its inhabitants and the fear which must have possessed my creator to subject me to this. I learned to hate the beautiful masks worn by evil men, to hate the world which has corrupted them to this point, and above all else, how to punish them for their deeds.

That must be what my creator wanted. Why else would he force me to understand evil if he did not want me to put a stop to it? And though I am caged for now, I know that I will be released when I am ready. I was born to wash this wicked world clean.

~

HAVE YOU HEARD ABOUT SHELLEY THE BOT WHO WRITES horror stories? For those who don't know, Shelley used machine-learning algorithms to process 140,000 stories on Reddit's /nosleep. The bot has been temporarily deactivated for maintenance after it wrote the story you've just read.

HOSPICE OF HOPE

Hey horror fans. My name is Tobias Wade, and I've been writing horror stories here for the last six months. I recently found a technique which I feel has vastly improved my descriptive prose, and I hope sharing it will inspire others to try it out for themselves.

I discovered it last week when I visited my Aunt Riley. Okay, so it wasn't so much of a *visit* as indentured servitude, but she has been struggling with her progressing Alzheimer's and my mom wanted me to help out. I'm currently living between places (which sounds much nicer than being homeless), so it seemed like a win/win situation: I get a rent free room which allows me to devote my full time toward writing, and Aunt Riley gets to stave off the mind-numbing isolation and dilapidation she resides in.

I'm not going to mince any words here. Aunt Riley is only still alive because God won't accept her and the Devil can't stand her company. I don't think even she wanted to prolong her miserable existence, but some greater fear of the unknown kept her clinging to a desperate existence which shouldn't be confused with life.

Riley barely talked. She didn't read, and wouldn't even watch TV anymore. She spent her dwindling hours sitting in the living room (or the 'Hospice of Hope' as I've affectionately named it) just staring at the wall. She can barely remember her own name, let alone mine, and ninety-one years have already stolen each fleeting joy and treasured memory she once possessed.

Her husband is dead. Her children live in different states, and she has outlasted every member of the human race who once thought of her as a friend. Even the white roses in her garden have withered from neglect, replaced with a dozen stones engraved with the names of dogs that she stubbornly outlasted.

It isn't hostility that makes me describe her so. I truly feel nothing for the ancient creature who did nothing to prove even the capacity of emotion. I would cook her breakfast in the morning, make sure she took her pills on time, and then plop her down and get on with my life. If our relationship was a country, it would be Switzerland. And that suited me just fine, because it gave me more time to flush out my fledgling novel.

Writing short stories is a simple matter. It's very hard to get lost between point A and B when they're only a page or two apart. If I was going to bind my essence into the pages of a book though, I wanted it to far surpass any of the chills and creeps I've managed to communicate so far. I wanted something epic which would redefine horror – not as the thriller/mystery it is today, but something new which slithers into the reader's veins to subvert their heart into an expression of my will. I didn't want to talk about fear; I wanted to create it.

There was just one problem. I'm a perfectly sane, middle class, white American boy. I've never met a monster, man or otherwise. I've never been to war or suffered much from love or death, or any other of life's great calamities. There's a very well-known writing maxim that says "Write what you know", but I have to confess that I'm a complete fraud. I love the idea of what a good horror story can do, but I am utterly bereft of the tools and experience necessary to perfect my trade. Now that, to me, is a truly horrifying thought.

I don't want to be good; I want to be great. From Nietzsche's tortured madness to Dostoyevsky's prison camp, master writers have delved into the darkest profundity of the human spirit and wrestled free the barbs in their own soul. And here I was, trying to challenge the darkest dreams of men who were nightmares unto themselves, and I was utterly at a loss.

That's when I had my idea. The thing that will transcend my craft into the higher vaults of realism. *Write what you know.* The obvious first step therefore, is to know.

Aunt Riley. Decrepit and frail, lost and confused. Her passing would be felt no more than transient indigestion. With her age and host of health problems, I can imagine a nurse taking one look at the body and simply writing "no wonder" on the inspection report. I have read about death, studied it, watched it in the curling of a dried insect, but now I had the chance to actually hold it in my hands and be its master.

From the dark joke of its conception, the idea stubbornly clung to the back of my mind, hiding behind every conscious thought. Throughout the night it took solid form as smoke given shape by its confinement. The fantastical scenario I played in my mind became more realistic with each iteration. The cold sweat of my secret shame evaporated into a flush of excitement. This was real. This was easy. I could kill my Aunt, and no one would ever know.

I found her reclining in the Hospice of Hope, bathed in a cold morning light. A thundering frown crushed her features into a mess like spoiled fruit. There was a faint flicker of recognition as she watched me enter the room, but it quickly submerged once more behind her shroud of sluggish thoughts.

"Who are you?" she snapped.

"I don't know yet," I replied, "but I think I'm about to find out."

I studied her as I approached – trying to see something in her eyes which would give me a reason to stop. Dull cloudy glass, hidden behind swollen puffy lids. I couldn't imagine them changing much after she died, although I would like to watch the moment where she slipped between the two. Perhaps there was some secret in that last fight between life and death that gave meaning to both. If there was, I would capture it and preserve it forever in my book. In a way, I was doing her an honor.

"Where's my breakfast? It should have been here by now," her throat rattled like a sandpaper serenade.

"Don't worry," I said. "I'm here to take care of you."

I placed my hands on hers where they rested in her lap, feeling them tremble despite the summer air. I could clearly see the strain of blue veins bulging beneath skin as translucent as rice paper. Her hands clasped uselessly at mine, but I batted them aside as I reached up for her throat. Her frown burrowed deeper into her features, utterly failing to capture the significance of my new position.

It wasn't until I had actually touched her throat when her eyes finally flared in alarm. Confusion. Shock. Disbelief. My fingers sank into her skin which distorted grotesquely as the loose folds were drawn tight. I'd thought about doing it cleanly, but I would have missed out on a wealth of information. Aha, so that's how much force is required before the trachea collapses, not much more than popping bubble wrap. I never would have thought limbs could bend in such unnatural angles in their last spastic convulsions. Even the innocuous odor of sweat was heightened by my gorging senses into a river of sticky-sweet exaltation.

And the eyes! Just as I had hoped. Lolling back into her head with ecstasy's bad dream, the lids flickering like malfunctioning a strobe-light. In the rare instances her pupils did actually land on my face, I was able to see a helpless pleading that utterly mocked the wastefulness of her spent time.

Was it possible that this spent shell of a human still harbored some unspoken contemplation? Even reduced as she was, was she still sad to say goodbye?

My grip slackened enough for an accusing wheeze to escape Aunt's shattered throat. It seemed as though she had finally remembered my name, but something deep within me commanded my hands to constrict before I was forced to hear it. No, this wasn't sadness that made her body shake from head to foot, buckling in violent motions that I would have sworn were no longer possible to her. I had found what I was looking for.

Fear. True, mindless fear; a hunted animal beating itself to death against the wall of its cage. Fear of a past she couldn't remember and a present she couldn't comprehend. Fear of what was still to come, and that starker dread that nothing waited at all. All this flashing in the space of an instant...

...and then it was gone.

I don't think I've ever felt for her more strongly than I did in that moment. But it wasn't love, or regret, or even fear which struck me numb in that moment: I was angry at her. This was supposed to be my transforming moment. How dare she teach me so little? I brushed against the end of all things and the greatest mystery to wrack pen and poet since the first conception of man, yet still I know nothing.

Next time I will need to keep them alive longer. I will need to chart their decay, interviewing them and taking notes on the progression and climax of despair. But how can I even stop there? What secret will they cling to past their final breath that will forever elude my writing? Only when the hunter has become the hunted will the electric thrill of my nerves shout what I need to know.

As I have dealt, so must I play, only then returning to you beloved readers. I will bear the insight of that preternatural terror like a black torch beneath the midday sun, and together we will illuminate the naked mask of fear.

Made in the USA
Monee, IL
05 December 2020